THE CITY
AND THE
MOUNTAINS

THE CITY AND THE MOUNTAINS

EÇA DE QUEIRÓS

*Translated from the Portuguese and with an
Afterword by* MARGARET JULL COSTA

A NEW DIRECTIONS BOOK

Published by arrangement with The Dedalus Press, London.

Originally published in Portuguese as *A cidade e as serras*.

The translator would like to thank Tânia Ganho and Ben Sherriff for all their help and advice.

Manufactured in the United States of America
New Directions Books are printed on acid-free paper.
First published as a New Directions Paperbook (NDP1117) in 2008.
Published simultaneously in Canada by Penguin Books Canada, Ltd.

Library of Congress Cataloging-in-Publication Data

Queirós, Eça de, 1845–1900.
[Cidade e as serras. English]
The city and the mountains / Eça de Queirós ; translated from the Portuguese by Margaret Jull Costa.
p. cm.
"A New Directions book."
ISBN 978-0-8112-1701-9 (paperbook : alk. paper)
I. Costa, Margaret Jull. II. Title.
PQ9261.E3C413 2008
869.3'3—dc22
2008022980

New Directions Books are published for James Laughlin
by New Directions Publishing Corporation,
80 Eighth Avenue, New York 10011

THE CITY
AND THE
MOUNTAINS

MY FRIEND JACINTO WAS BORN IN A PALACE, with an annual income of one hundred and nine contos in rents from the vineyards, grain, cork trees and olive groves planted on his lands.

In the Alentejo, in Estremadura and the two Beiras—Baixa and Alta—the fields of this ancient landed family—who were already storing grain and planting vines in the days of King Dinis—were bounded by dense hedges which undulated over hill and dale, and by good high stone walls, and by streams and roads. Their estate in Tormes, in Baixo Douro, took in a whole mountain range. Rents flowed in from the estates they owned between Tua and Tinhela, an area covering five leagues, and their thick pine woods darkened the Arga hills all the way down to the sea at Áncora. However, the palace in which Jacinto was born, and where he had always lived, was in Paris, on the Champs-Elysées, No. 202.

One evening in Lisbon, before Jacinto was born, his very plump, very rich grandfather—also named Jacinto, but known to everyone by the nickname Dom Galeão, "Sir Galleon"—was walking down Travessa da Trabuqueta beside a garden wall shaded by a vine trellis, when he slipped on a piece of orange peel and landed flat on his back on the ground. At that precise moment, there emerged from a low door in the wall a swarthy, clean-shaven man, wearing a thick green wool coat and high boots like a picador's. Smiling and apparently without the slightest effort, he promptly helped the vast Jacinto to his feet, even picking up the gold-handled walking-stick that had skittered away into the gutter. Then, fixing him with dark, thick-lashed eyes, he said:

"Come now, Jacinto 'Galeão,' what are you doing, rolling around in the road at this hour?"

And it was then that a stunned and grateful Jacinto recognized the Infante—Dom Miguel!

From that day forth, he loved the good Infante as—for all his gluttony and his devotion—he had never loved his dinner or his God! In the splendid hall of his house (in Calçada da Pampulha), he hung upon a damask wall the portrait of "his saviour," adorned with palm leaves as if it were a *retabla*, and displayed beneath it the walking stick which those same magnanimous royal hands had raised up from the dirt. While his adorable, beloved Infante languished in exile in Vienna, the paunchy gentleman rattled about Lisbon in his yellow carriage, bustling from Zé Maria's bar in Belém to Plácido's in Algibebes, bemoaning the fate and plotting the return of his "angel." On that most blessed day when *The Pearl* appeared in the harbor, bearing the returned Messiah, Jacinto garlanded his house with flowers and erected a monument made out of cardboard and canvas in which Dom Miguel, transformed into St. Michael, appeared all in white, with the halo and wings of an archangel, mounted on an Alter stallion and driving his spear into the Dragon of Liberalism, which, as it writhed in its death agony, was depicted vomiting up the Charter of 1826. During the war with "that pretender and freemason," Dom Galeão sent muleteers to Santo Tirso and to São Gens, to provide the King with fine hams and sweetmeats, bottles of his own Tarrafal wine, and silk purses crammed with coins which he rubbed with soap to make the gold shine more brightly. And when Jacinto "Galeão" learned that Dom Miguel, with only two battered old trunks and a mule, had set off along the road to Sines and his final exile, he ran through his house, shutting all the windows as if for a family funeral, and crying out angrily:

"All right! Then I'm not staying here either!"

For he had no wish to remain in that perverse land which the plundered and banished King of Portugal—that picker-up of Jacintos—was now leaving. He embarked for France with his wife, Senhora Dona Angelina Fafes (of the famous Fafes da Avelã), his son, Jacintinho—a sallow sickly child, sorely afflicted by pimples and boils—the nursemaid, and a black servant-boy. Off the Cantabrian coast, the ship met with such rough seas that Senhora Dona Angelina, kneeling on the bed in her cabin, her hair all disheveled, prayed fervently to Our Lord of the Stations of the Cross in Alcântara, promising him a crown of thorns made of gold and adorned with drops of blood made of Pegu rubies. In Bayonne, where they put into harbor, Jacintinho fell ill with jaundice. Next, on a particularly wild night on the road to Orléans, the axle of their coach snapped, and the plump gentleman, the delicate lady from the house of Avelã, and the boy had to trudge for three hours through the rain and mud of exile until finally they reached a village, where, after knocking like beggars at various silent doors, they ended up sleeping on tavern benches. And in the Hotel des Saints Pères in Paris, they had to endure a further horror: a fire broke out in the stables immediately beneath Jacinto's room, and the worthy nobleman, stumbling down the stairs in his nightshirt to the courtyard, stepped with his bare foot on a sliver of glass. Bitterly shaking one hairy fist at the heavens, he roared:

"Enough is enough!"

That same week, without looking any further, Jacinto "Galeão" bought the palatial residence at No. 202 Champs-Elysées from a Polish prince, who, after the fall of Warsaw, had chosen to take orders and became a Carthusian monk. And beneath the lavish gold of No. 202's stucco ceilings and amid its sprigged silks, Dom Galeão took refuge from all these vicissitudes in a life of utter idleness and good food, in the company of a few fellow emigrés (Judge Nuno Velho, the Count de Rabacena, and other minor figures), until, one day, he died of indigestion brought on by a dish of pickled lamprey sent to him by his agent in Montemor. Their friends assumed that Senhora Dona Angelina Fafes would return at once to Portugal; the good lady, however, feared the journey, the sea, and those carriage axles all too prone to snap. Nor did she wish to leave her confessor or her doctor, who understood her scruples and her asthma so very well.

"Much as I miss the good water of Alcolena, I'm going to stay here in No. 202," she declared. "I'll leave it to Jacintinho to decide what to do once he's grown up."

Jacintinho *had* grown up. Thinner and paler than a wax candle, he was a silent, lank-haired, large-nosed youth permanently bundled up in baggy black clothes a size or so too large for him. At night, unable to sleep for coughing and choking, he would wander the rooms of No. 202 in his nightshirt, carrying a candle; the servants always referred to him as "The Shadow." When the period of mourning for his father came to an end, there surfaced in his silent, hesitant soul an intense desire to take up wood-turning; then, somewhat later, in the sweet flower of his twentieth year, another entirely different sentiment sprang up in him: one of love and admiration for Judge Velho's daughter—round and plump as a pigeon—who had been brought up in a convent in Paris and was a girl of many talents, for she could enamel and gild, mend clocks, and make felt hats. In the autumn of 1851, when the chestnut trees in the Champs-Elysées were already beginning to lose their leaves, Jacintinho began to cough blood. The doctor, stroking his chin and furrowing his vast brow, advised the lad to set off at once for Golfe Juan or for the warm sands of Arcachon.

Jacintinho, however, tenacious as a shadow, could not bear to leave Teresina Velho, after whom he did, indeed, trail across Paris like a slow, silent shade. Then, shadow-like, he married, turned a few more pieces of wood, spat up a little more blood, and passed on—like the shadow he was.

Three months and three days after his funeral, my Jacinto was born.

His grandmother scattered fennel and amber over his cradle to ward off bad luck, and Jacinto grew with all the confidence, vigor and sap of a pine tree growing in the dunes.

He caught neither measles nor worms. Literature, mathematics, and Latin poured into him as easily as sunlight through a window. In the playground, whenever he raised his tin sword and bellowed out a command to his schoolmates, he was always the victor, the adored king, to whom the booty of afternoon tea was always surrendered. At an age when most boys are reading Balzac and Musset, he was never troubled by the torments of the over-sensitive; on hot evenings, he never lingered alone at a window, tortured by formless, nameless desires. His friends (there were three of us, including his old black valet, Cricket) always felt for him a pure and genuine friendship, unsullied by thoughts of acquiring a share of his wealth or dampened by signs that there was also a more selfish side to his nature. Lacking sufficient heart to feel any very strong passion, and quite content with this liberating incapacity, he only ever tasted love's honey—the honey that love reserves for those who gather it as lightly and quickly as bees buzzing by. He was rich and robust, indifferent to both the State and the Government of Men; and his sole ambition, as far as we knew, was to gain a thorough grasp of General Ideas; and his intelligence, in those jolly days of controversies and schools of thought, slipped in and out of the most complex philosophies like a lustrous eel through the clear waters of a pond. His very real, 24-carat value never went unrecognized or unappreciated; and his every opinion or merest facetious remark was immediately met with a wave of sympathy and agreement that lifted him up to the heights and held him there, cosseted and resplendent. Even inanimate objects served him with docility and affection; I cannot recall a single one of his shirt buttons popping off, or some vital piece of paper mischievously hiding from his eyes, or a drawer treacherously sticking when confronted by his haste and vivacity. When, one day, laughing skeptically at Fortune and her Wheel, he bought a lottery ticket from a Spanish sacristan, Fortune, sitting brisk and smiling at her Wheel, immediately ran to him in a flash and presented him with four hundred thousand pesetas. And if, in the heavens, the slow, heavy-laden clouds espied Jacinto out and about without his umbrella, they would hold back their waters until he had passed. Ah, yes, Senhora Dona Angelina's fennel and amber had triumphantly and forever banished bad luck from his destiny! His adorable grandmother (who, by the time I knew her, had a beard and was extremely fat) often used to quote a birthday sonnet composed by Judge Nunes Velho with the salutary line:

Remember, Madam, that Life is a river . . .

And a summer river, gentle and translucent, flowing harmoniously over soft, white sand, past happy villages and fragrant groves of trees, could not have offered more security or more sweetness to someone stepping down into a cedar boat—a well-shaded and well-cushioned boat, with fruit to eat and champagne on ice, with an angel at the helm and other angels keeping firm hold of the tow-rope—than that which Life offered to my friend Jacinto.

It was for this reason that we named him "the Prince of Great Good Fortune."

Jacinto and myself—Zé Fernandes—met and became friends in Paris, at the *Grandes écoles* in the Latin Quarter, where I had been sent by my good uncle Afonso Fernandes Lorena de Noronha e Sande, when the miserable wretches at Coimbra University expelled me for having slapped the vile face of Dr. Pais Pita during an afternoon procession down Rua da Sofia.

Around this time, Jacinto had come up with an idea, namely, that "a man can only be superlatively happy when he is superlatively civilized." And by "civilized" my friend meant the kind of man who, by honing his thinking skills on all the philosophy acquired from Aristotle onwards and multiplying the physical strength of his organs by using all the mechanisms invented since Theramenes created the wheel, could make of himself a magnificent, near-omnipotent, near-omniscient Adam ready to reap—

within a particular society and within the limits of Progress (at least as far as Progress had gotten in 1875)—all the pleasures and all the advantages that spring from Knowledge and Power. That was how Jacinto spoke, at length, about his Idea, when we discussed human aims and destinies, sipping our somewhat grubby glasses of beer beneath the awning of some philosophical café-bar on the Boulevard St-Michel.

Jacinto's "Idea" greatly impressed the other members of our "clan," who—having emerged into intellectual life between 1866 and 1870, that is, between the battle of Sadowa and the battle of Sedan, and having been told constantly ever since by technicians and philosophers that the needle musket had won at Sadowa and the schoolmaster at Sedan—were more than prepared to believe that the happiness of individuals, like the happiness of nations, could be achieved by the unfettered development of Mechanics and Erudition. And in order to condense the brilliance of Jacinto's idea and to spread it more widely, one of these young men, our inventive friend Jorge Carlande, boiled it down into an algebraic formula:

Absolute Knowledge x Absolute Power = Absolute Happiness

And for days afterward, from the Odéon to the Sorbonne, the positivist youth of the time praised Jacinto's metaphysical equation to the skies.

For Jacinto, however, his concept was not merely metaphysical—created for the sheer elegant pleasure of exercising his speculative reasoning powers—it constituted a very real and useful rule, one that could determine one's conduct and mold one's life. And so, in accord with his Idea, he purchased the *Shorter Encyclopedia of World Knowledge* in sixty-five volumes and installed a telescope in a glass observatory built on the roof of No. 202. Indeed, one hot sleepy August night, it was the telescope that first made his Idea real to me. In the distance, lightning flashed languidly across the sky. Fiacres—slow, open, indolent, and filled to overflowing with pale dresses—were rolling along the Champs-Elysées toward the coolness of the Bois.

"Here, Zé Fernandes," Jacinto said, leaning at the observatory window, "you will find conclusive proof of the theory that rules my life. For with these keen, quick eyes of ours, received from Mother Nature herself, we can barely see the lit window in that shop over there, on the other side of the avenue. Nothing more. However, if I add to my eyes the two simple lenses of a pair of horse-racing binoculars, I can see through the glass to the hams, cheeses, jars of jam and boxes of prunes. I conclude, therefore, that it is a grocer's shop. This, I believe, gives me a positive advantage over you who, with your naked eye, can see only the lit window. However, if, instead of those two simple lenses, I were to use my more scientifically advanced telescope, I could see beyond all that to Mars, with its seas and snows and canals, could see the outline of its gulfs, the whole geography of a planet that exists thousands of leagues from the Champs-Elysées. And what about another still more brilliant idea! Here you have the primitive eye, the eye of Nature, raised by Civilization to its maximum power of vision. As regards eyes, clearly I, the civilized man, am happier than the uncivilized man because I can discover the realities of the Universe about which he knows nothing and of which he is, therefore, deprived. If you apply that proof to all the organs, you will understand my principle. As for intelligence and the happiness one gains from it through the endless accumulation of ideas, I ask only that you compare Renan and Cricket, my manservant.

It becomes clear then that we must surround ourselves with the maximum possible amount of Civilization in order to enjoy to the maximum the joy of being alive, don't you agree, Zé Fernandes?"

It did not seem to me irrefutably true that Renan was necessarily happier than Cricket, nor could I see what spiritual or temporal advantage was to be gained from being able to peer through space at the smudgy spots on a planet—or across the Avenue des Champs-Elysées at the hams hanging in a grocer's shop window. Nevertheless, I assured him that, of course, I agreed with him, because I'm a good fellow and would never try to dislodge from another man's mind any idea in which he finds security, discipline, and a source of energy. I unbuttoned my waistcoat and, indicating the café and its lights down below, declared:

"Let's go downstairs and drink the maximum possible amount of brandy and soda—with ice!"

Naturally enough, Jacinto's idea of Civilization was inseparable from the image of the City, an enormous City with all its vast organs in powerful working order. My super-civilized friend could not even comprehend how nineteenth-century man could possibly savor the delight of living far from the stores employing three thousand cashiers, the markets receiving the produce from the gardens and fields of thirty provinces, the banks clinking with universal gold, the factories frantically spewing out smoke and smart new inventions, the libraries bursting with the paperwork of the centuries, the long miles of streets crisscrossed in all directions by telegraph wires and telephone wires, by gas pipes and sewage pipes, the thunderous lines of buses, trams, carriages, velocipedes, rattletraps, and deluxe coach-and-pairs, and the two million members of its seething wave of humanity, panting as they scrabble to earn their daily bread or under the vain illusion of pleasure.

When, in his bedroom in No. 202—its balconies open to the lilac trees in the garden—Jacinto unfurled these images to me, he grew larger and positively glowed. What an august creation the City was! "Only in the City, Zé Fernandes, can Man proudly affirm that he has a soul!"

"But what about religion, Jacinto? Doesn't religion prove the existence of the soul?"

He shrugged. Religion! Religion was merely the over-development of a rudimentary instinct common to all creatures, namely, terror. A dog licking its owner's hand, from which he might receive either a bone or a beating, is basically a devotee in primitive form, prostrated in prayer before the one God who offers him Heaven or Hell! But the telephone! The phonograph!

"Yes, take the phonograph! Even the phonograph, Zé Fernandes, gives me a real sense of my superiority as a thinking being and distinguishes me from the beasts. Believe me, Zé Fernandes, there is only the City and nothing but the City!"

Besides (he added), only the City gave him a sense of human solidarity, as necessary to life as warmth. When, at No. 202, he thought of the huddled masses living in the houses of Paris, two million people sweating and laboring in order to create Civilization (and to maintain the natural dominion of the Jacintos of this world!), he felt a sense of relief and reassurance comparable only to that of the pilgrim who, as he crosses the desert, sits up on his dromedary and sees, ahead of him, the long line of the caravan, bristling with lights and weapons.

Impressed, I murmured:

"Gosh!"

It was so very different in the countryside where the indifference and impassivity of Nature made him tremble for his fragile, solitary state. It was as if he were lost in a world with which he had no fraternal bonds; no bramble bush would draw in its thorns to let him pass; if he were groaning with hunger, no tree, however heavy-laden, would hold out a compassionate branch to offer him its fruit. Besides, surrounded by Nature, he became suddenly and humiliatingly aware of the uselessness of all his superior faculties. In the company of plants and animals, what was the point of being a genius or a saint? The wheat fields do not understand *The Georgics*; and it took God's eager intervention, the overturning of all natural laws, and an outright miracle for the wolf of Gubbio not to devour St. Francis of Assisi, who smiled at the creature and held out his arms and addressed it as "Brother Wolf." In the country, all intellect grows sterile, and there's nothing left but bestiality. In the crass kingdoms of Vegetable and Animal only two functions remain—feeding and breeding. Alone and with nothing to do, surrounded by snouts and roots that never cease to graze and suck, suffocating in the warm breath of universal fecundation, his poor soul shriveled up, became a little crumb of a soul, a tiny guttering spiritual spark on a poor scrap of matter; and in that poor scrap of matter only two instincts stirred, urgent and imperious—the instincts of appetite and procreation. After a week in the country, all that would remain of his noble being would be a stomach and, below, a phallus! And what of the soul? It was swamped by the beast! He needed then to run back to the City and plunge into the purifying waves of Civilization, to wash himself clean of that vegetable crust and emerge re-humanized, re-spiritualized and fully Jacintic!

My friend's elegant metaphors expressed genuine feelings to which I myself was witness and which tickled me immensely on the one trip we made into the countryside together, to the pleasant and friendly forest of Montmorency. Jacinto's encounter with the Natural World had all the makings of a farce! As soon as he left wooden floors and macadamized roads, any surface that his feet touched filled him with distrust and terror. Any stretch of grass, however parched, seemed to ooze some mortal dampness. In each lump of earth, in the shadow cast by each stone, he feared attack by scorpions, snakes, and other creeping, viscous things. In the silence of the woods he heard only the gloomy depopulation of the universe. He could not bear the over-familiarity of the branches that brushed his sleeve or cheek. Scrambling over a hedge seemed to him a degrading act that took him straight back to the very first ape. He was convinced that any flower he had not previously seen in a garden, domesticated by long centuries of ornamental servitude, was sure to be poisonous. And it seemed to him, too, that there was a kind of fickle melancholy about the forms and shapes of certain inanimate things: the futile sprightly haste of streams, the bald rocks, the contorted trunks of trees, and the silly solemn muttering of leaves.

After an hour in that honest Montmorency forest, my poor friend was left terrified and gasping for breath, already experiencing the slow shrinking and vanishing of the soul that would soon reduce him to being a mere beast among other beasts. He only cheered up when we returned to the flagged sidewalks and gaslamps of Paris, where our victoria was almost smashed to pieces by a near-collision with a rumbling omnibus crammed with fellow citizens. He begged to be let out of the carriage when we reached the boulevards, in order to allow their rude sociability to dissipate that sense of having been transformed into gross matter, with a head as heavy and vague as that of an ox. And he demanded that I go with him to the Théâtre des Variétés so as to drive out with a few choruses from the operetta *La Femme à Papa* the importunate memory of the blackbirds singing in the tall poplars.

My delightful friend Jacinto was, at the time, twenty-three years old, and a superb-looking young man in whom the strength of all those past rural Jacintos had re-emerged. The only part of his body that seemed to belong to the more delicate sensibilities of the nineteenth century was his fine, pointed nose with its near-transparent nostrils, which were never still, as if constantly engaged in sniffing out perfumes. His hair, as in more primitive ages, was curly, indeed, almost woolly; and his moustache, like that of a Celt, grew in silky threads which he had to trim and curl. His suits, his thick dark satin ties pinned with a pearl, his white antelope-skin gloves, and the polish for his boots all arrived from London in cedar-wood boxes; and he always wore a flower in his buttonhole, not a real flower, but one skillfully concocted by his florist from the petals of several different flowers—carnations, azaleas, orchids, or tulips—all bound together on one stem, along with a sprig of fennel.

In 1880, one gray, chilly, rainy February morning, I received a letter from my good uncle, Afonso Fernandes, in which, after many complaints about his age—he was seventy—his hemorrhoids, and the heavy responsibility of managing his estate—"which calls for a younger man with stronger legs"—he ordered me back to the family mansion in Guiães in the Douro valley! As I leaned against the cracked marble mantlepiece, where, the night before, my mistress Nini had left her stays wrapped up in a copy of the *Journal des Débats*, I severely censured my uncle for thus nipping in the bud—before it had even opened—the flower of my Juridical Knowledge. In a post-script to his letter, he added: "The weather here is grand, almost perfect you might say, and your dear aunt sends you her very best wishes from the kitchen, because today we are celebrating thirty-six years of marriage, and the parish priest and Quintais are coming for supper, and she wants to make her special golden soup."

Putting a log on the fire, I thought how good Aunt Vicência's golden soup would be. It was years since I had tasted it, or her roast suckling pig, or her rice pudding! And if the weather really was "grand," the mimosa trees in our garden would be bent low beneath the weight of their yellow blooms. Into the room came a patch of blue sky, the blue of Guiães—for there is no softer, more lustrous blue—and traced green grass, brooks, daisies and clover on the threadbare melancholy of the carpet; my eyes swam with tears. From behind my wool curtains there wafted in a fine, bracing air, smelling of mountains and of pine woods.

Whistling the sweet tune of a *fado*, I took my old suitcase from beneath the bed and tenderly placed among my trousers and my socks a treatise on Civil Law in order that I might at last, in idle village moments spent lying beneath the beech tree, learn about the laws that govern men. Later that afternoon, I announced to Jacinto that I was leaving for Guiães. My friend drew back, uttering a soft moan of horror and pity:

"To Guiães! Oh, Zé Fernandes, how awful!"

And all that week, he kept solicitously reminding me of various comforts that I really ought to take with me in order to preserve, in that wilderness so far from the City, at least a little of my soul in a little of my body. "Take an armchair! Take the *General Encyclopaedia*! Take a few boxes of asparagus!"

As far as Jacinto was concerned, being torn from the City made of me an uprooted tree that would never revive. He accompanied me to the train as sorrowfully as if he were attending my funeral. And when he closed the carriage door for me as gravely and finally as if he were closing the iron gate of my tomb, I almost sobbed— out of grief for myself.

I reached Guiães. There were still flowers on the mimosas in the garden; I delightedly drank Aunt Vicência's golden soup; I put on clogs and helped bring in the crop of maize. And what with harvests and work in the fields, getting burned by the sun at threshing-time, hunting for partridge in the frozen scrub, slicing open fresh melons in the dust of village fairs, eating roast chestnuts around open fires, working by lamplight, building bonfires for St. John's night, making creches for Christmas-time, I happily spent seven whole years there, years so busy that I didn't have a moment to open my treatise on Civil Law, and years so uneventful that the only thing I can remember happening is that, on the eve of St. Nicholas, the parish priest fell off his mare. From Jacinto I received the occasional note, written in haste amid the hurly-burly of Civilization. Then, one very warm September, while out picking grapes, my good uncle Afonso Fernandes died as easily— and may God be praised for this grace—as a little bird falls silent at the end of a day spent in full song and full flight. I exhausted the village's stock of mourning clothes. My god-daughter got married at the village's annual killing and roasting of the pig. The roof on our house had to be repaired. And I returned to Paris.

: II :

I T   W A S   A N O T H E R   G R A Y , chilly, late-February afternoon when
I strolled down the Champs-Elysées in search of No. 202. Ahead
of me walked the slightly bowed, hunched figure of a man who
positively exuded elegance and a familiarity with the finer things
of life—from the tips of his gleaming boots to the elegantly curved
brim of his hat, beneath which one caught just a glimpse of rebellious curls. He was strolling along with his white-gloved hands
behind his back and carrying a sturdy walking-stick topped with a
glass knob. And only when he stopped at the door of No. 202 did I
recognize the pointed nose and the long, silky moustache.

"Jacinto!"

"Zé Fernandes!"

We embraced so enthusiastically that my hat fell off into the
mud. And as we went inside, both of us, overcome by emotion,
kept murmuring:

"Seven years!"

"Seven years!"

And yet during those seven years, nothing had changed in the
garden of No. 202! The same two neat, sandy paths bordered the
same circular lawn, as smooth and clean-swept as a carpet. In the

middle of the lawn, a Corinthian vase waited to be filled, first with the tulips that would burst forth in April and then with the marguerites that would flower in June. And beside the steps, shielded by a glass awning, stood the two slender stone goddesses from the days of Jacinto's grandfather, "Dom Galeão," still holding aloft the same opaque-glass lamps in which the gas was already whistling.

Inside, however, in the hall, I was astonished to find that Jacinto had installed a lift, even though No. 202 only had two floors linked by a staircase so undemanding that it hadn't even troubled Senhora Dona Angelina's asthma! The spacious, carpeted lift offered numerous comforts during the seven-second journey: a divan, a bearskin rug, a street map of Paris, and a cabinet containing cigars and books. In the antechamber, where we disembarked, the temperature was as mild and warm as a May afternoon in Guiães. A servant—who paid as close attention to the thermometer as a pilot to the compass needle—was dexterously adjusting the heater's golden vent. And among the palm trees, as on some holy terrace in Benares, censers exhaled a beneficent vapor that perfumed and humidified the delicate, superfine air.

From the depths of my astonished self, I murmured:

"*This* is Civilization!"

Jacinto pushed open a door and we entered a majestic, shadowy temple which I only realized was a library when I bumped into a monstrous pile of new books. My friend brushed his finger lightly against the wall and a circle of electric lights, which glowed against the carved wooden ceiling, lit up the monumental ebony shelves. These were filled by over thirty thousand books—bound in white, scarlet and red, with just a few touches of gold—

as stiff and erect in their pomp and authority as an assembly of learned doctors.

I could not contain my amazement.

"What a storehouse, Jacinto!"

"Well, one has to read . . ."

I noticed then that my friend had grown thinner, and that his nose, flanked by two deep lines, like those on the face of a weary actor, had grown more pointed. The locks of woolly hair tumbling over his brow were now sparser, and his brow itself had lost its look of serene polished marble. He was no longer curling his moustache, which drooped in pensive threads. I realized, too, that he had a slight stoop.

He lifted a tapestry curtain and we passed into his study—a most disturbing room. The somber carpets were so thick that the sound of our footsteps vanished, along, it seemed to me, with reality itself. The damask wall-coverings, the divans, the woodwork, were all green, a dark laurel green. There were green silk shades on the electric lights, which were placed in such low, squat lamps that they looked like stars fallen onto the tables, where they lay cooling and dying: only one shone out, naked and bright, atop a tall, square, slender set of shelves, as solitary as a tower or a melancholy beacon in the middle of a plain. A green lacquer screen, grass-green this time, covered the sea-green marble fireplace, in which the embers of some aromatic wood were slowly burning out. And everywhere, among all these greens, on pedestals and pillars, glinted the most extravagant array of machinery—gadgets, blades, wheels, tubes, gears, spindles, all made of cold, rigid metal.

Jacinto patted the cushions on the sofa, where he plumped himself down with a weariness I had never known in him before.

"Sit down, Zé Fernandes, sit down! After a separation of seven years we have a lot to catch up on! Seven years in Guiães! What on earth did you do there?"

"And what about you, Jacinto, what have you been up to?"

My friend gave a slight shrug. He had lived; he had serenely fulfilled all the necessary functions, both material and spiritual.

"And you've certainly acquired more Civilization, Jacinto! No. 202 is quite extraordinary!"

He glanced around with eyes that no longer sparkled with their old vivacity.

"Yes, it's comfortable enough, but there's still much that's lacking. Humanity is so badly equipped, Zé Fernandes . . . and life, well, life resists."

Suddenly, in one corner, a telephone bell tinkled. And while my friend bent over the mouthpiece, impatiently repeating "Hello? Hello? Are you there?" I proceeded to investigate his vast desk and its strange legion of miniature machines in nickel, steel, copper and iron, all equipped with teeth, blades, rings, hooks and pincers—all highly expressive, but whose uses remained a mystery. When I picked one up and tried to make it work, a malevolent barb immediately pricked my finger. Then, from another corner, came an urgent, almost frantic tick-tick-tick. Jacinto, his mouth still pressed to the phone, said to me:

"It's the telegraph machine . . . next to the divan. There should be a strip of paper coming out of it."

And indeed, on top of a column perched a glass dome containing a lively, diligent machine, busy dribbling onto the carpet a long tapeworm of paper with letters on it, which I, rustic that I was, immediately snatched up in astonishment. The line of blue-printed letters was announcing to my friend Jacinto that the Russian frigate *Azoff* had put in at Marseilles with mechanical problems.

Jacinto had by now given up on the telephone. I asked anxiously if the problems encountered by the *Azoff* affected him directly.

"The *Azoff*? Me? No! It's just a bit of news."

Then, consulting the monumental clock that stood at the far end of the Library and marked the time in all the capitals of the world and the positions of all the planets, he announced:

"I have to write a letter, just six lines or so. You'll wait, won't you, Zé Fernandes? You'll find all the newspapers from Paris, last night's editions, and this morning's papers from London. Oh, and there are some pictures in that leather folder with the metal clips."

I, however, preferred to take an inventory of the study, which, in my profane rustic state, I found as thrilling as an initiation. On either side of Jacinto's chair hung thick speaking tubes, through which he doubtless issued his orders to the staff of No. 202. From the foot of the desk, soft, fat cables snaked over the carpet, scurrying into the shadows like startled cobras. On a bench, and reflected in its varnished surface as if in the water of a well, stood a Writing Machine, and further off a vast Adding Machine, with rows of holes from which protruded stiff, metal numbers, patiently waiting. Then I was drawn back to the strange, lone, four-sided bookshelf I had noticed before, standing as if in the middle of a plain like a tower with a beacon on top. The whole of one side was packed with Dictionaries, the other with Manuals, the third with Guides, among which, as I discovered when I opened it, was a street map of Samarkand. It was a solid tower of information! On other shelves I found other pieces of apparatus, each more incomprehensible than the last: one was made from sheets of gelatine, between which the lines of what might have been a love letter lay limp and fading; another had a fearsome chopping blade suspended above a poor, half-bound book, as if primed and ready to decapitate it; another propped up the gaping mouth of a tube, wide open to the voices of the invisible. Gleaming wires clung to lintels, coiled around architraves, then disappeared up through the ceiling into space. They were all either tapping into universal forces or else transmitting them. Nature was meekly marshalling all its energies in order to serve my friend in his own home!

Jacinto cried out impatiently:

"Oh, these wretched electric pens!"

As he angrily crumpled up the letter he had begun, I escaped, breathless, into the Library. What a storehouse of the products of Reason and the Imagination! There lay more than thirty thousand volumes, all doubtless essential to anyone wishing to be considered a cultivated human being. At the entrance I noticed, in gold on a green spine, the name of Adam Smith. This, then, was clearly the Economists' section. I ventured further in and walked, wondering, past more than twenty-six feet of Political Economy. Then I spotted the Philosophers and their commentators, who filled a whole wall, from the pre-Socratics to the Neo-Pessimists. These shelves were piled high with over two thousand systems of thought, all contradicting each other. You could guess the doctrines from the bindings: Hobbes, near the bottom, was heavy in black leather; Plato, up above, glowed in soft white calf. Further on began the ranks of Universal Histories, but these shelves were obscured by an immense pile of books smelling of fresh ink and paper, like alluvial soil covering a centuries-old river bank. I skirted this hill and headed into the Natural Sciences, wandering, with growing incredulity, from Orography to Paleontology, and from Morphology to Crystallography. This shelf came to an end next to an ample window that once looked out over the Champs-Elysées. I drew back the velvet curtains and behind it discovered another portentous mound of books—treatises on the History of Religions and Religious Exegesis—which climbed mountain-like up to the highest panes, thus blocking out, on bright mornings, the Good Lord's air and light.

Beyond, though, in pale morocco leather, glowed friendlier shelves devoted to the Poets. Like a respite for the spirit grown weary of all that positive knowledge, Jacinto had created a cosy corner, with a divan and a lemonwood table as glossy as the finest enamel and covered with cigars, oriental cigarettes and eighteenth-century snuffboxes. On a smooth wooden box, some-one had left a dish of dried damsons from Japan. I surrendered to the seduction of the cushions, bit into a damson and opened a book; I could hear beside me an odd buzzing sound, like the noise of some insect borne on harmonious wings. I smiled at the thought that they might be bees making honey out of that florile-gium of verses. Then I noticed that this distant, drowsy whisper was coming from that apparently innocent mahogany box. I pushed aside a copy of the *Gazette de France* and discovered, emerging from a hole cut out of the box, a string to which was attached, at the other end, an ivory funnel. Out of curiosity, I held the fun-nel to my trusting ear, which was still attuned to simple, country sounds, and suddenly, a very gentle yet very confident voice—taking advantage of my curiosity in order to invade and take over my mind—whispered slyly: "And so by studying the way in which the diabolical cubes are arranged, I can then calculate the hyper-magical spaces . . ."

I shrieked and leaped to my feet:

"Jacinto, there's a man in here! A man inside the box, talking!"

Accustomed to such prodigies, my friend did not so much as blink an eye.

"Oh that, it's the Conferencephone; it's the same as the Theaterphone, except that it's linked up to the lecture halls at the universities. It's frightfully convenient. What's the man saying, Zé Fernandes?"

Still wild-eyed, I stared at the box.

"I don't know, something about diabolical cubes and magical spaces, all kinds of nonsense . . ."

In the other room, I sensed Jacinto's superior smile.

"That'll be Colonel Dorchas: 'What Positive Metaphysics can teach us about the Fourth Dimension.' Pure conjecture and a total bore! Listen, Zé Fernandes, do you want to have dinner tonight with me and a couple of friends?"

"Certainly not, Jacinto. I'm still wearing the Sunday suit my country tailor made for me!"

And I went back into the study to show my friend the thick flannel jacket and the scarlet-spotted tie that I wore on Sundays in Guiães to visit the House of Our Lord. Jacinto told me that his guests—both of whom were artists—would find such rustic simplicity interesting. Who were these guests? The author of *The Triple Heart*—a transcendently intelligent psychologist with feminist leanings and an experienced teacher of and authority on the Sentimental Sciences—and Vorcan, a painter of myths, who, a year ago now, had managed to tune into the ether and channel the rhapsodic symbolism of the siege of Troy into one vast composition, entitled *Helen the Destroyer*.

I was scratching my beard:

"No, Jacinto, no. I've only just come back from Guiães, from the mountains. I need to re-enter Civilization slowly and cautiously, because if I don't, I'll explode. Electricity, the conferencephone, hypermagical spaces, a feminist psychologist, not to speak of destructive, ethereal symbolism—it's all too much for one evening. I'll come back tomorrow."

Jacinto was slowly folding up his letter, in which he had included, quite openly (as befitted our fraternal friendship) two white violets taken from the flower that adorned his buttonhole.

"Tomorrow, Zé Fernandes, before lunchtime, I want you to take a cab and bring yourself and all your luggage to No. 202, so that you can move into your room here. Staying in a hotel is so awkward and uncomfortable. Here you have the telephone, the theaterphone, books . . ."

I accepted at once without a murmur. And Jacinto put his mouth to one of the many speaking tubes and whispered:

"Cricket!"

The damask-lined wall suddenly and silently split asunder, and out of it emerged his old manservant, Cricket (the same little black boy who had come to Paris with Dom Galeão), and who, I was cheered to see, was in robust health and blacker than ever, looking venerable and resplendent in his stiff cravat and white, gold-buttoned waistcoat. He was equally glad to see me—"Master Fernandes"—again, and when he learned that I was to take up residence in Grandpa Jacinto's room, he positively beamed at me and at his master, pleased to be provided once more with a family to take care of.

"Cricket," Jacinto was saying, "have this letter delivered to Madame d'Oriol. Oh, and telephone the Trèves household and tell them that the spiritualists are only free on Sunday. Oh, and I'll have a shower before dinner, warm, about seventeen degrees. Followed by a friction massage with essence of mallow."

Then, falling dully back onto the divan, he gave a slow gaping yawn.

"Yes, my dear friend, here we are again after seven years, in old Paris . . ."

I, however, stayed where I was at the table, wanting to finish what I had started.

"But Jacinto, what *is* the point of all these machines? One of the wretches even pricked me. They seem almost malevolent. Are they of any real use?"

Jacinto made a vague, languid gesture indicating their sublime utility. "They're essential, my boy, absolutely essential, because they do so simplify one's work. Look . . ." And he listed them one by one. This one was for removing old nibs, this one for paginating manuscripts; that one over there erased emendations. . . . And there were others for sticking down stamps, printing dates, melting sealing wax, binding documents . . .

"But you're right," he went on, "it is a terrible bore. All those springs and pointed ends do inflict the occasional wound. Occasionally I've had to discard a letter because it was covered in bloody fingerprints! A dreadful nuisance!"

Then, seeing my friend glance up again at the vast clock, I thought it best not to keep him from the consolation of that warm shower and mallow friction rub.

"Right, Jacinto. I feel better now that I've seen you again, and I'll be back tomorrow—with my luggage."

"Zé Fernandes, please, wait a moment. First, take a look at the dining room. You might be tempted!"

From the Library, we went into the dining room, which charmed me with its air of cool, calm luxury. The walls were lined with lacquered white wood that had the soft sheen of satin and encircled medallions of damask, the color of ripe crushed strawberries; the sideboards, discreetly carved with flowers and rocaille work, glowed with the same snow-white lacquer; and the ample white chairs, upholstered in strawberry damask, were clearly made for those with slow, delicate, intellectual appetites.

"Bravo, my Prince! This, Jacinto, is the most comprehensive and most restful of dining rooms!"

"Then stay to dinner, man!"

I was already beginning to grow uneasy, for at each place setting there were six forks, each more cunningly designed than the last, and my anxiety only grew when Jacinto revealed that one was for oysters, another for fish, another for meat, another for vegetables, another for fruit and yet another for cheese! However, with a sobriety that Solomon himself would have praised, there were only glasses for just two wines—the Bordeaux rosé in glass pitchers and the Champagne chilling in silver buckets. The whole of one dresser, though, groaned beneath an entirely unnecessary and almost frightening array of bottled waters—oxygenated water, carbonated water, phosphated water, sterilized water, soda water, as well as others in pot-bellied bottles with therapeutic treatises printed on the labels.

"Good heavens, Jacinto! I see you're still a great drinker of water! An 'aquatic' as our Chilean poet and translator of Klop-stock used to call you."

He cast a disconsolate eye over all that glassware with its metal caps and clips.

"No, that's not the reason. It's because the waters of the City are so contaminated; they're positively heaving with microbes; but I have yet to find a really good water that suits me, that satisfies me. So much so that I sometimes go thirsty."

Then I felt curious to know what the psychologist and the symbolist would be eating that night; the menu was written in red ink on slivers of ivory placed beside each setting. It began respectably enough with classic Marennes oysters, then came artichoke and carp roe soup. . . .

"Is that good?"

Jacinto gave a bored shrug:

"Oh, yes . . . not that I ever have any appetite myself . . . well, I haven't for a long time, not for years."

All I could make of the next dish was that it contained chicken and truffles. Afterwards, his gentlemen guests would be savoring a venison fillet marinated in sherry and served with walnut jelly. And for dessert, iced oranges in ether.

"Why in ether, Jacinto?"

My friend hesitated and made a rippling gesture with his fingers as of an aroma being wafted away.

"It's a new thing. Apparently the ether develops and brings out the soul of the fruit."

I bowed my ignorant head and murmured to myself:

"This is true Civilization!"

And as I walked down the Champs-Elysées, bundled up in my overcoat and pondering that symbolic dish, I considered the coarseness and backwardness of Guiães, where, for centuries, in all the orange groves that shaded and perfumed the valley from Roqueirinha to Sandofim, the souls of oranges had remained undiscovered and unused inside their succulent segments! Now, thank God, in the company of a great connoisseur like Jacinto, I would come to understand the true refinement and power of Civilization.

And (as a still better aid to my friendship) I would see that rare thing, a man who had not only conceived an idea of how Life should be, but had actually realized that Idea, and through it and because of it, achieved perfect happiness.

Jacinto truly was the Prince of Great Good Fortune!

: III :

AT No. 202, AT NINE O'CLOCK EACH MORNING, when I
had drunk my hot chocolate and was still in my slippers, I would
go into Jacinto's room. There I would find my friend duly bathed,
shaved and frictioned, wearing a white robe—fashioned from Tibetan goatskin—and seated at his dressing-table (made entirely
of glass for fear of microbes), which was crammed with those
utensils of tortoiseshell, ivory, silver, steel, and mother-of-pearl
so vital to nineteenth-century man if he is to play his part in Civilization's sumptuary harmony and not disgrace it. The brushes in
particular never failed, each morning, to amaze and delight me,
for they came in all shapes and sizes: as large as the wheel on a Sa-
bine chariot; as narrow and curved as a Moor's scimitar; concave,
like a rustic roof tile; pointed, like an ivy leaf; some with hair as
stiff as boar's bristles and others as soft as pigeon down! Like a
master who scorns none of his slaves, Jacinto faithfully used all
of them. And thus, gazing into a mirror framed with silver leaves,
my Prince would spend fourteen minutes brushing his hair with
those other creatures' hair.

Meanwhile, behind the brocaded silk screens from Kyoto,
Cricket and another valet would be manipulating, with skill and

energy, the various implements of the washroom—a miniature version of the Bathroom and its monumental machines, which were No. 202's greatest marvel. Amid all the marble there were just two spouts graded from zero to one hundred degrees; two showers, one gentle and one more vigorous (the latter for washing one's hair); a spring of sterilized water for cleaning one's teeth; a bubbling fountain in which to shave; and then there were discreet buttons which, at the slightest touch, could unleash jets of water, singing cascades or a light summer dew. From this dread place—in which all that violent, boiling water was kept disciplined and enslaved in some alarmingly slender pipes—Jacinto would finally emerge, drying his hands first on a soft towel, then on a linen towel, then on a towel made of plaited cord to stimulate his circulation, and finally on a soft silk towel to burnish his skin. Once this ritual was over, Jacinto, sighing and yawning and recumbent on a divan, would leaf through his diary, in which were listed, in Cricket's hand or his own, the day's duties, often so numerous that they covered two whole pages.

All these duties had to do either with his social life, with his highly complex sense of Civilization, or with the interests nurtured by my Prince over the past seven years in order that he might live in more conscious communion with the City's many functions. (Jacinto was, in fact, president of the Fencing and Shooting Club; a shareholder in the newspaper *Le Boulevard*; a director of the Telephone Company of Constantinople; an associate of the United Bazaars of the Spiritualist Arts; a member of the Committee for Initiation into Esoteric Religions, etc., etc.) It seemed, however, that none of these occupations gave my friend any pleasure at all, for, despite his usually mild, harmonious manner, he would often—in the rebellious gesture of a free man—hurl to the floor the diary that was enslaving him. On one such morning (of wind and snow), when I picked up the oppressive book—bound in kid leather in a tender tone of faded rose—I learned that, after lunch, Jacinto had to make a visit to Rue de l'Université, another to Parc Monceau, and yet another to the remote groves of La Muette; then, as a matter of loyalty, he had to vote in an election at his club, accompany Madame d'Oriol to an exhibition of fans, choose an engagement present for the niece of the Trèves family, attend the funeral of old Count de Malville, and preside at a court of honor over a matter of alleged cheating by some gentlemen playing écarté. Above and in between these entries were further notes scribbled in pencil by Jacinto: Coachman—Five o'clock tea with the Efraims—The girl from the Théâtre des Variétés—Deliver letter to the newspaper. . . . I looked at my Prince. Lying stretched out on the divan, his eyes closed in despair, he was yawning a vast silent yawn.

But Jacinto's obligations began in No. 202 itself, immediately after his bath. From eight o'clock onwards, the telephone bell kept ringing and ringing impatiently, almost angrily, like someone summoning a tardy servant.

Still barely dry from his bath and still wearing his Tibetan goatskin robe or his thick plush old gold pajamas, he was also constantly going out into the corridor to hold whispered conversations with men who were in such a hurry that they did not even have time to put down their sopping umbrellas, which dripped onto the carpet. One of the most frequent visitors (doubtless someone from the Telephone Company of Constantinople) cut a most alarming figure. Gaunt, swarthy, and with bad teeth, he was always carrying the same fat grimy folder under one arm and wore the collar of his mangy fur coat turned right up, so that his small, sinister, predatory eyes seemed to be peering fiercely out from the entrance to his lair. Ceaselessly, inexorably, a valet would come and go, bearing notes on a tray.

Then there were the purveyors of Industry and Art; rubicund horse-dealers in white overcoats; inventors with large rolls of paper; antiquarian booksellers carrying in their pocket "an almost unbelievable find"—a "unique" edition by Ulrich Zell or "Lapidanus." Inside No. 202, a befuddled Jacinto scurried back and forth, scribbling at his desk, making telephone calls, nervously untying packages, eluding, as he came and went, some man waiting in ambush for him and who would emerge out of the darkness of the antechamber brandishing like a blunderbuss a petition or a catalogue!

At midday, a silvery, melancholy gong would sound, calling us to lunch. With *Le Figaro* or *Les Nouveautés* open before me on my plate, I always had to wait at least half an hour before my Prince would come tearing in, consulting his watch and, with a look of exhaustion on his face, give vent to his eternal complaint:

"Yet another dreadful night beset by dreams! I tried sulfural, I summoned Cricket to rub me with turpentine, but nothing worked!"

He surveyed the contents of the table with an already jaded eye. No dish, however rare, tempted him, and since, in his morning tumult, he smoked innumerable cigarettes that dried his throat, he would then start gulping down a great glass of water—oxygenated, carbonated or sparkling—mixed with a very rare, extremely expensive and disgustingly sweet brandy made from Syracuse moscatel. Reluctantly, with the hesitant point of his knife, he would pick disconsolately at a sliver of ham or a morsel of lobster and then call impatiently for coffee—Moka coffee dispatched each month by a man in Dedjah, and made very thick, Turkish style—which he would then stir with a cinnamon stick.

"And what about you, Zé Fernandes, what are you going to do?"

"Me?"

Leaning easily back in my chair, my thumbs hooked in the arm-holes of my waistcoat, I said:

"Oh, I'm just going to mooch around like the idle dog I am."

My solicitous friend, still stirring his coffee with the cinnamon stick, diligently listed the many delightfully civilized things I could do in the City, but each time he mentioned an exhibition, a lecture, a historical monument, a walk, he would immediately give a disconsolate shrug and say:

"No, don't bother, it's probably not worth it!"

He would light another of his Russian cigarettes, which bore his name emblazoned in gold on the cigarette paper. He would stand for a moment at the Library door, nervously twirling the ends of his moustache and listening to what his administrator, the sleek and majestic Laporte had to say; then, followed by a manservant and carrying under his arm a huge bundle of newspapers for the journey, the Prince of Great Good Fortune would get into his coupé and plunge into the City.

On days when Jacinto's social calendar was less packed, and the March sky charitably bestowed on us a scrap of watery blue, we would set off after lunch for a stroll through Paris. These slow, aimless walks had, in our student days, been one of Jacinto's greatest pleasures, because it was while out walking that one could most intensely and most minutely savor the City. Now, however, despite my company, these strolls only irritated and fatigued him, in desolate contrast to the state of glowing ecstasy they had once provoked in him. With some alarm (even with a degree of sorrow, for I am a good man and it always saddens me to see a belief destroyed), I realized, on the first of our afternoon strolls down the Boulevards, that the seething mass of humanity on the pavements and the somber flow of carriages along the streets distressed my friend with the sheer brutality of their haste, their egotism and their noise. Leaning on, nay, clinging to my arm, this new Jacinto began to regret that the streets of Civilization were not surfaced with rubber, for rubber clearly represented to my friend a discreet substance that would dull the coarse rumble and roar of things. Amazing! Jacinto wanting rubber to insulate his sensibility from the workings of the City! He would not even allow me to stand gawping before the same gilded and mirrored shops he had once described as "precious museums of the nineteenth century."

"It's a waste of time, Zé Fernandes. Such poverty of imagination, such a lack of invention! Always the same Louis XV fleurons, the same plush fabrics. It's a waste of time!"

And I would stare wide-eyed at this transformed Jacinto. What shocked me most of all was his horror of the Crowd, of certain effects of the Crowd, which only he noticed and which he called "grooves."

"You won't be aware of them, Zé Fernandes, because you've just come up from the country. But these 'grooves' represent the one real inconvenience of Cities! It could be the strong, brazen perfume some woman gives off as she passes and which lodges in your sense of smell and contaminates the air for the rest of the day. It could be a phrase overheard in a group of friends and which reveals a world of deceit or pedantry or stupidity that remains stuck to your soul, like a spatter of mud, reminding you of the vastness of the swamp yet to be traversed. Or, my friend, it could be an individual whose unbearable pretentiousness or bad taste or impertinence or vulgarity or hardness of heart presents you with a vision of such repellent ugliness that you simply cannot shake it off. These grooves, Zé Fernandes, are quite dreadful, but then again, they are the minor miseries one has to put up with in an otherwise delicious Civilization!"

All this was specious, possibly puerile, but it revealed to me a cooling of that devotee's passionate commitment to the City. That same afternoon, if I remember rightly, we penetrated into the very depths of Paris: the long streets, the miles of houses, all of them the color of brownish rubble and bristling with chimneys clad in black lead, all of them with their windows closed, their skimpy curtains drawn, suffocating and smothering the life within. Nothing but brick, iron, mortar, and plaster, straight lines and sharp corners—barren and rigid. And from ground to rooftop, covering the façades and balconies and devouring the walls, were signs and hoardings and more signs and hoardings.

"Jacinto, this Paris of yours is nothing but a vast vulgar bazaar!"

And more out of a desire to probe my Prince's feelings than out of any real conviction, I indicated the ugliness and sadness of these buildings—harsh warehouses, whose floors were actually shelves crammed with humanity, a humanity pitilessly catalogued and filed away: the better-looking and the more expensive on the freshly varnished bottom shelves, the vulgar and the workaday on the top, in the garrets, on bare pine shelves, with the dust and the silverfish.

Jacinto, a look of horror on his face, murmured: "Yes, it is ugly, very ugly!" Then, waving one buff-colored glove in the air, he immediately added:

"But what a marvelous organism, eh, Zé Fernandes! What solidity! What productivity!"

Where Jacinto had most changed, it seemed to me, was in his once quasi-religious love of the Bois de Boulogne. As a young man, he had constructed large and complicated theories around the Bois and would declare, with the shining eyes of the fanatic, that the City went to the Bois each afternoon in order to reinvigorate itself, receiving from the presence there of Duchesses, Courtesans, Politicians, Financiers, Generals, Academicians, Artists, Club members, and Jews, the consoling certainty that all of its personnel were just as numerous, vital, and active as ever, and that not one contributory element to its grandeur had disappeared or died. "Going to the Bois" became, then, an act of conscience for my Prince. And he would return, proudly asserting that the City still had all its planets, thus guaranteeing the eternal nature of its light!

Now, however, it was only apathetically and reluctantly that he would accompany me to the Bois, where, taking advantage of the mild April weather, I would try vainly to satisfy my longing for large groves of trees. While Jacinto's groomed and glossy horses proceeded at a leisurely trot along the Champs-Elysées and the Avenue du Bois de Boulogne—the latter rejuvenated by the tender grass and the cool green of new shoots—Jacinto, blowing his cigarette smoke out of the open windows of the coupé, remained a good and amiable companion with whom it was pleasant to philosophize as we crossed Paris. However, as soon as we had passed the gilded gates of the Bois and entered the Avenue des Acacias and joined the long line of elegant carriages and cabs, and the decorous silence—broken only by the squeak of brakes and the slow crunch of wheels over sand—my Prince would fall silent and shrink back into the cushioned interior of the coupé, rarely opening his mouth except to give a wide world-weary yawn. Faithful to his old habit of verifying the comforting presence of "the personnel, the planets," he would still occasionally point out another coupé or victoria creaking past us in another slow line and murmur a name to me. Thus I came to know the curly Hebraic beard of the banker Efraim; the long patrician nose of Madame de Trèves which gave shelter to her perennial smile; the flaccid cheeks of the Neoplatonist poet Dornan, who sat, chest puffed out, in some hired fiacre; the long, dark Pre-Raphaelite locks of Madame Verghane; the smoked glass monocle of the editor of *Le Boulevard*; the triumphant little moustache of the Duke de Marizac, enthroned in his war-like phaeton; the various fixed smiles, Renaissance goatees, drooping eyelids, prying eyes, and powdered skin, which all belonged to one or other of my Prince's illustrious friends. When we reached the top of the Avenue des Acacias, we would start back down again, at a restrained trot, crunching slowly over the sand. In the sluggish line of carriages still driving up the avenue, chaise upon landau, victoria upon fiacre, we would inevitably see again the dark monocle of the man from *Le Boulevard*, the fiercely black locks of Madame Verghane, the prominent chest of the Neoplatonist poet, the Talmudic beard, in short, each and every one of those same figures, motionless as waxworks, and all too familiar to my friend Jacinto— figures he had passed and re-passed every afternoon, year after year: always the same smiles, always the same face powder, always the same wax-like immobility. At this point, Jacinto, unable to contain himself any longer, would shout to the coachman:

"Home, and make it quick!"

And the horses—feeling as exasperated as Jacinto by the soporific pace enforced on them in the Bois, with brakes always squealing, and in the company of other mares whom they, too, knew far too well—would positively gallop back down the Avenue du Bois de Boulogne and the Champs-Elysées.

I would occasionally test Jacinto by speaking ill of the Bois:

"It's not as much fun as it used to be. It's lost its glow."

And he would venture timidly:

"No, no, it's very pleasant; what could possibly be more pleasant, it's just that . . ."

And he would blame the cool afternoon breeze or the tyranny of his many obligations. We would return then to No. 202, where, sure enough, Jacinto would soon be wrapped once more in his white robe, and where, seated at the glass dressing-table before his legions of brushes, with all the electric lights on, he would begin to adorn himself for that evening's social duties.

It was on just such a night (a Saturday) that we experienced, in that safest and most civilized of rooms, one of those violent and ferocious terrors that can only be produced by the wildness of the Elements. It was getting late (we were to dine with Marizac at the club before accompanying him to a performance of *Lohengrin* at the Opera) and Jacinto was hurriedly tying his white tie, when, in the washroom, either because a pipe had burst or because a tap had come unsoldered, the hot water suddenly started pouring forth in a furious torrent, smoking and steaming. A dense mist of steam dimmed the lights and, lost in that mist, we could hear, amid the screams of Cricket and the valet, the devastating rush of water beating against the walls, splattering everything with a scalding rain. Beneath our feet, the sodden carpet turned to burning mud. And as if all the forces of Nature, hitherto subordinated to Jacinto's service, were rising up and taking courage from that watery rebellion, we heard dull snarls coming from inside the walls and saw threatening sparks springing from electric cables! I had fled into the corridor where the thick mist was spreading. No. 202 was filled by the tumult of disaster. At the front door, attracted by the clouds of steam escaping from the windows, I found a policeman and a crowd of other people. And on the stairs, I bumped into a reporter—hat pushed back on his head, notebook open—asking urgently if there had been any deaths.

Once the water had been tamed and the mist had cleared, I found a gray-faced Jacinto dressed only in his underwear, standing in the middle of his room.

"Oh, Zé Fernandes, all our hard work! And we're powerless, powerless! This is the second such disaster we've had! And we'd installed new machinery, put in place a whole new system . . ."

"Well, I've been well and truly drenched by your new system! And that was my one and only tailcoat!"

Around us, the fine embroidered silks, the Louis XIII brocatelles—all covered in black stains—were still steaming. My Prince, pale with shock, was wiping dry a photograph of a very décolletée Madame d'Oriol. I was thinking angrily how different things were in Guiães; there the water was heated in nice safe saucepans and brought up to my room by the sturdy Catarina in nice safe jugs! We did not dine with the Duke de Marizac at the club. And at the Opera—pinched and oppressed as I was in the tailcoat lent to me by Jacinto and which cut into my armpits and gave off a befuddling whiff of Flowers of Nessari—I did not enjoy Lohengrin with his white soul, his white swan and his white armor.

Very early next day, Cricket—whose hands, badly scalded on the previous evening, were bandaged in silk—came into my room, drew the curtains, sat down on the edge of the bed and, with his usual radiant smile, announced:

"We're in *Le Figaro*!"

He triumphantly opened the newspaper. So magnificently and so publicly did our waters roar and gush through twelve lines in the society column that I too smiled delightedly.

"And the phone, Senhor Fernandes, hasn't stopped ringing all morning," exclaimed Cricket, his ebony skin aglow. "Everyone wants to know what happened: 'Is he there?' 'Was he scalded?' The whole of Paris is worried sick, Senhor Fernandes!"

The telephone was, indeed, insatiably ringing and ringing. And when I came down to lunch, the table cloth was buried beneath a mound of telegrams, which my Prince was ripping open with a knife, frowning and fulminating against this "unnecessary nuisance." His face only brightened when he read one of these small blue pieces of paper and flung it down on my plate with the same gratified smile that Cricket and I had exchanged that morning.

"It's from the Grand Duke Casimiro, the dear fellow, the poor soul!"

Over my eggs, I savored each word of His Highness' telegram.

What! My Jacinto flooded out! Very chic and in the Champs-Elysées too! The next time I visit No. 202 I'll bring a life buoy! Condolences, Casimiro.

I deferentially echoed Jacinto's words: "The dear man, the poor soul!" Then, slowly turning over the pile of telegrams that extended as far as my glass, I asked:

"By the way, Jacinto, who *is* this Diana who's always writing to you, telephoning you, sending you telegrams, and . . ."

"Diana? Oh, you mean Diana de Lorge. She's a cocotte, *une grande cocotte!*"

"And she's yours?"

"Mine? No, I only have a piece of her."

And when I lamented the fact that even a rich, fine, proud gentleman like my Prince could not afford his own trough, but had to wallow around in the public one, he merely shrugged and speared a prawn with his fork.

"You're from the country, Zé Fernandes, you wouldn't understand, but a city like Paris needs courtesans of great style and luxury, and to set up a cocotte in this ridiculously expensive city of Paris and furnish her with the requisite clothes, diamonds, horses, lackeys, boxes at the theater, parties, house, publicity and insolence, you have to combine several large fortunes and form a syndicate! There are seven of us in the Club. I pay my part, but only out of a sense of civic duty, in order to bestow upon the city a cocotte on the grand scale. Otherwise, I don't wallow at all. Poor Diana! I wouldn't know if, from the shoulders down, her skin was the color of snow or the color of lemons."

I looked at him, amused.

"That's from the shoulders down, but from the shoulders up?"

"Oh, from the shoulders up, she's pure powder! But she really is a terrible pest. Always writing me notes, telephoning and sending telegrams. And she costs me three thousand francs a month, and that's not counting the flowers I have to buy for her. Dreadful!"

And as he bent over his salad, the two lines on either side of my Prince's sharp nose were like two sad valleys at evening.

We had just finished lunch, when the valet, in a discreet murmur, announced Madame d'Oriol. Jacinto calmly put down his cigar, and I almost choked on a hasty sip of coffee. Dressed all in black—the smooth austere black of Holy Week—she appeared through the strawberry damask door curtains, indicating to us prettily with her muff that we must not disturb ourselves on her account. Then, in sweet, voluble, trilling tones, she said:

"I won't stop. Don't get up. I was just passing on my way to La Madeleine, and I couldn't help myself, I simply had to see the damage. A flood in Paris, in the Champs-Elysées! Such a thing could only happen to Jacinto. It even appeared in *Le Figaro*. I was so worried when I telephoned. Imagine! Boiling water, like the lava out of Vesuvius. It's quite thrilling. And then, of course, the ruined fabrics, the carpets. . . . I'm simply dying to have a peek at the scene of devastation!"

Jacinto, who seemed neither touched by nor grateful for her interest, smilingly took up his cigar again.

"Everything is dry now, my dear lady, quite dry. The best part was yesterday, with all that steaming, roaring water. It's just a shame that, at the very least, a wall didn't collapse!"

But she insisted. It wasn't every day in Paris that you could view the aftermath of a flood. *Le Figaro* had described the whole thing. It was a truly delightful escapade—a house in the Champs-Elysées scalded!

Her whole person, from the little feathers that curled about her hat to the shining tips of her patent leather boots, trembled and vibrated like the fragile branch on which a singing bird is perched. Only her smile, through her thick veil, remained bright and still. And from her energy, her elegance, there emanated a scent, a sweetness, that filled the air.

Jacinto, meanwhile, had gaily given in to her request. I could hear Madame d'Oriol, as she proceeded down the corridor, still praising the delightful *Le Figaro* and telling Jacinto how she had trembled for him. I returned to my coffee, mentally congratulating the Prince of Great Good Fortune on that perfect flower of Civilization perfuming his life. Still pondering the refined grace with which that flower moved, I rushed to the mirror in the antechamber to check my hair and the knot in my cravat. Then I withdrew to the dining room and positioned myself by the window, where I stood, languidly leafing through a copy of *The Review of the Century*, in a pose redolent of elegance and high culture. They returned almost at once, and Madame d'Oriol, still smiling, declared that she had been robbed, having found not a trace of those furious waters, and she paused by the table, where Jacinto was about to offer her some Malta tangerines, some glazed chestnuts or a cake dipped in Tokai.

She declined, keeping her hands in her muff. She was neither tall nor strong, but every fold of her dress or curve of her cape formed the most harmonious and undulating of lines, perfection upon perfection. Beneath the dense veil covering her face, I could make out only the whiteness of her powdered skin and the darkness of her large eyes. And everything about her—the black silks and velvets, the lock of fair hair, warm gold in color, that lay tightly curled on the dark furs worn about her neck—breathed delicate refinement. I could not help but think of her as a flower of Civilization and I pondered the centuries of labor and the superior methods of cultivation required for that flower and its perfume to open and unfurl, all the lovelier for being a forced hothouse bloom containing in its petals already just a hint of decadence and decline.

Meanwhile, with her bird-like volubility, twittering brightly first to me and then to Jacinto, she was charmingly astonished when she saw the pile of telegrams on the tablecloth.

"And all these came this morning because of the flood?! Jacinto is clearly the man of the moment, the only man in Paris! Did many *women* send telegrams?"

Languidly, his cigar still smoking, my Prince pushed the Grand Duke's telegram over to her. Madame d'Oriol uttered a grave heartfelt "Ah!" She carefully re-read His Highness' note, caressing the paper with a kind of greedy reverence. Then, still grave-faced, still serious, she said:

"Brilliant!"

Indeed, everything about that disaster had passed off quite brilliantly and in grand Parisian style. The delicious creature, though, could not stop a moment longer. She had reserved a place at La Madeleine for the sermon!

Jacinto innocently exclaimed:

"For the sermon! Is it the season for sermons already?"

Madame d'Oriol made a grimace of tenderly amused scandal and pain. Had even he failed to notice that it was Lent? Not that she was surprised—Jacinto was little better than a Turk! And she began praising the preacher, a Dominican friar, Père Granon! He was so eloquent, so intense! In his last sermon, he had preached about love and the fragility of earthly love. And he had said such inspiring, such brutally true things! And the gestures he made, raising one hand as if to deliver a crushing blow, and the way his sleeve fell back to reveal a superb bare arm, so white and so strong!

Behind the veil, her smile shone palely beneath her dark eyes. And Jacinto, with a laugh, said:

"A fine arm for a father confessor! Ready to give those souls a good thrashing!"

She, however, exclaimed:

"No, no! Père Granon, alas, does not take confession!"

And suddenly she changed her mind and accepted a cake and a glass of Tokai. She needed a little something to fortify herself against Père Granon's powerful emotions! Jacinto and I both rushed to help, one grabbing the bottle, the other offering her the plate of cakes. She rolled her veil up as far as her eyes and hurriedly nibbled the cake, having first dipped it in her glass of Tokai. And when Jacinto, happening to notice the hat she was wearing, bent over it, curious and intrigued, Madame d'Oriol's smile vanished, and she adopted a suitably grave expression for such a serious subject.

"It's very elegant, don't you think? An entirely new creation by Madame Vialo. A combination of the somber and the seductive—now that we're in Lent."

She included me in her gaze, inviting me, too, to admire her hat. I approached with my mountain-man's snout to contemplate this supremely glamorous Lenten creation. And it really was a marvel! Delicately poised on the velvet, nestling amid the somber curled feathers and lace and fixed in placed by a hat pin, was a Crown of Thorns made entirely of jet!

We were both entranced. Then with a gesture and a smile that seemed to exude yet more perfume and brilliance, Madame d'Oriol hurried off to La Madeleine.

My Prince paced thoughtfully and slowly up and down the carpet. Then, suddenly, straightening his back with a look of immense determination, as if he were shrugging off a whole world, he said:

"Zé Fernandes, let's spend this Sunday doing something simple and natural."

"What, for example?"

Jacinto looked about him, wide-eyed, as if anxiously scouring Universal Life for one natural, simple thing. Finally, he turned those same wide eyes on me, eyes that seemed to be returning, weary and rather hopeless, from some far distant place.

"Let's go to the Jardin des Plantes and see the giraffe!"

: IV :

ONE NIGHT DURING THAT SAME FECUND WEEK, we were on our way back from the Opera when Jacinto announced with a yawn that there was to be a party at No. 202.

"A party?"

"In honor of the Grand Duke, poor soul. He's going to send me a very rare and delicious fish which is only ever caught off the coast of Dalmatia. I'd have preferred a brief lunch myself, but the Grand Duke demanded a supper. He's a barbarian at heart, steeped in the literature of the eighteenth century, a man who still believes in suppers—in Paris! So this Sunday, just to amuse him, I've invited a few ladies and ten or so typically Parisian gentlemen. You should come too. It will be like leafing through a list of the great and the good of Paris society. But it really is the most frightful bore!"

Since Jacinto was not himself looking forward to the party, he took few pains to make it a brilliant success. He merely ordered a gypsy orchestra (in those far-off days, Parisians were still excited by the sight of gypsies in their short scarlet jackets and by the harshly melancholic strains of the czardas, the Hungarian national dance), and, in his desire to cater for all tastes from the tragic to the picaresque, he arranged to have the Theaterphone in the Library linked up to the Opéra, the Comédie Française, the Alcazar, and the Théâtre des Bouffes Parisiens. Later, on Sunday evening, we inspected the supper table, resplendent with Dom Galeão's old dinner service. And the lavish profusion of orchids—for upon the silk-embroidered cloth whole forests of them had been arranged around the Saxe fruit bowls made of cut glass and filigree of gold—gave off such a refined sense of luxury and good taste that I found myself murmuring: "God bless money!" For the first time, too, I visited the abundantly and minutely equipped pantry, and admired, in particular, the two lifts that traveled up from the depths of the kitchen, one for fish and meat—heated by hot water pipes—and the other for salads and ices—lined with refrigerating panels. Ah, No. 202!

At nine o'clock, however, on my way down to Jacinto's study to write a letter to my Aunt Vicência, while Jacinto remained at his dressing-table where the manicurist was engaged in polishing his nails, we experienced yet another fright in that delightful palace festively decked out with flowers! All the electric lights, throughout the whole of No. 202, suddenly went out! In my immense distrust of these universal forces, I immediately raced for the door, stumbling in the darkness and bleating a "Help! Help!" that positively reeked of rustic Guiães. Up above, Jacinto, still in his pajamas, was calling out too, while the manicurist clung fearfully to him. Then the lights slowly flickered on again, like a laggardly servant who appears only when summoned, dragging his slippers. Nevertheless, my ashen-faced Prince, who had come downstairs by then, gave orders to send for an engineer from the Central Company for Domestic Electricity, and, just in case, another servant was dispatched to the grocery store to buy a few packets of candles, while Cricket disinterred from the cupboards the abandoned candelabra and heavy, archaic candlesticks from the unscientific days of Dom Galeão. These were the sturdy veteran reserve troops to be used in the awful eventuality that later, over supper, the inexperienced forces of Civilization should again treacherously fail. The electrician, who arrived out of breath, assured us, however, that the Electricity would stand firm and throw no further tantrums. Ever cautious, I slipped two candle stubs into my pocket.

The Electricity did, indeed, stand firm and tantrum-free. And when I came down from my room (late, because I had lost my dress waistcoat, which I found, after a furious search and much cursing, fallen behind the bed!), the whole of No. 202 was aglow, and the gypsies in the antechamber—tossing their hair and furiously bowing their violins—were playing a waltz so irresistible that the larger-than-life characters in the tapestries on the walls—Priam, Nestor and sly Ulysses—were all lifting their venerable feet in time to the music and panting!

Tugging nervously at my shirt cuffs, I crept timidly, noiselessly into Jacinto's study. I was greeted at once by the perennial smile of the Countess de Trèves, who, in company with the illustrious historian Danjon (of the Académie Française), was marveling at my super-civilized Prince's sumptuous collection of machines and instruments. Never had the Countess seemed to me more majestic than in those saffron silks, her décolletage edged with lace, her curly, reddish hair caught back over her magisterial brow, and her curved patrician nose sheltering that ever-glittering smile, just as the arch of a bridge shelters the flow and shimmer of a stream.

Erect as a throne and with her long tortoiseshell lorgnette held to her small, dull blue eyes, she stood first before the Graphophone and then before the Microphone, listening as if to some superior melody as Jacinto, with pained politeness, gave a garbled explanation of their workings. And each wheel, each spring elicited from her cries of wonder and finely turned compliments, as, with a mixture of shrewdness and candor, she attributed all these scientific inventions to Jacinto himself. The mysterious implements crowding his ebony desk were for her like a stirring rite of initiation. A paginating machine! A sticker-on of stamps! The metals grew warm beneath the gentle caress of her dry fingers. And she begged Jacinto for the addresses of the manufacturers so that she herself could purchase these adorably useful items! For thus equipped, one's life would be so much easier! But it was, of course, necessary to have Jacinto's taste and talent in order to choose and to "create!" Nor did she offer the honey of flattery only to Jacinto (who received it with resignation). Caressing the Telegraph machine with the handle of her lorgnette, she praised Danjon's eloquence. As we stood by the Phonograph, she even managed to flatter me (whose name she did not even know) by saying how sweet it was to be able to record and collect the voices of one's friends—a plump and luscious compliment which I sucked on as if it were a piece of celestial candy. Like a good farmer's wife, she threw grain to all the hungry chickens, maternally feeding other people's vanity as she went. Eager for more candy, I followed the whispering saffron train of her dress. She paused next to the Adding Machine, and Jacinto patiently provided her with an erudite description of its uses. She again ran her fingers over the holes concealing the black numbers, and with the same rapturous smile murmured: "It really is quite remarkable, this electric printing press of yours!"

Jacinto spluttered:

"But it's a—"

Still smiling, Madame de Trèves had, however, already moved on. She had failed to understand the function of each of my Prince's machines! She had not listened to a single one of his explanations! In that room filled with sumptuous machinery, her sole concern had been to exercise, with profit and perfection, the Art of Pleasing Others. Everything about her was sublimely false. I confessed my astonishment to Danjon.

The eloquent academician rolled his eyes:

"Oh, she has such taste, such intelligence, such allure! Besides, one dines so well at her house! What coffee! She is, dear sir, a truly superior woman!"

I sidled away into the Library. At the entrance to that temple of erudition, a few gentlemen stood talking next to the shelf housing the Fathers of the Church. I stopped to greet the editor of *Le Boulevard* and the feminist psychologist, author of *The Triple Heart*, whom I had met the day before over lunch at No. 202. The latter greeted me paternally and, as if he urgently required my presence there, greedily clasped my large, coarse, country paw in his illustrious, glitteringly beringed hand. Everyone there, in fact, was celebrating his novel, *The Cuirass*, which had been launched that week to little yelps of pleasure and an excited rustle and flurry of skirts. An overcoat, with a vast head of hair—which resembled a wig coiffed à la Van Dyck—was standing on tiptoe and proclaiming that the scalpel of experimental psychology had never before penetrated so deeply into that ancient thing, the human soul! And everyone agreed and pressed closer to the psychologist and addressed him as "Maître." I had never so much as glimpsed the book's yellow cover, but finding myself the object of those imploring eyes, hungry for more honey, I murmured sibilantly:

"Yes, absolutely delicious!"

And the psychologist, face aglow, lips moist, neck pinched by a high collar around which coiled an 1830s-style cravat, modestly confessed that he had dissected the souls who appeared in *The Cuirass* with "some care," basing himself on documentary evidence, on scraps of still-warm, still-bleeding life. And it was then that Marizac, the Duke de Marizac, his hands in his pockets, remarked, with a smile sharper than the glint on the blade of a straight razor:

"And yet, my friend, in this carefully researched book there is one mistake, a very strange, very curious mistake."

The psychologist threw back his head and squeaked:

"A mistake?"

Yes, a mistake. And a most unexpected one in a man of the Maître's great experience. The mistake consisted in attributing to *The Cuirass*'s splendid heroine—a Duchess with exquisite taste—*a black satin corset*! This black satin corset made its appearance in an otherwise fine and passionately perceptive passage in which she was getting undressed in Ruy D'Alize's bedroom. And Marizac, still with his hands in his pocket, but looking serious now, appealed to the other gentlemen. Was it likely that an aesthetic, Pre-Raphaelite woman like the Duchess, who bought her clothes from such intellectual couturiers as Doucet and Paquin, would wear a black satin corset?

The psychologist was struck dumb, caught out, wounded! Marizac was the supreme authority on the underwear of duchesses, and he knew that when spending the afternoon in a young man's bedroom, a duchess would—for purely idealistic reasons and in keeping with the dictates of her yearning soul—always wear a white corset and a white petticoat. The editor of *Le Boulevard* then weighed in pitilessly, declaring confidently that only an uneducated grocer's wife would ever think that the combination of plump flesh and black satin could possibly be attractive. And in order that they would not think me inexperienced in such expensive, ducal adulteries, I smoothed my hair and said:

"Black, of course, would only be suitable if the woman happened to be in deep mourning!"

The poor author of *The Cuirass* accepted defeat. His reputation as an authority on Female Elegance lay in tatters, and the whole of Paris would now assume that he had never seen a duchess unfastening her corset in his psychologist's boudoir! Moistening his lips grown dry with fear, he acknowledged his mistake and contritely attributed it to a moment of unthinking improvisation.

"It does indeed strike a completely false note. How could it possibly have escaped my notice, I mean a black corset, it really is absurd! At the very most—as a reflection of the duchess' state of mind—it could have been lilac or possibly the very palest of yellows, with just a touch of old Malines lace. I can't understand how I could have made such a blunder! I have my notebook of interviews, all carefully annotated and documented!"

In his distress, he ended up begging Marizac to broadcast his confession everywhere, at the club and in all the salons. It had been purely and simply an artistic lapse, for true artists, of course, are always working at such a fever pitch of inspiration, lost in the black depths of the souls they are probing! He hadn't even noticed the corset or its color. Arms outstretched, he declared to the editor of *Le Boulevard*:

"I am ready, dear friend, to give an interview and to make a full and frank declaration to my public! Send me one of your reporters. Tomorrow at ten o'clock! Yes, we will hold an interview and decide there and then what should be the correct color—which, naturally, should be lilac. Yes, send me one of your men, dear friend! It would also give me an opportunity to list, out loud, the many services *Le Boulevard* has done for the psychological sciences and for feminism!"

With his back pressed against the spines of the Holy Fathers on the shelves, he continued in this supplicant vein. I hurried off to the far end of the Library, where Jacinto was engaged in a heated discussion with two men.

They were Madame de Trèves' "two men"—her husband the Count de Trèves, a descendant of the kings of Candia, and her lover, the formidable Jewish banker, David Efraim. And so earnestly were they arguing with my Prince that they failed even to recognize me, both offering me a vague, limp handshake and addressing me as "dear Count"! As I rummaged around on the lemonwood table for a box of cigars, I realized at once that they were talking about the Burma Emerald Company, a forbidding enterprise that glittered with potential millions and to which these two confederates of bourse and bed had been trying, since the beginning of the year, to recruit Jacinto's name, influence, and money. Bored with business and distrustful of those emeralds buried in some obscure valley in Asia, Jacinto had so far resisted. The Count de Trèves, a very tall, thin man with a gaunt, bristly, sparsely-bearded face and a domed yellow head like a melon, was bent on assuring my poor Prince that, as the current prospectus made clear in setting out the sheer scope of the endeavor, it would outshine the *Thousand and One Nights*. More important still, any truly cultivated mind would see in the excavation of those emeralds a powerful civilizing force. It would bring a whole stream of Western ideas flowing into Burma and thereby educate the country. He himself had taken on the directorship of the company for purely patriotic reasons.

"Besides, a business involving gems, art, and progress should only be carried out by the very cream of society, among friends."

And on Jacinto's other side, the formidable Efraim smoothed his beautiful beard—a beard curlier and blacker than that of any Assyrian king—with one small, plump hand and declared that, given the powerful forces backing it—Nagaiers, Bolsans, Saccart— the success of the enterprise was guaranteed.

Jacinto, weakening, wrinkled his nose.

"You have, I presume, at least carried out the necessary studies? It has been shown that there are emeralds to be found?"

Efraim found such naivety exasperating.

"Emeralds? Of course there are emeralds! Wherever there are shareholders to be had there are emeralds!"

And I was still admiring the boldness of this maxim when one of No. 202's regular visitors arrived, out of breath and unfurling a highly perfumed handkerchief. This was Todelle—Antoine de Todelle—a young man prematurely bald, but a man of many talents, for he could lead a quadrille, imitate the singers at the café-concerts, concoct unusual salad dressings, and tell you all the latest Paris gossip.

"Is he here? Has the Grand Duke arrived yet?"

No, His Highness had not arrived. And where was Madame de Todelle?

"She can't come . . . can't leave the sofa . . . grazed her leg."

"Oh, dear!"

"Oh, it's nothing really. She fell off her velocipede!"

Jacinto was immediately all ears.

"Madame de Todelle rides a velocipede?!"

"Well, she's learning to. She doesn't actually own one herself, but during Lent, she's been practicing on one belonging to Father Ernesto, the priest at St. Joseph's. However, yesterday, in the Bois, crash, over she went! Grazed her leg. Just here."

And with his finger he indicated on his own leg the exact location of the graze. Efraim said rather coarsely, but very seriously: "The best place, dammit!" But Todelle did not even hear him, for he was already scuttling over to the editor of *Le Boulevard*, who was approaching, slow and paunchy, wearing his black monocle like an eyepatch. The two men met and stood pressed against a bookshelf, whispering earnestly.

Jacinto and I went into the billiard room, whose walls were lined with old Cordoban leather and where smoking was allowed. The great Dornan—that Neoplatonist poet and mystic and subtle master of all the meters—was sitting slumped among the cushions on a divan, one foot resting on his fat thigh, like an Indian god, two buttons of his waistcoat undone, and his pendulous double chin concealing his collar, as he puffed majestically on a vast cigar. Seated near him was an old man I had never seen before at No. 202, a slender figure, with white ringlets pushed back behind his ears; his face was heavily powdered, and he sported a small, very

black, very curled moustache; he had clearly just finished telling some salty anecdote, for Joban, that theater critic supreme,
was standing beside him, roaring with laughter, his bald head
scarlet with pleasure, and a red-haired young man (a descendant of Coligny), with a profile like a parakeet, was flapping his
short arms about like wings and squawking: "Delicious! Divine!"
Only the idealistic poet, in his plump majesty, remained utterly
impassive. However, as we approached, that same master of the
meter, having first blown out a great cloud of smoke and greeted
me with a slow lifting of his eyelids, began in a rich, metallic-
sounding voice:

"Oh I know a better story than that, infinitely better. You all
know Madame Noredal, don't you? Well, Madame Noredal has the
most enormous buttocks . . ."

Alas, Todelle rushed into the room at that moment, loudly calling for Jacinto. The ladies wanted to hear an aria by Patti on the
Phonograph! My friend shrugged and said irritably:

"An aria by Patti . . . oh, I don't know. The rolls are all in a mess.
Besides, the Phonograph doesn't work very well. No, what am I
saying? It doesn't work at all. I've got three of them and not one
of them works."

"Not to worry!" exclaimed Todelle gaily. "I'll sing 'Pauvre fille'
instead. It's better suited to a supper party anyway. Oh, la pauv',
pauv', pauv' . . ."

And with that, he linked arms with me and dragged me and my
rustic shyness into the faded pink salon, where, like goddesses
in one of Olympus' choicest circles, Madame d'Oriol, Madame
Verghane, and the Princess de Carman were waiting, resplendent, along with another very fair-haired woman, who wore large

diamonds in her long hair, and had such bare shoulders, such bare arms, and such a bare bosom that her white dress edged with pale gold seemed more like a chemise about to slip off. Impressed, I grabbed Todelle and growled softly: "Who's that?" But the jolly man had already scurried over to join Madame d'Oriol, with whom the Duke de Marizac—with easy, superior familiarity—was enjoying a joke, along with a young man whose soft downy beard was the color of maize, and who was rocking back and forth on his heels, like an ear of wheat in the wind. I was left stranded by the piano, slowly rubbing my hands, trying to quell my embarrassment; then Madame Verghane got up from the sofa where she had been talking to an old man (who wore the Grand-Croix de St. André pinned to his chest) and advanced, nay, glided toward me across the carpet, a small, brilliant figure, dragging behind her the long dark-green velvet train of her dress. So tiny was her waist, between the fecund roundness of her hips and the vastness of her bare, mother-of-pearl bosom, that I feared she might break in two as she slowly swayed toward me. Her famous, furiously black hair, parted in the middle and combed smoothly down on either side, entirely covered her ears; and on a large gold circlet glittered a diamond-studded star, as if on the brow of a Botticelli angel. Doubtless knowing my position of authority in No. 202, she threw me a smile—like a beneficent bolt of lightning—that made her liquid eyes still more liquid. She murmured:

"The Grand Duke *is* still coming, isn't he?"

"Of course, Madame, he's coming for the fish."

"For the fish?"

And at precisely that moment, the Rákóczy March burst forth

in the antechamber with a triumphant roll on the drum and much furious scraping on the violins. It was he! In the Library, our majordomo boomed out:

"His Highness, the Grand Duke Casimiro!"

Madame de Verghane uttered a brief, excited sigh and pushed out her chest, as if to provide the Grand Duke with a better view of her marble magnificence. And the editor of *Le Boulevard*, the old fellow wearing the Grand-Croix, and Efraim, almost pushed me out of the way as they charged the door in their eagerness to see the Royal Personage.

The Grand Duke entered, preceded by Jacinto. He cut an imposing figure, slightly balding and with a neat, pointed, graying beard. For a moment, he hesitated, rocking slowly back and forth on his small feet, which were shod in flat shoes almost entirely concealed by his very wide trousers. Then, leisurely and smiling, he went over to shake hands with the ladies who had sunk into their velvets and silks as they performed a low curtsey. Then, clapping Jacinto jovially on the shoulder, he asked:

"And how's that fish coming along? You did use the recipe I sent you, didn't you?"

Jacinto murmured a reassuring reply.

"Just as well, just as well!" exclaimed the Grand Duke in his loud commanding voice. "Because I've had no dinner you know, not a crumb! Well, one eats so badly at Chez Joseph! I don't know why anyone bothers to dine there at all? Whenever I come to Paris, I ask: 'Where's the best place to dine now?' And everyone tells me: 'Chez Joseph.' Nonsense! Today, for example, they were serving snipe! Absolutely foul! They haven't the faintest notion how to cook snipe!"

His rather murky blue eyes glinted and grew wide with indignation.

"Paris is losing all its finest qualities. One can't dine well anywhere in Paris nowadays!"

Around him, the other guests all glumly nodded their agreement. The Count de Trèves defended Le Bignon, where they still kept up the noble traditions. And the editor of *Le Boulevard*, leaning toward His Highness, attributed the decadent state of cooking in France to the Republic, to the crude democratic taste for cheapness.

"At Paillard's you can still . . ." began Efraim.

"At Paillard's!" thundered the Grand Duke. "But the Burgundy there is appalling, simply appalling!"

He let his arms hang limp and dejected by his side. Then he carefully smoothed the lapels of his tailcoat and, with the slow rolling gait of an old sea captain, went over to greet Madame d'Oriol, every part of whom seemed to glitter: her smile, her eyes, her jewels, each fold of her salmon-pink silk dress. However, no sooner had the pale, soft creature begun to chatter, fluttering her fan like a bright bird's wing, than His Highness noticed the Theaterphone positioned among some flowers on a table, and he summoned Jacinto:

"In communication with the Alcazar by any chance? A Theaterphone, is it?"

"It certainly is, sir."

Excellent! Perfect! He had regretted having had to miss Gilberte singing that new song "*Les Casquettes*." Half past eleven! That was just the time she was due to sing it in the final act of *La Revue Électrique*! He clamped the two "receivers" from the Theaterphone to his ears and stood there, engrossed, an earnest frown on his stern face. Suddenly, he issued a command:

"It's her! Shh! Come and listen. It's her! Everyone, come over here! Princess, you too! All of you! It's her! Shh!"

Then, since Jacinto had been so prodigal as to install *two* Theaterphones, each equipped with twelve lines, all the ladies and gentlemen present hurriedly pressed a receiver to one ear and stood, motionless, enjoying "*Les Casquettes*." The faded pink salon and the Library filled with an august silence, and I alone remained disconnected and instead stood idly by, my hands in my pockets.

On the monumental clock, which marked the time in all the capitals of the world and the positions of all the planets, the delicate hands fell asleep. Like some icy, melancholy sun, the Electricity blazed down on the silence and on the pensive immobility of all those backs and all those décolletages. From each attentive ear, cupped by a hand, hung a black wire, like a piece of intestine. Dornan, slumped across the table, had closed his eyes, like a fat monk at his meditations. The historian of the Dukes d'Anjou was gravely performing his palace duty, delicately holding the "receiver" between the tips of his fingers and holding his sad, sharp nose aloft. Madame d'Oriol was smiling languidly as if the wire were murmuring sweet-nothings in her ear. To stir myself, I risked taking one timid step, but was immediately halted by a fierce "Shh!" from the Grand Duke. I withdrew behind the curtains to hide my idleness. The psychologist and author of *The Cuirass* was standing some way from the table, the long wire drawn taut, and he was biting his lip in the sheer effort of concentration. Reclining in a vast armchair, His Highness was in seventh heaven. Beside him, Madame Verghane's bosom rose and fell like a milky wave. And my poor Jacinto, ever conscientious, was bent over the Theaterphone as sadly as if it were a tomb.

Confronted by this vision of superior, civilized beings devoutly and silently drinking in the obscenities Gilberte was bleating down the line at them from beneath the soil of Paris, through wires buried in the gutters, close by the sewers, I thought about my sleeping village. The same crescent moon accompanied by one tiny star that was racing through the clouds over the rooftops and the black chimneys of the Champs-Elysées would also be racing over the pine woods there, but shedding a softer, brighter light. Far off in the deeps of the Dona, the frogs would be croaking. Up on the hill, the little church of São Joaquim would be glowing white, bare and innocent.

One of the women muttered:

"That's not Gilberte!"

And one of the men said:

"That's a cornet, isn't it?"

"Now they're applauding."

"No, it's Paulin!"

The Grand Duke uttered another ferocious "Shh!" In the court-yard of my house in Guiães, the dogs were barking. From beyond the river, João Saranda's dogs answered. Now I was walking down a narrow lane, beneath the trees, with my staff on my shoulder. And there among the silk curtains, I sensed in the fine, soft air the smell of pine logs crackling in hearths, the warmth from the sheep-pens that penetrated even the high surrounding hedges, and the sleepy whisper of the streams.

I awoke to a shout that came neither from the sheep-pens nor from the shadows. It was the Grand Duke who had leaped to his feet with a furious shrug of the shoulders.

"I can't hear a thing! Nothing but squeaks and buzzes! What a bore! But what a song, eh?

> "*Oh les casquettes,*
> "*Oh les casqu-e-e-ttes!*"

Everyone lay down their wires, proclaiming Gilberte to be simply divine. And the good majordomo, opening wide the two leaves of the door, announced:

"*Monseigneur est servi!*"

At the table, whose splendid orchids drew loud praise from His Highness, I sat between the ethereal poet Dornan and the young man with the blond fuzz of beard, the one who swayed like an ear of wheat in the wind. After unfolding his napkin and arranging it on his ample lap, Dornan disentangled a large lorgnette from his watch chain in order to study the menu, which met with his full approval. He leaned toward me with his fat apostle's face and muttered:

"If this is Jacinto's 1834 port, it must be authentic, don't you think?"

I assured the Master of the Meters that the port had indeed been aged in Dom Galeão's cellars. By way of preparation, the poet carefully brushed aside the long, thick hairs of the moustache that covered his large mouth. A cold consommé with truffles was served. And the corn-colored young man, looking up and down the table with his gentle, blue eyes, murmured, half-regretful, half-amused:

"What a shame! All that's lacking are a general and a bishop!"

And he was right! The Ruling Classes were all there, eating Jacinto's truffles. Opposite us, Madame d'Oriol gave a laugh as melodious as bird-song. The Grand Duke had noticed among the forest of orchids surrounding his plate one particularly sinister and ugly one, resembling a green scorpion with lustrous wings, fat and tumescent with venom; very delicately he handed this monstrous flower to Madame d'Oriol, who, warbling with laughter, solemnly placed it in her décolletage. Next to that soft flesh—like fine cream—the "scorpion" had grown still greener and its wings trembled. All eyes lit up, fixed on that lovely bosom, to which the misshapen, poisonous-looking flower only gave an added piquancy. Madame d'Oriol glowed, triumphant. The better to accommodate the flower, she adjusted the neckline of her dress, thus revealing further beauties and showing the way to all those male eyes, which, aflame with curiosity, were slowly undressing her. Jacinto's frowning face stared down at his empty plate. And the lyric poet of *Mystic Twilight* stroked his beard and snarled scornfully:

"She's a beautiful woman right enough; scrawny hips, though, and no bottom at all, I bet!"

Meanwhile, the young man with the downy beard had returned to his theme. It was such a shame not to have a general with his sword there and a bishop with his crosier!

"But for what purpose, sir?"

The young man made a delicate gesture that made all his rings sparkle.

"Why, for a dynamite bomb. Here we have a splendid bouquet of the flowers of Civilization, including a Grand Duke. Imagine the effect if someone lobbed a bomb through the door! What a fine end to a *fin-de-siècle* supper!"

And when I merely stared at him in amazement, he, taking sips of his Chateau d'Yquem, declared that the one genuine, truly refined pleasure would be to destroy Civilization. Neither science nor the arts, neither love nor money could bring such real, intense pleasure to our satiated souls. Any pleasure that could be had from *creating* had long since been exhausted. Now all that remained was the divine pleasure of *destroying*!

He uttered several more such enormities, his pale eyes twinkling. However, I was no longer listening to this genteel pedant, for something else was troubling me. I noticed that suddenly, all around me, as in the tale of the Petrified Palace, all service had ceased. The next dish should have been the famous fish from Dalmatia, His Highness's fish, the inspiration for the party! Jacinto was nervously crushing a flower between his fingers. And every one of the servants had vanished!

Fortunately, the Grand Duke was busy regaling the table with a story about a hunting party on a game reserve in Sarvan, during which a lady, the wife of a banker, had suddenly leaped from her horse when they reached a clearing. He and all the other hunters had stopped, and the gallant lady, ashen-faced, had caught up her riding habit and disappeared behind a rock . . . However, we never found out what the banker's wife was doing in that clearing, crouched behind a rock, because, just then, the majordomo appeared, his face glistening with sweat, and whispered something to Jacinto, who bit his lip in horror. The Grand Duke fell silent. Everyone looked at each other in bright expectation. Then my Prince, patiently, heroically, forcing a pale smile, said:

"My friends, something most unfortunate has occurred—"

Dornan leaped up from his chair:

"Is there a fire?"

No, there was no fire. The dumb waiter had unexpectedly gone wrong and got stuck halfway, with His Highness' fish inside!

The Grand Duke flung down his napkin. His politeness cracked like badly applied enamel.

"This is too much! I had the devil's own job getting hold of that fish! That, after all, is why we've come here for supper. How ridiculous! Why didn't they just bring it up by hand? Stuck halfway? Honestly! Let me see. Where's the pantry?"

And he stumped angrily off toward the pantry, led by the stumbling majordomo, who was cowed by the Grand Duke's terrifying rage. Jacinto followed, like a shadow, carried along in His Highness' wake. Unable to restrain my curiosity, I went with them down to the pantry to witness the disaster, while Dornan kept slapping his thigh and demanding that we finish our supper without the fish.

The Grand Duke was already there, peering into the black well of the lift and holding a candle that made his flushed face seem still redder. I looked over his royal shoulder. Down below, in the darkness, on a large platter, surrounded by slices of lemon, lay the precious fish, white and gleaming, the steam still rising from it. Jacinto, looking as white as his own tie, was desperately fiddling with the lift's complicated springs. Then it was the Grand Duke's turn, and with his hairy hands, he gave the cables a tremendous shaking. In vain. The machine was stuck fast, as inert as eternal bronze.

There was a rustle of silk at the pantry door. It was Madame d'Oriol and behind her Madame Verghane, eyes flashing, curious to know what was happening to this fish about which the Grand Duke clearly cared so passionately. Our friend Marizac appeared too, smiling and proposing that a ladder be lowered into the shaft. Then the psychologist joined us and duly psychologized, attributing wise motives to that stubborn fish. And in response to each of them, the scarlet-faced Grand Duke pointed, with one tragic finger, at his fish lying in the bottom of that black hole! They all peered over and muttered: "Yes, there it is!" Todelle, in his haste, almost tumbled in. Coligny's parakeet descendant flapped his wings, squawking: "Doesn't it smell delicious!" In the crowded pantry, the ladies' décolletages rubbed up against the lackeys' uniforms. The heavily powdered older man accidentally put his foot in a bucket of ice and uttered a feral yelp! And above them all, the historian of the Dukes d'Anjou moved his sad, pointed nose back and forth.

Suddenly, Todelle had an idea:

"It's perfectly simple! We must fish for the fish!"

The Grand Duke gave his thigh a triumphal slap. Of course! They must fish for the fish! And he so enjoyed this comical suggestion, so unusual and so novel, that his anger vanished, and he became once more the amiable nobleman, magnificently polite, asking the ladies to take a seat in order to watch this miraculous bit of fishing! He himself would be the fisherman! All that was required for this diverting exploit was a walking-stick, a piece of thread and a hook. Madame d'Oriol excitedly offered one of her hairpins. Everyone crowded around her, conscious of her perfume and the warmth of her skin, and praised such sweet dedication. And the psychologist proclaimed that never had such a divine hook been used for fishing!

When two astonished servants returned bearing a walking-stick and some string, the Grand Duke, radiant now, bent the hairpin to form a hook. Jacinto, still pale, held a lamp over the darkness of the deep shaft. And the more serious gentlemen—the historian, the editor of *Le Boulevard*, the Count de Trèves, the man with the Van Dyck hairstyle—stood in the doorway, showing a reverent interest in His Highness' little fancy. Madame de Trèves, meanwhile, was serenely examining the contents of the pantry. Only Dornan had not risen from the table. With his clenched fists resting on the cloth and his fat neck bowed, he looked as sullen and bored as a caged beast whose lump of meat has just been snatched away.

Meanwhile, His Highness continued his fervent fishing! To no avail. The rather blunt hook, dancing about on the end of the thin soft thread, failed to catch hold.

"Jacinto, lift that light up higher!" he cried, his face puffy and perspiring. "Higher! Now! Yes! It has to catch the gill, that's the only place the hook can get some purchase. Yes! Oh, no, dammit! It won't work!"

He looked up from the shaft, breathless and weary. It was impossible. What they needed was a crew of carpenters with crowbars! And we all urged him anxiously to abandon the fish.

The Grand Duke, smiling and rubbing his hands, agreed that it had, in the end, turned out to be more fun fishing for the fish than eating it! And the elegant group returned eagerly to the table, to the sound of a Strauss waltz, which the gypsies attacked with languid ardor. Only Madame de Trèves hung back in order to tell my poor Jacinto how much she admired his pantry. It was perfect! What an acute understanding of life it revealed, what a keen appreciation of comfort!

His Highness, the Grand Duke, who was feeling rather hot after his efforts, energetically downed two glasses of Chateau-Lagrange. Everyone declared him a fisherman of genius. And the valets served the "Baron de Pauillac"—a lamb dish from the Bordeaux region, the preparation of which involved almost sacred rituals, and which had been given this grand, sonorous name and thus elevated to the nobility of France.

I ate with the appetite of a Homeric hero. The Champagne, like water flowing from a winter fountain, sparkled and spurted unceasingly into my glass and into Dornan's. When they served the *ortolans géles*, which melted in the mouth, the divine poet, to my delight, murmured his sublime sonnet to Santa Clara. And since, on my other side, the young man with the fair, downy beard was still insisting on the destruction of the old world, I agreed with him as well, and together, sipping Champagne so cold it had almost coagulated into a sorbet, we cursed Civilization, the Century, and all the proud inventions of Science! Peering across through the flowers and the lights, I was also keeping a close eye on the breathless billowing of Madame Verghane's vast bosom as she laughed like a bacchante. I didn't even feel sorry for Jacinto who, with the meekness of St. Jacinthus with his head on the executioner's block, was longing for an end to his torment and to his party.

The party did finally end. I can still remember, at three o'clock in the morning, the Grand Duke standing in the antechamber— red-faced and unsteady on his small feet, unable to get his arms in the sleeves of the fur coat despite help from Jacinto and myself—and effusively inviting my friend to go hunting one day on his estates in Dalmatia.

"I owe my friend Jacinto a fine fishing trip, and I want him to owe me an equally fine shooting party!"

And as we accompanied him to the door, past the ranks of servants, down the vast staircase, preceded by the majordomo bearing a three-branched candlestick, His Highness kept repeating over and over:

"Oh yes, we'll put on a fine shooting party for you . . . and Zé Fernandes must come too! Good old Zé Fernandes! An excellent supper, Jacinto! The 'Baron de Pauillac' was divine! I reckon we should promote him to Duke. Yes, Duke de Pauillac! Another slice from the Duke de Pauillac's leg, if you please. No, no, don't come out! You'll catch cold!"

And from the coupé, as it set off, he was still shouting:

"Don't forget to rescue that fish, Jacinto! It'll be excellent for lunch, served cold with a green sauce!"

Climbing wearily back up the steps, drowsy with Champagne and sleep, my eyes drooping, I said softly to my Prince:

"Oh, that was fun, Jacinto! And what a gorgeous woman that Madame Verghane is! Shame about the dumb waiter . . ."

And Jacinto, in a dull voice that was half-yawn, half-roar, replied:

"A disaster! A complete fiasco!"

Three days after the party at No. 202, my Prince unexpectedly received some important news from Portugal. A devastating storm of wind, lightning and rain had struck his house and estate in Tormes and, indeed, the whole area. With the heavy rain, "or for some other reason that the experts have yet to reveal" (in the words of his evidently distraught administrator, Silvério), a section of the hillside that overhung the Vale da Carriça had collapsed, dragging with it the old church—a little rustic chapel built in the sixteenth century, and in which Jacinto's male forebears had had their final resting-place ever since the days of King Manuel. The venerable bones of all those Jacintos now lay interred beneath a shapeless mound of earth and rock. Silvério had already set to work with the young men on the estate to uncover the "precious remains." He was, however, anxiously awaiting orders from Jacinto.

Jacinto turned pale with shock. The sudden collapse of that ancient mountain soil, which had stood firm and steady since the Goths! Those peaceful tombs thunderously hurled, in the midst of storm and darkness, into the dark depths of the valley! Those bones, the remnants of individuals each of whom had once had a name, a date and a history, now lying jumbled together like so much rubble!

"How strange! How very strange!"

And all that evening, he kept asking me about the mountains and about Tormes, which I had known as a child, because the mansion, with its noble avenue of ancient beech trees, was only two leagues from our house, on the old road from Guiães to the station and to the river. The caretaker at Tormes, kindly Melchior, was the brother-in-law of our administrator at Roqueirinha, and, given my friendship with Jacinto, I had often entered that robust granite mansion to admire the grain piled up in its echoing rooms and to taste the new wine in its vast cellars.

"And what about the church, Zé Fernandes? Did you ever go into the church?"

"No, never, but it was very picturesque, with a squat, square, black tower, where a family of storks have lived for many years. It will be a terrible upheaval for them too!"

"How strange!" my Prince was murmuring, still filled with foreboding.

And he sent a telegram to Silvério telling him to clear away the rubble, collect together the bones, rebuild the church, and to spend on this work of piety and reverence whatever was necessary, as if money were as boundless as the waters of a great river.

: V :

MEANWHILE, JACINTO, DRIVEN TO despair by so many
humiliating disasters—taps coming unsoldered, dumbwait-
ers getting stuck, steam condensing and electricity vanishing—valiantly decided to overcome the final resistance put up
by Matter and Force with some still newer and more powerful
Machines. And in the weeks of April, while the roses were coming into bloom, our agitated household—unlike the other houses
in the Champs-Elysées lazing peacefully in the sunshine—was
ceaselessly trembling and ringing to the brutal sound of pick-
axe on stone and the clink of hammer on metal and permanently
swathed in dust from brick and rubble. The silent corridors,
where I used to enjoy a pensive cigarette before lunch, were
now crowded, from dawn onwards, with gangs of workmen in
white smocks, whistling *"Le Petit Bleu"* and making me feel
rather intimidated in my nightshirt and slippers on the way to
the bathroom or to other such places of retreat. No sooner had
I skilfully negotiated the scaffolding blocking the doors than
I would trip over a pile of planks, a basket of tools, or a huge
bucket of mortar. And the bits of flooring taken up revealed
the sad sight, laid bare like a dissected corpse, of No. 202's

innards—its bone structure, its sensitive wire nerves, its black cast-iron intestines.

Each day a slow cart would draw up outside the front door, and shirt-sleeved workmen would unload wooden crates and canvas bundles, which they would pry open or unstitch in an asphalt-floored shed erected at the bottom of the garden behind the lilacs. And every so often I would be summoned by my Prince to admire some new machine that would make our lives easier and confirm our dominion over Substance. With the arrival of the hot weather, which grew hotter after Ascension Day, we hoped to be able to cool our mineral water, soda water and light Medoc wines in one of the three "freezers" that had accumulated in the pantry, but, one after the other, all three let us down. With the new season's straw-berries came a clever little hulling-machine. Then we received another prodigious tool, all silver and glass, for frenetically toss-ing salads, but the first time I tried it, all the vinegar spurted out, temporarily blinding my Prince, who retreated howling. He did not give up though. Jacinto now relied on Dynamics to make even the most elementary of actions easier or faster. He even used a machine to button up his underwear.

And simultaneously, whether as a way of keeping faith with his idea, or because he was ruled by the despotism of habit, he con-tinued, ceaselessly, along with the machines he had already ac-cumulated, to accumulate erudition. The number of books that continued to invade No. 202! Singly, in pairs, in packages, in boxes, slender and fat and all replete with knowledge, wrapped in plebeian yellow wrappers or bound in morocco leather and gold, they flowed, perpetually and torrentially, through the wide doors and into the Library, where they lounged on the carpet, lolled on the soft chairs, lorded it over sturdy tables and, above all, scrambled up windows in greedy piles, as if suffocated by their own multitudes and reaching anxiously for space and air! This erudite space, where only a few of the higher windowpanes remained clear and unobstructed by books, was filled by a thick, perennial, pensive Autumn twilight while outside June blazed. The Library had, by then, overflowed into all the other parts of No. 202! You couldn't open a cupboard anywhere without a pile of books tumbling out on top of you. You couldn't draw aside a curtain without uncovering a hefty mound of books! And I was extremely indignant when, one morning, running urgently to the water-closet and already loosening my braces, I found the door blocked by a vast collection of books on Social Studies!

However, I recall even more bitterly the historic night when I returned tired and weary from a trip to Versailles, my eyelids dusty and heavy with sleep, and, cursing roundly, found myself obliged to remove from my own bed a terrifying Dictionary of Industry in thirty-seven volumes! At that point, I felt well and truly satiated with books. I punched the pillows and rained down curses on both the printing press and human loquacity. And just as I was luxuriously stretching out and drifting off to sleep, I almost broke my precious kneecap on the spine of a volume that had craftily made its nest between the wall and the bedcovers. Letting out a furious bellow, I grabbed the offending tome and flung it across the room, and, in doing so, upset a vase and spilled water all over an expensive rug from Dagestan. And I'm not even sure that I did manage to sleep afterward, because my feet, which made no sound, not even a murmur—as if I were being carried along by a gentle breeze—kept stumbling over books as I made my way down the dark corridor and walked along the sandy garden paths white in the moonlight, then along the Champs-Elysées, which was as crowded and noisy as if for some civic celebration. And, O miracle, the houses on either side were made out of books. And all the men and the elegant ladies were wearing printed paper, with titles on their backs, and their faces were not faces, but open books whose pages were turned by the softest of breezes. At the far end, in Place de la Concorde, I spotted a steep mountain of books, which I attempted to scale, panting hard, now sinking deep into flaccid layers of verse, now stubbing my toe on the pebble-hard spines of volumes of exegesis and criticism. So high did I climb, beyond the Earth, beyond the clouds, that, to my amazement, I found myself among the stars. There they were rolling serenely by, huge and silent, thickly encrusted with books, whence emerged, here and there, through a crack between two volumes that did not quite meet, a tiny ray of smothered, much-needed light. Thus I ascended into Paradise. And it clearly was Paradise because with my eyes of mortal clay I saw the Ancient of Days who knows neither morn nor night. Bathed in the light that he himself gave off—the brightest of all possible lights—surrounded by high, golden shelves crammed with codices, the All-High sat reading, perched upon the most antique of folios, the threads of his infinite beard spreading out over reams of pamphlets, brochures, gazettes and catalogues. The super-divine brow that had conceived the World was resting on the super-strong hand that had created the World, and the Creator was reading and smiling. Shivering with sacred horror, I dared to peer over his gloriously coruscating shoulder. The book was bound in paper and must have cost, at most, three francs. The Eternal One was reading a cheap edition of Voltaire and *smiling*! A door glimmered and creaked open, as if someone were entering Paradise. I thought it must be some saint newly arrived from Earth, but it was Jacinto, smoking a cigar, wearing a posy of carnations in his buttonhole and carrying under his arm three racy novels lent to him by the Princess de Carman!

During one of these busy weeks, however, my attention was suddenly drawn away from the fascinating Jacinto. As a guest at No. 202, I kept my luggage and my clothes at No. 202 and, encamped beneath the banner of my Prince, I still occasionally ate from his sumptuous board. But my soul, my brutish soul, and my body, my brutish body, now inhabited No. 16 Rue du Helder, fourth floor, first door on the left.

I'd been walking along Boulevard de la Madeleine one afternoon, feeling utterly at peace as regards ideas and sensations, when I spotted, standing outside the omnibus station and prowling the asphalt with slow, feline step, a rather skinny woman, so dark as to be almost swarthy; she had sad, deep, taciturn eyes and, beneath an old hat adorned with black feathers, a tangle of curly, yellowish, rebellious hair. I stopped, as if seized by a sudden griping in my intestines. The creature passed by with her prowling step, like a scrawny black cat on the eaves of a roof on a moonlit January night. Two deep wells could not have gleamed more darkly or more taciturnly than her dark, taciturn eyes. I cannot remember (God be praised!) how I came to brush against her silk dress, the folds of which were shiny with grease, nor how I managed to mutter a plea from between grinding teeth, nor how we both ended up in a warm, drab room above Café Durand, having ascended the stairs more slowly and more silently than condemned prisoners. Once in the room, the creature stood in front of the mirror and, as painstakingly as if she were performing some sad ritual, took off her hat and her beaded cape. The threadbare silk of her bodice was torn where her sharp elbows poked through. And her vast hair, as coarse and thick as a lion's mane, was in two tones of yellow, one more golden, the other more parched, like the crust of a pie hot from the oven.

With a tremulous smile, I grasped her long, cold fingers:

"So what's your name?"

And she in a serious, almost grave voice replied:

"Madame Colombe, 16 Rue du Helder, fourth floor, first door on the left."

And I (wretched Zé Fernandes) felt equally serious, filled by a grave emotion, as if, in that upstairs room in a café, we were enfolded by the majesty of a sacrament. The door opened softly and a shiny-faced waiter came in. I ordered lobster, duck cooked with sweet peppers, and Burgundy wine. And only when we had finished off the duck did I get to my feet, nervously crumpling my napkin, and tremblingly, tremulously kiss her on the mouth—a deep and terrible kiss that mingled saliva and the taste of sweet peppers! Then, in an open carriage, beneath the soft breath of a stormy, easterly wind, we drove up the Avenue des Champs-Elysées. Outside the gates of No. 202, I said quietly, hoping to astonish her with my wealth: "This is where I live!" And when, in order to get a proper look at the mansion, she bent forward and brushed her golden hair against my beard, I yelled desperately to the coachman to gallop straight to 16 Rue du Helder, fourth floor, first door on the left!

I loved that woman. I truly loved her—with all the Loves that exist in Love—Divine Love, Human Love, Bestial Love, as St. Anthony loved the Virgin, as Romeo loved Juliet, as a billy-goat loves a nanny-goat. She was stupid and sad. I deliciously quenched my joy in the ashes of her sadness and with ineffable pleasure plunged my reason into the depths of her stupidity. For seven furious weeks, I lost all consciousness of myself as Zé Fernandes—Fernandes de Noronha e Sande from Guiães! One moment I imagined myself to be a piece of wax melting with vile voluptuousness in a roaring, scarlet furnace, at another, I was a hungry bonfire on which a bundle of dry twigs flamed and crackled and was consumed. Of those sublimely sordid days I retain only a vague impression of a bedroom lined with grubby cretonnes, a lilac woolen dressing gown with black braiding, the vague shapes of beer bottles on the marble washstand, a swarthy body that creaked and had hair on its nipples. I also retain the sense I had of incessantly and delightedly plundering my own self, of throwing into a lap that lay between a flaccid belly and a pair of bony knees, my watch with its chain and trinkets, my rings, my sapphire cuff-links, and the one hundred and ninety-seven gold *libras* I had brought with me from Guiães in a chamois leather money-belt. All that remained of that once solid, well-provided Zé Fernandes was a carcass wandering through a dream, loose-limbed and drooling.

Then, one afternoon, I bounded with my usual eagerness up the stairs in Rue du Helder, only to find the door locked and the card bearing the name *Madame Colombe* gone, the card which I always read so devotedly and which was the equivalent of her signboard. My whole being trembled as if the ground of Paris itself were shaking! The door of the World had been slammed shut in my face. Beyond it lay people, cities, life, God and Her, and there was I all alone on the landing of not-being, outside that locked door, the only creature excluded from the World! I stumbled down the stairs with all the incoherent clatter of a stone, and went into the small room occupied by the concierge and her man, who were playing cards in blissful idleness, as if that terrible earthquake had not dismantled the whole Universe!

"Madame Colombe?"

The bearded old gossip slowly picked up her hand of cards:

"She doesn't live 'ere any more. She buggered off this morning to some other town with some other slut!"

To some other town! With some other slut! Empty, black, and empty of all thought, of all feeling, of all desire, I bobbed and drifted like an empty barrel on the rushing current of the Boulevard, until I finally ran aground on a bench in Place de la Madeleine, where I covered my face so as not to feel the fever, and covered my eyes so as not to show my tears. Late, very late, when the shops were noisily closing their iron shutters, there emerged from among the confused ruins of my being, the one eternal survivor of all ruins— the idea of dinner. I went into the Café Durand, clumsily dragging my feet like one brought back from the dead. And even though the memory of that first supper seared my soul, I ordered lobster, duck and Burgundy wine! When I loosened my collar, drenched with sweat from the heat of that July afternoon spent in the dust of Place de la Madeleine, I thought disconsolately: "Great God, but it's given me a thirst, this misfortune!" And I furtively signaled to the waiter: "Before the Burgundy, bring me a bottle of Champagne with plenty of ice and a large glass!" That Champagne had, I believe, been bottled in Heaven where the cool fountain of Consolation perennially flows, and a good long draught from that ineffable font had clearly been added to it before the cork was put in. Ah, what transcendent pleasure I drew from that noble glass, frosted, icy, foaming, sparkling and glinting like gold! Followed by a bottle of Burgundy! Followed by a bottle of brandy! Followed by a little iced mint tea! Followed by an ardent desire to give that slut who had run off with another slut a sound beating with my sturdy Guiães walking-stick made from quince wood. Inside the cab that carried me off at a gallop to No. 202, I did nothing to suppress that holy impulse, and with my rustic fists I loudly thumped the pillows, where I could *see*, I could actually *see* the great thicket of yellow hair in which my soul had got lost one afternoon and in which it had been thrashing about for a whole three months and by which it had been forever soiled. When the cab drew up outside No. 202, I was still beating the ungrateful creature so hard that, summoned by the coachman's shouting, two young men rushed to assist him and hold me down, receiving on their shoulders and their servile necks the weary remnants of my wrath.

Upstairs, I rejected all attempts at solicitude on the part of Cricket, who was trying to impose on Master Zé Fernandes, on Zé Fernandes of Guiães, the immense indignity of a cup of camomile tea! Lying on Dom Galeão's bed, with my boots on the pillow, my top hat over my eyes, I laughed a painful laugh at this burlesque, sordid world of Jacintos and Colombes! Then suddenly I felt a terrible pang of fear. It was Her! It was Madame Colombe who had sprung from the candle flame and leaped onto my bed and unbuttoned my waistcoat and wrenched open my ribcage, and plunged bodily, her and her filthy skirts, inside my chest, where she had fastened her lips on my heart and was slowly sucking out my heart's blood, as she had in Rue du Helder! Convinced that I was dying and calling out for Aunt Vicência, I hung over the edge of the bed, ready to dive into my tomb, which, through the final mist, I could just make out on the carpet—small and round and shiny, made of porcelain and with a handle. And leaning thus over my tomb, which bore an unseemly resemblance to my own chamber pot, I vomited up the Burgundy and the duck and the lobster. Finally, in a superhuman effort, with a roar, feeling as if I were emptying out not only my intestines, but my entire soul, I vomited up Madame Colombe! I fell back on Dom Galeão's bed. I put my hat over my eyes again so as not to see the sun's rays. It was a new sun, a spiritual sun, that was rising over my life. And I fell asleep, like a little baby gently rocked in a wicker cradle by his Guardian Angel.

In the morning, I washed my skin clean in a long bath, perfumed with all the aromas of No. 202, from Indian lemon verbena to essence of French jasmine, and I washed my soul clean with a long letter from my Aunt Vicência that had just arrived, and in which she, in her large hand, told me all about our house, and how promising the vines were this year, and about the lovely bonfire they had built in the courtyard on St. John's night, and about the very chubby little baby with very thick hair which, as if heaven-sent, had been born to my god-daughter. Then, with soul and body cleansed, I donned a white silk jacket and sat by the window, drinking tea from Nai Po and breathing in the scents from the roses in the garden refreshed by the dawn rain; and with a sense of amused wonder, I realized that for seven long weeks I had been demeaning myself in Rue du Helder with a very thin, very swarthy hussy of a woman. I concluded that I had been suffering from a form of intermittent fever, a fever of the flesh, a fever of the imagination, picked up from some Paris puddle, from one of those puddles that form all over the City, full of the stagnant water, slime, rubbish, mold, and worms of a putrefying Civilization.

Then, fully restored, my whole spirit, like a needle pointing north, immediately turned its attentions to my complicated Prince, who, in the glimpses I had caught of him during the final weeks of my sentimental infection, had always been slumped on sofas or wandering through the Library among his thirty thousand volumes, yawning long yawns of inertia and vacuity. In my unworthy haste, I had merely thrown him a distracted "What's wrong?" And he, in his slow state of despair, had replied with a muttered: "It's the heat!"

And on the morning of my liberation, when I went into his room before lunch, I found him sitting there, with *Le Figaro* open on his belly, his diary abandoned on the carpet, his whole face in shadow, and his feet, in a pose of sovereign sadness, given over to the pedicurist who was buffing his nails. My Prince was doubtless impressed by the clear, bright light in my eyes and the whiteness of my flannels, both of which reflected the serenity of my feelings, as well as the utter harmony in which my whole being visibly moved. And raising himself up limply on one limp arm, he asked with an acuteness never dulled even by melancholy:

"So what's happened to that wild caprice of yours?"

I unleashed on him the full blaze of my victorious smile.

"Dead! Like the Duke of Marlborough—dead and buried! May she rest in peace or, rather, roll in peace; in fact, she's probably rolling about in some sewer even as we speak!"

Jacinto yawned and muttered:

"Ah, Zé Fernandes de Noronha e Sande!"

And my name, my worthy name spoken with such indifference and such irony and enfolded in a yawn, was the sum total of my

Prince's interest in the grubby storm in which my heart had been caught up! Not that I was offended by such consummate egotism. I could see that Jacinto was walking through a dense fog of tedium, so dense-and he so deep inside that formless fog—that the glories or torments of a friend could not move him, as if they were too remote, too intangible, and separated from his own sensibility by great layers of cotton wool. Ah, my poor Prince of Great Good Fortune lying inert on the sofa, his feet in the pedicurist's lap! Into what muddy tedium had he fallen after so valiantly renewing No. 202's erudite and mechanical contents in his battle against Force and Matter? And once we had resumed our usual communion of life and soul from which I had so foolishly torn myself one afternoon outside the omnibus station, in the puddle that was the Place de la Madeleine, he made no attempt to conceal from his old friend Zé Fernandes that great sense of tedium.

He never openly confessed his feelings to me. Jacinto, elegant and reserved, did not wring his hands and moan: "Oh accursed life!" It was more the look of satiety on his face; a gesture angrily dismissing the importunate nature of things; the way in which he would sometimes sit immobile, as if in protest, on a divan from which he would not stir, as if he wished those moments of repose to be eternal; then there were the yawns, the gaping yawns with which he underlined each thing he did, and yet which, out of weakness or out of an unavoidable sense of duty, he continued to do; and, above all, it was the murmured comments that had become continual and natural in him: "Oh, what's the point?" "It's not worth it." "What a bore!"

One night in my room, as I was taking off my boots, I consulted Cricket:

"Jacinto is so depressed, so low in spirits. What do think is wrong, Cricket?"

The venerable servant declared with absolute certainty:

"What my master is suffering from is surfeit."

Of course, surfeit! My Prince was being smothered by the surfeit of Paris; and in the City, the symbolic City, outside of whose strong, cultivated life (as he, face aglow, once used to say) nineteenth-century man could never fully enjoy the "pleasure of living," he could now no longer find a way of life—spiritual or social—that interested him, that would make it worth his while setting off on even the shortest of carriage rides! Poor Jacinto! An old, worn and faded newspaper, read and re-read seventy times from the society page to the advertisements, could not have bored the solitary man—who, in his solitude, had only that one source of intellectual food—more than Paris and Parisianism bored my dear friend! If, during that summer, I craftily lured him to a *café-concert* or to the jolly Pavillon d'Armenonville, my dear Jacinto, would plump himself down heavily in his chair—a marvelous spray of orchids in his buttonhole, his slender hands resting dully on the handle of his walking stick—and sit there all night, with the same weary air of gravity, until I took pity and liberated him, enjoying his eagerness to escape, like that of a caged bird suddenly set free. Only rarely (and with the kind of vehement determination required by someone about to jump a ditch) did he venture out to one of his clubs at the far end of the Champs-Elysées. He no longer participated in any of his many societies and companies, not the Telephone Company of Constantinople, not the Society of Esoteric Religions, not even the Spiritualist Bazaar, whose unopened letters lay in a pile on the ebony table until Cricket finally swept them sadly up like the detritus left behind by a life that was over. He slowly detached himself from all his social engagements. The pages of his faded pink diary remained blank and unfilled, and when he did submit to a trip by mail-coach or to an invitation to some friendly chateau on the outskirts of Paris, he did so with such lethargy and reluctance that he always reminded me of a man who—stomach bursting after a vast provincial dinner—still, out of politeness and obedience to social dogma, forces himself to eat a large slice of very sweet cake!

It would have been a great solace to my Prince simply to recline at home, safe behind closed doors, protected from all worldly intrusions, if his very own No. 202, stuffed to the gills with Civilization, had not filled him with a painful sense of being smothered, choked! July was scalding hot, and he found the brocades and rugs, the plump, soft furniture, the metal machinery and the books so oppressive that he was always flinging open windows to get more space, more light, more fresh air. But then, of course, warm gusts of dirty, acrid dust would come rolling in, and he would exclaim angrily:

"Oh, the amount of dust in this city!"

"Then why don't we go to Fontainebleau or Montmorency or . . ."

"What? Go to the country? The country!"

And after this howl of outrage, a look of such indignation would flicker across his frowning face that I would humbly bow my head, regretting having so outrageously affronted my beloved Prince. Poor unhappy Prince! Holding his golden Yaka cigar, he would slowly, dejectedly wander the rooms, like someone walking through a strange land where he knows neither affections nor occupations. His disaffected, unoccupied steps brought him monotonously back to his center, to the green study, to the ebony Library, where he had accumulated the maximum amount of Civilization in order to enjoy, to the maximum, the joy of living. He would look around him with jaded eye. No twinge of curiosity or interest tempted his hands which he kept buried in the pockets of his silk trousers in an attitude of defeat and inertia. Rendered thus null and void, he would give a dispirited yawn. There was nothing sadder or more instructive than to see this supremely nineteenth-century man—surrounded by all kinds of apparatus intended to aid and strengthen his bodily organs, and by all those wires and cables intended to bend to his service the Universal Forces, and by those thirty thousand volumes replete with the knowledge of the centuries—standing stock still, hands plunged dejectedly in his pockets, expressing in the look on his face and in the indolent indecision of a yawn the difficulty and discomfort of living!

: VI :

Every afternoon at four o'clock—keeping up one of those intimate relationships that still manage to hold our interest when nothing else does—Jacinto visited Madame d'Oriol with devout regularity, for even after the Grand Prix race had been run, that flower of Parisianism had remained in Paris, languishing in the heat and dust of the City. On one such afternoon, however, the telephone rang urgently to advise Jacinto that his sweet friend was dining with the Trèves at Enghien-les-Bains. (The couple spent their summers by the lake there, in a house that belonged to the banker Efraim, a white house covered in white roses.)

It was a soft, silent, misty Sunday, conducive to the voluptuous pleasures of melancholy. And I (in the interests of my soul) suggested to Jacinto that we go up to see the Basilica of Sacré Coeur that was then in the process of being built on the heights of Montmartre.

"Oh, it's such a bore, Zé Fernandes."

"Damnation, Jacinto, I've never seen the Basilica."

"All right, all right, you *homme fatale*, we'll visit the Basilica!"

And finally, once we had begun to penetrate, beyond St. Vincent de Paul, into an area of steep, narrow streets filled with a provincial quiet—small country gardens surrounded by old stone walls; women, their hair still uncombed, sitting sewing at their doors; carts standing unhitched outside taverns; chickens pecking at the rubbish; nappies drying on canes—my bored friend smiled at such freedom and simplicity.

The victoria stopped by the street of broad steps that cuts across narrow rural lanes and climbs up to the esplanade where, swathed in scaffolding, the vast Basilica rises up. At the top of each flight of steps there were stalls lined with red cloth and devoted to the sale of images, scapulars, crucifixes, silk-embroidered hearts of Jesus, and bright bundles of rosaries. Old ladies crouched at street corners, mumbling their Hail Marys. Two priests were coming down the steps, laughing and enjoying a pinch of snuff. A slow bell was tolling in the gray sweetness of the afternoon. Jacinto sighed and said contentedly:

"Hm, most curious!"

But the Basilica itself proved of no interest to us, barricaded as it was by planks and scaffolding, its new stark white stone still lacking any soul. Jacinto, in a very Jacintian impulse, strode eagerly over to the edge of the terrace and gazed down on Paris. The City lay all in gray on the gray plain, beneath the gray sky, like a vast, thick layer of rubble and roof tiles, and in all that mute immobility the only visible sign of its magnificent life was an occasional curl of smoke, thinner and more tenuous than smoke from the dying embers of a fire.

I smilingly teased my Prince. There was the City, Humanity's august creation! There it was, Jacinto! On Earth's gray crust—a layer of even grayer rubble! And yet when, only moments before, we had left, it had been prodigiously alive, full of strong people, with all its powerful organs working, stuffed with wealth, resplendent with knowledge, in the triumphal plenitude of its pride, like the Queen of the World crowned with Grace. And there were we, having climbed a hill, handsome Jacinto and I, peering down, straining eyes and ears, and yet not a murmur, not a flicker reached us of the City's strident, radiant Civilization. And what of No. 202, splendid No. 202, with its wires, its apparatus, its magnificent Machinery, its thirty thousand books? Vanished, lost in that confusion of roof tiles and ashes! Is it for this easily obliterated human creation, when seen from three hundred feet up, that the human worker so painfully labors and struggles? Is it, Jacinto? Where are the shops served by three thousand cashiers? And the banks clinking with universal gold? And the libraries crammed with the knowledge of the centuries? Everything had dissolved into a brown stain sullying the Earth. To the feeble eyes of a Zé Fernandes—smoking a cigarette and strolling up one of the City's remoter hills—the sublime edifices of the Ages seemed nothing more than a silent dunghill, of the same texture and color as the final dust. What, then, must it seem to the eyes of God?

And in response to these complaints, intended in a friendly, mischievous way to goad my Prince, he muttered thoughtfully:

"Yes, perhaps it's all just an illusion, and the City the greatest of all illusions!"

Finding victory so easy, I redoubled my eloquence. Yes, my Prince, it *was* an illusion! And the most bitter of illusions, too, because Man believes the City to be the very basis of his greatness, when in fact it is the source of all his misery. Do you see, Jacinto! In the City, Man has entirely lost the strength and harmonious beauty of his body and become, instead, either desiccated and scrawny or obese and drowning in his own fat, with bones as soft as rags and nerves as tremulous as wires; a being reduced to wearing glasses, wigs, dentures made of lead; a twisted, hunchbacked creature with no blood, no muscle and no vigor; a thing in whom a horrified God would barely recognize his slender, strong, noble Adam! Man's moral freedom ended in the City: each morning it imposed on him a new need, and each new need impelled him further into dependency; poor and subaltern, he found his life had become a round of begging, flattering, cringeing, fawning and making do; when it came to a wealthy, superior man like Jacinto, Society immediately entangled him in traditions, social expectations, etiquettes, ceremonies, customs, and rituals—far harsher disciplines than one would find in a prison or a barracks. And where, Jacinto, was Man's peace of mind (a treasure so great that God gave it as a reward to the saints)? Lost forever in the desperate battle for bread or reputation or power or pleasure or for that elusive roundel of gold! What joy can there be in the City for those millions of beings so tumultuously engaged in the exhausting business of *wanting* and who, finding their wants never satisfied, are left in a permanent state of disappointment, despair, or defeat? In the City, the most genuinely human feelings are immediately dehumanized! Don't you see, Jacinto? They're like flames that the rough winds of society will not allow to burn serenely and brightly; one moment, they cause the flame to shiver and tremble, the next, they cruelly snuff it out or make it flare up with unnatural violence. Friendships are never more than alliances, which—at the anxious hour of defense or the eager hour of attack—self-interest hurriedly fastens with a piece of cord, alliances that break down at the first sign of rivalry or pride. And what about Love in the

City, dear Jacinto? Consider the vast shops with their mirrors, where the noble flesh of Eve is offered for sale, priced like a cow at so much per pound! Regard the old god Hymenaeus, who carries not the flaming torch of Passion but the stingy money-bag of the Dowry. See the multitude fleeing from the broad, open paths—on which, according to the good natural law, Fauns make love to Nymphs—and seeking out instead the gloomy corners of Sodom and of Lesbos! But the City has its most deleterious effects on Man's Intelligence, which it either imprisons in banality or drives into wild extravagance. In the dense, ever-present layer of ideas and formulae that constitutes the mental atmosphere of cities, the man who breathes it in and is surrounded by it only ever thinks thoughts that have been thought already, only expresses ideas that have been expressed already, or else—in order to stand out from dull, boring routine and climb the rickety scaffolding of vainglory—he invents, with much moaning and wailing and racking of brains, a misshapen novelty that startles and attracts the crowd like a freak at a fair. In intellectual terms, all of these men are sheep treading the same track, bleating the same bleat, their snouts in the dust through which they troop, always stepping in the footsteps of others; and just a few are monkeys, swinging from the tops of brightly colored poles, pulling faces and turning somersaults. Thus, my dear Jacinto, in this highly unnatural creation where the ground is made of wood and felt and tar, where coal-smoke conceals the sky, and people live piled up in buildings like rolls of cloth in a store, where the light is channelled through pipes, and where lies are whispered down wires, man seems a non-human creature, without beauty, strength, freedom, laughter or feeling, a creature carrying within him a spirit that is as passive as a slave's or as impudent as an actor's. And that, my fine Jacinto, is your fine City!

And before these grizzled and venerable arguments—boomed out with great regularity by all bucolic moralists throughout the centuries, from Hesiod on—my Prince bowed his docile neck as if, on the heights of Montmartre, those arguments had sprung, unexpected and fresh, from some superior Revelation.

"Yes, you're right. Perhaps the City is just a perverse illusion!"

I talked garrulously on, tugging at my cuffs and enjoying my easy philosophizing. If the illusion of the City could at the very least make all the people who maintained it happy, but it patently fails! Only a narrow, lustrous caste enjoys the special pleasures the City can provide. The others, the vast, dark populace, find only the pain and suffering peculiar to the City. From this terrace, next to this splendid Basilica consecrated to the Heart that so loved the Poor and for whom it spilled its life blood, we have a clear view of the dismal houses where the populace remains weighed down by that ancient opprobrium from which neither religions or philosophies or morality, nor their own brute strength, will ever be able to free them! There they lie, scattered about the City, like some kind of vile human manure. The centuries roll by, and the same immutable rags cover their bodies, and beneath those rags, through the long day, the men will labor and the women will weep. And the wealth of the City, dear Prince, is built on the labor and tears of the poor. There it lies, full of houses in which they cannot live, stacked high with cloth and fabrics they cannot use to make warm clothes for themselves, crammed with food of which they cannot eat their fill. For them there is only the snow, when the snow falls and benumbs and buries the little children huddled on the benches in the squares or beneath the arches of the bridges of Paris. The snow falls, silent and white in the darkness; the little children freeze in their ragged clothes; and the police do their rounds to ensure that nothing troubles the warm sleep of those who love the snow because it means they can go skating on the lakes in the Bois de Boulogne wearing fur coats worth three thousand francs. What do you say to that, Jacinto? Your Civilization is always insatiably demanding more pomp and more pleasure, which it can only obtain in this climate of bitter social disharmony if Capital, in payment for each laborious effort, gives to Labor only a measly crumb. It is inevitable, then, that the populace must always serve and suffer. The City's serene splendor depends on their hard-won poverty. If their bowls were filled with their fair ration of steaming soup, the lavish portions of foie gras and truffles served on silver platters, which are the pride of Civilization, would simply not be possible. There are rags in garret rooms so that the likes of the beautiful Madame d'Oriol, resplendent in silks and lace, can ascend the stairs at the Opéra with suitably soft and swaying step. There are frozen hands held out and thin lips that mouth words of gratitude for the magnificent gift of a single *sou* so that the Efraims of this world may have ten million francs in an account at the Bank of France, and may warm themselves by a fine fire piled high with aromatic wood, and may distribute sapphire necklaces to their mistresses, the grand-daughters of the Dukes of Athens. And a whole people weeps for hunger and for the hunger of their little ones so that, in January, bored and yawning Jacintos can nibble at iced strawberries in Champagne, spiced up with a dribble of ether and served on Saxe porcelain!

"And I've eaten those strawberries too, Jacinto! We're both of us wretches!"

He muttered glumly:

"Yes, it's all horribly true, we have both eaten those strawberries. And for what? Probably for a mere illusion!"

He walked pensively away from that spot on the terrace, as if the presence of the City, stretched out on the plain below, were offensive to him. And in the gray indolence of the afternoon, we strolled along philosophizing and pondering why there could be no human cure for the iniquity created by human effort. Ah, the Efraims and the Trèves, the voracious, shadowy sharks of the human sea, would only cease or slacken their exploitation of the populace if some celestial influence, through some new miracle, superior to all the old miracles, were to convert their souls! Hardened in sin, the bourgeois revels in his strength, and against him all the tears of the Humanitarians, the reasoned arguments of the Logicians and the bombs of the Anarchists are impotent. Only divine grace can soften such granite. And so the world once more places its hopes in the coming of a Messiah! The Messiah who descended once before from the great Heavens made it quite clear what his mandate was by quietly entering the world through a stable door. Alas, his sojourn among men was so brief! A gentle sermon on a mount at the end of a gentle afternoon; a mild reprimand to the Pharisees in charge of the equivalent of Le Boulevard; a few lashes with the scourge for those Efraim-like money-changers; and then a swift exit through the door of Death to escape jubilantly up to Paradise! That adorable son of God was in rather too much of a hurry to get back to his Father's house! And the men whom he charged with continuing his work soon came under the influence of the Efraims, the Trèves, and the people from Le Boulevard, and quickly forgot the lessons taught them on the Mount and on Lake

Tiberias; they ended up donning purple, declaring themselves bishops and Popes, and thus became part of the oppression and even reigned over it, building their kingdom on the misery of the breadless and the homeless! And so the work of Redemption must begin all over again. Jesus or Gautama or Krishna or any one of those sons whom God occasionally plucks from a Virgin's womb or from the quiet gardens of Asia will have to descend once more to the land of servitude. Will he come, the long-desired One? Perhaps some grave-faced king of the Orient has already woken in the night, seen a star, taken the myrrh in his royal hands and pensively mounted his camel. At night, on the outskirts of this hard City, while Caiaphas and Mary Magdalene are dining on lobster at Paillard's, is some watchful angel flying low overhead, looking for a stable? Somewhere far off, with no herdsman to call them, are the cow and the donkey trotting eagerly forward in anticipation of a divine encounter?

"Do *you* know, Jacinto?"

No, Jacinto didn't know, and what's more, he needed a light for his cigar. I provided him with a match. We were still wandering up and down the terrace, throwing out into the air more such solid ideas, which dissolved at once into nothing, when, just as we were about to go into the Basilica, a plump sacristan, wearing a velvet biretta, slammed the door shut, and a priest walked past us, thrusting his old breviary into his pocket with a final, weary gesture.

"All this philosophizing has given me the most tremendous thirst, Jacinto!"

We went down the steps, which looked even more like a devout country fair. My thoughtful friend bought an image of the Basilica. And we were just about to jump into the victoria when someone called out in loud surprise:

"Jacinto!"

Equally astonished, my Prince spread wide his arms:

"Maurice!"

And in great excitement, he crossed the street to a café, beneath whose striped awning a sturdy-looking man with a pointed beard was sitting stirring his absinthe, a straw hat pushed back on his head, with no cravat, and a light jacket on over his silk shirt, just as if he were relaxing on a bench in the shade of his garden.

And both men, as they shook hands, remarked on how unusual it was that they should meet on the heights of Montmartre on a summer Sunday.

"This is my home now!" Maurice exclaimed gaily. "You find me *en famille* and in my slippers! I moved up to these peaks of Truth three months ago. But what's a profane man like you from the plains and from the streets of Israel doing on this Holy Hill?"

My Prince introduced me.

"I'm on a pilgrimage to the Basilica with my friend here. Fernandes Lorena, this is Maurice de Mayolle, an old comrade of mine."

Monsieur de Mayolle (whose long face and large, noble nose were reminiscent of François de Valois, King of France) raised his straw hat to me. And drawing up another chair, he insisted that we make ourselves comfortable and join him in a drink of absinthe or a beer.

"Have a beer, Zé Fernandes!" said Jacinto. "You're the one who was dying of thirst!"

"I was keeping that thirst for dinner later, with a nice chilled wine!"

Maurice nodded in silent admiration of such shrewdness. Then he turned to my Prince.

"It must be three years since I've seen you, Jacinto. How is that possible in the little village of Paris where you're normally impossible to avoid?"

"Life, Maurice, dispersive life. But, you're right, it must be three years since we met at the Lamotte-Orcels' house. Do you still visit that sanctuary?"

Maurice made a grand, scornful gesture as if taking the world by the scruff of the neck and shaking it.

"No, I've had nothing to do with that bunch for a year now. They're an undisciplined, heretical rabble, Jacinto! No fixity of purpose, just blind dilettantism and a complete and quite laughable lack of any scientific basis. What was in vogue when you used to go to the Lamotte-Orcels' house and to the Parola at 37 and to *La Bière Idéale*?"

Jacinto combed his moustache with his fingers as he sifted through his memories.

"Let me see ... well, there was Wagner and Eddic Mythology, and Ragnarök and the Nornies ... There was a lot of Pre-Raphaelitism around too, and Montagna, and Fra Angelico. And when it came to morals, Renanism was all the rage."

Maurice gave a dismissive shrug. All that belonged to an ancient, almost prehistoric past! By the time Madame de Lamotte-Orcel had refurnished her salon with William Morris velvets—great fat artichokes against a saffron background—Renanism was already passé, as forgotten as Cartesianism.

"Were you around for the cult of the Ego?"

My Prince sighed and smiled:

"Yes, and I was even a follower myself for a while."

"Well, after that came Hartmannism and the philosophy of the Unconscious. Then came Nietzscheism and Spiritual Feudalism. Then Tolstoyism took over, and neo-cenobitic renunciation was all the rage. I can still remember a dinner where a great monster of a Slav appeared, hair all dirty and disheveled, and when he wasn't casting lewd glances at the poor Countess d'Arche's décolletage, he was wagging his finger and growling: 'We seek the light deep down, in the very dust of the earth!' And over dessert we all drank to the delights of humility and servile labor with that iced Champagne St. Marceaux that Matilde always gave us on special occasions served in glasses in the shape of the Holy Grail! Then came Emersonianism. But the worst was Ibsenism—a real plague! In short, my friend, a veritable Babel of Ethics and Aesthetics. It was as if Paris had gone mad. Some lost souls even strayed into Luciferism. And a few of our little female friends, poor things, fell into Phallicism, a pseudo-mystical hodgepodge preached by that poor man, La Carte, who later became a White Monk and is now to be found wandering somewhere in the desert. Quite dreadful! And then one afternoon, out of the blue, they all seized on Ruskinism!"

I clung on to my walking stick, the end planted firmly in the ground, for I felt a tornado whirling inside my head! And even Jacinto, equally dazed, could only stammer:

"Ruskinism?"

"Yes, old Ruskin . . . John Ruskin!"

Then my fortunate Prince understood.

"Oh, Ruskin! *The Seven Lamps of Architecture*, *The Crown of Wild Olive*, the cult of Beauty and all that."

"Exactly! The cult of Beauty," said Maurice. "But by that time, I was thoroughly fed up with it all and had descended from those foolish clouds. I was treading on safer and more fertile ground."

He took a slow sip of his absinthe, closing his eyes as he did so. Jacinto was waiting, the nostrils of his fine nose dilated, as if to sniff the Flower of Novelty about to unfurl.

"And then?"

But Maurice only murmured vaguely and secretively:

"Then I came to Montmartre. I have a friend here, a man of real genius, who has traveled all over India. He's lived there with the Toddas, spent time in the monasteries of Garma-Khian and Dashi-Lumbo, and studied with the Gegen Chutuktu in the holy sanctuary of Urga . . . The Gegen Chutuktu was the sixteenth incarnation of Gautama and, therefore, a Bodhisattva . . . We work, we seek . . . These things are not visions exactly, but facts, very ancient experiences, which date back perhaps to the times of Krishna . . ."

As he spoke these names, which gave off the sad perfume of archaic rituals, he pushed back his chair. Standing up and distractedly throwing down on the table a few silver and copper coins to pay for his absinthe, he remained still for a moment—his eyes apparently fixed on Jacinto, but in fact absorbed in some private vision—and murmured:

"In the end, everything comes down to the supreme development of the Will within the supreme purity of Life. Therein lies the knowledge and strength of the great Hindu teachers. But the real struggle, the real obstacle lies in attaining absolute purity of life! Even the desert isn't enough, even the forest surrounding the oldest temple in high Tibet isn't enough. Nevertheless, Jacinto, we've already obtained some very strange and interesting results. You know Tyndall's experiments with sensitive flames? Well, he, a mere chemist, in his attempts to demonstrate sound vibrations, almost opened the doors of esoteric truth. But what can you expect? He was a man of science and therefore stupid, and so he remained on this side of those doors, among his electrodes and his retorts! We, however, went through the doors. We discovered the *undulations of the Will*! Using only my colleague's fluctuating energies and following his commands, we watched as a flame, three yards away, flickered, drooped, flared up, touched the high ceiling, roared black and furious, glowed erect and silent—and then abruptly died, reduced to ashes!"

This strange man, his straw hat still pushed back on his head, stood there, absolutely motionless, arms wide and eyes staring, as if re-experiencing the astonishment and shock of that marvel. Then resuming his calm, easy ways and slowly lighting a cigarette, he said:

"One of these days, Jacinto, I'll come and have lunch with you at No. 202, and I'll bring my friend too. He eats only rice, a little salad and some fruit. And we can talk. As I recall, you had a copy of the *Sepher-Zerijah* and the *Targum d'Onkelus*, both of which I really need to take a look at."

He shook my Prince's hand, said goodbye to me—a bewildered Zé Fernandes—and calmly walked off down the quiet street, his hat pushed back on his head, his hands deep in his pockets, like a natural man among natural things.

"Who is that wizard, Jacinto? Tell me! For the love of God, who *is* he?"

Leaning back in the victoria, straightening the crease in his trousers, my Prince gave me a concise biography. Maurice was a loyal, noble young man, very rich and very intelligent, from the ancient house of Mayolle, a descendant of the Dukes de la Septimanie. Then, yawning his customary yawn, Jacinto muttered:

"The supreme development of the Will. Theosophy and esoteric Buddhism. Aspirations and disappointments. I've tried them all. What a bore!"

In silence and amid the clammy warmth of a summer evening, we crossed Paris to go and dine in the Bois, at the Pavillon d'Armenonville, where the gypsies, as soon they spotted Jacinto, struck up the Portuguese national anthem, which they played with an odd mixture of passion and languor, as if it were a sad, discordant Hungarian czardas.

And unfolding my napkin, I said:

"Right, bring on that chilled wine to slake my glorious thirst! I certainly deserve it, for I philosophized quite superbly. And I believe that I have definitively established in Senhor Jacinto's mind a salutary horror of the City!"

My Prince was stroking his moustache as he ran his eye down the wine list, while the waiter hovered reverently beside him.

"Tell them to put two bottles of Champagne St. Marceaux on ice, but first an old Barsac, very lightly chilled. And Evian water, no, from Bussang! No, wait, bring us some Evian *and* some Bussang! And to start with, a beer."

Yawning and slowly unbuttoning his gray frock coat, he said:

"I rather fancy building a house in Montmartre, with a mirador on top, all in glass and iron, where I could sit in the afternoons and look out over the City."

: VII :

JULY ENDED WITH SOME REFRESHING, consoling rain, and
I began thinking that I really should make the pilgrimage to the
great cities of Europe that I had been putting off since the Spring,
delayed by the surprises sprung on me by the World and the Flesh.
Suddenly, though, Jacinto started urging me to go with him every
afternoon to the house of Madame d'Oriol. And I realized that
(in the manner of the divine Achilles, who always kept his friend
Patroclus with him in his tent when in the company of the pale,
insipid, docile Briseis) my Prince wished to have, in that lovers'
retreat, the presence, comfort and aid of Friendship. Poor Jacinto!
Each morning he would telephone Madame d'Oriol to arrange a
time for that hour of sweet peace. And thus we would always find
that highly refined lady, forewarned and alone in her room in Rue
de Lisbonne, where there was scarcely enough space for Jacinto
and myself, overwhelmed as we were by the profusion of baskets
of flowers and gold rocaille, by monsters from Japan and the gallant fragility of Saxe porcelain, by the skins of wild animals that
lay stretched out at the feet of slumbering sofas, and by Aubus-
son screens arranged to form pleasant, languid alcoves. Nestled
on a white lacquered bamboo chair, among cushions perfumed

with Indian verbena, and with a novel resting on her lap, Madame d'Oriol awaited her friend in a pose of gentle, passive indolence that always reminded me of the Orient and of harems. Then again, when dressed in cool Pompadour silks, she also resembled a little marchioness from Versailles, weary of the Grand Siècle, or even, when in dark brocades and broad studded belts, a Venetian lady dressed for the doge. My intrusion into the intimacy of these afternoons did not seem to bother her in the least; rather it brought her a new vassal, another pair of eyes to contemplate her. I was already her *"cher Fernandez"*!

And she had only to open her lips, as red as a fresh wound, and begin chattering, to enfold us at once in the buzz and murmur of Paris. She could only talk about her own person, which was a summation of her whole Class, and about her life, which was a summation of her Paris; and her life, since marriage, had been devoted to bringing all her vast knowledge to bear on the adornment of her lovely body; to affecting a perfect entrance and lighting up a room; to handling fabrics and holding deep conversations with the great couturiers; to driving through the Bois in her carriage in which she sat as still and posed as a wax image; to wearing décolleté dresses and keeping her throat and neck powdered and white; to nibbling on a leg of woodcock at banquets; to threading her way through the wealthy throngs in crowded ballrooms; to falling asleep with her vanity exhausted; to reading, over her hot chocolate, the gossip and society columns of *Le Figaro*; to murmuring occasionally to her husband: "Oh, is that you?"; and, in the twilight, on a sofa, to uttering a few brief sighs in the arms of someone to whom she remained true. That year, my Prince occupied that place on the sofa. All these duties of City and Caste she performed with a smile

on her lips. She had smiled so much since she had been married that there were now two indelible lines on either side of her
mouth. But her soul and her skin showed no other signs of fatigue.
Her visitor's book contained one thousand three hundred names,
all of them from the Nobility. During all that furious socialising,
however, a few General Ideas had managed to take up residence
in her brain (into which must have seeped some of the powder
with which she had been plastering her face ever since she was
at school). In Politics she was in favor of the Princes; and all the
other "horrors"—the Republic, Socialism, the great unwashed
Democracy—she laughingly brushed aside with a flick of her fan.
In Holy Week, she added a bitter crown of thorns to the lace on
her hat because for high-born people those were days of peni-
tence and sorrow. And confronted by any book or any painting,
she felt whichever emotion and delicately formulated whichever
opinion it was considered elegant to formulate and to feel in her
World in that particular week. She was thirty years old. She had
never become entangled in the torments of passion. With strict
regularity, she kept a note of all her expenses in an account book
bound in sea-green plush. Her personal religion (more genuine
than the other religion that carried her to mass each Sunday at
St. Philippe du Roule) was Order. In Winter, as soon as homeless
children began to die of cold beneath the bridges of that amiable
City, she would, with touching attention to detail, prepare her
skating outfits. She had special outfits for Charity too, because
she was good-hearted and attended bazaars, concerts and tom-
bolas, whenever these were sponsored by the Duchesses who belonged to her "set." Then, in Spring, very methodically, she would
sell her Winter clothes and capes to a second-hand clothes dealer,

haggling over the price. Paris considered her to be one of the supreme flowers of Parisianism.

And thus we spent our July afternoons, breathing in the scent of this soft, fine flower, while all other flowers drooped and withered in the heat and the dust. However, even in intimate contact with that perfume, Jacinto did not seem to find the contentment of soul that never palls when all else does. He ascended Madame d'Oriol's cool, silent, palm-flanked stairs with the patient slowness with which one climbs all Calvaries, however sumptuously carpeted. When, in order to entertain him, the alluring creature devotedly unfurled her vivacity, much as a peacock unfurls its tail, my poor Prince would pull at his drooping moustache in the limp posture of one who, on a May morning, while the blackbirds are singing in the bushes, finds himself obliged to attend a funeral service for a prince. And, when they parted, there was always a great deal of alacrity and relief in the murmurous kiss he placed on his sweet friend's hand.

However, the next day, in the early afternoon, having wandered aimlessly through the Library and the Study—occasionally plucking dully at the tape issuing forth from the telegraph machine, having already glumly telephoned someone to leave a message or cast a dejected eye over the immense knowledge contained in those thirty thousand books or flicked through the mound of newspapers and reviews, Jacinto would finally summon me, with the lethargic air of a man undertaking a feat not of his choosing.

"Let's go to Madame d'Oriol's house, shall we? There were six or seven things I intended to do today, but I just can't, it's such a bore! So let's go to Madame d'Oriol's house instead! At least there one can enjoy a little coolness and peace!"

And it was on just such an afternoon, when my Prince was desperately seeking "a little coolness and peace," that, halfway up the lavish palm-flanked staircase, we encountered Madame d'Oriol's husband. I knew him by sight already, because Jacinto had pointed him out to me one night in the Grand Café, where he was having supper with some dancers from the Moulin Rouge. He was a flabby, indolent fellow, with pale skin the color of lard and a prominent and very shiny bald pate, which he constantly caressed with plump, beringed fingers. On that afternoon, however, he looked scarlet-faced and agitated, angrily pulling on his gloves. When he saw Jacinto, he stopped and, not even bothering to shake his hand, gestured upwards.

"Are you going to see Joana? Well, you'll find her in the very foulest of moods. We've just had the most tremendous row."

He gave another desperate tug at one already torn straw-colored glove.

"We live separate lives; we each do as we please, and that's fine. But there's a limit to everything. She bears my name, and I simply cannot allow her—in Paris and in the full knowledge of everyone—to take a footman as her lover. Lovers taken from our own circle, yes, but a lackey, no! If she wants to sleep with the servants then she should head off to the provinces, to her house in Corbelle. She can sleep with the animals there, for all I care! And I told her so. That's when she really saw red."

Then he shook hands with Jacinto, who was "one of their circle," and waddled off down the stairs, florid head held high. My Prince did not move, but kept his eyes downcast and continued slowly to stroke his limp moustache. Then, looking at me like a man so saturated with tedium that not a single drop more tedium could be squeezed in, he said:

"Shall we go up, then?"

It was after this that I set off joyfully on my longed-for pilgrimage to the cities of Europe.

My intention was to travel, and I certainly traveled. Thirty-four times, panting and red-faced, I packed and unpacked my case. Eleven times I spent the whole day in a train carriage, surrounded by dust and smoke, choking, gasping, dripping with sweat, and leaping out at every station to suck desperately on warm lemons that subsequently played havoc with my digestion. Fourteen times, I followed a servant up the unfamiliar steps of a hotel and glanced nervously around an unfamiliar room; I slept badly in unfamiliar beds from which I rose wearily and called out in unfamiliar languages for a white coffee that tasted of beans or for a bath in a bathtub that smelled of mud. Eight times I got into a fray with coachmen who were trying to swindle me. I lost a hat-box, fifteen handkerchiefs, three pairs of underwear, and two boots, one white and the other patent leather, both from the right foot. At more than thirty tables, I waited gloomily to be served a dish of *boeuf à la mode*, cold and with a coagulated sauce, and for the waiter to bring me a bottle of Bordeaux wine which, after just one sip, I would reject with a grimace of distaste. In the cool shade of granites and marbles, I padded softly and respectfully around twenty-nine cathedrals. With a slightly stiff neck, I trudged dully through fourteen museums, one hundred and forty rooms hung from floor to ceiling with Christs, heroes, saints, nymphs, princesses, battles, buildings, meadows, nudes, and dark smudges of pitch—ah, the sadness of static shapes! My most enjoyable day was spent in Venice, in the pouring rain, when I met an old Englishman with a very large nose who had lived in Oporto and knew Ricardo, José Duarte, the Viscount do Bom Sucesso, and the Limas from Boavista. In all, I spent six thousand francs. I had traveled!

Finally, one blessed October morning, along with the first chills and mists of Autumn, it was with a feeling of tender excitement that I saw the silk curtains of No. 202—still drawn! I patted the porter on the back. On the landing, where I rediscovered the soft warm air I had left behind me in Florence, I embraced Cricket's excellent old bones.

"And Jacinto?"

The worthy Cricket muttered from above his high, shiny collar:

"My master still goes out and about, but he's terribly bored and fed up. He came home late last night from a ball held by the Duchess de Loches. It was an engagement party for Mademoiselle de Loche. Before retiring, he drank a glass of iced tea, scratched his head and said: 'What a bore! What a bore!' "

At ten o'clock, after a bath and some hot chocolate, and wrapped cosily in a velvet dressing-gown, I burst into my Prince's room, eager arms held wide.

"Jacinto!"

"Ah, the traveler returns!"

We shared a long embrace, and afterward, I drew back to look at his face—and thus at his soul. Hunched in a mauve jacket edged with marten fur, his moustache limp, the two lines on either side of his mouth etched still deeper, his broad shoulders bowed, my friend seemed already bent beneath the weight, burden and terror of the coming day. I smiled in order to make him smile.

"So, my brave Jacinto, how's life been with you?"

He replied serenely:

"More like death."

I forced a laugh, as if his troubles were of little importance.

"Pretty boring, eh?"

My Prince made such a despairing gesture and uttered such a weary "Oh" that I took pity on him, embracing him once again, more tightly this time, as if to communicate to him some part of the pure, solid joy I received from my God!

From that morning on, Jacinto made absolutely no attempt to hide from me the tedium with which existence itself filled him. All his attention and all his efforts were channelled into investigating and describing that tedium in the hope that he could overcome it once he understood its origins and its power. And thus my poor Jacinto played the rather drab role of the Melancholic who does nothing but ponder his own Melancholia! In these ponderings, he always started from the obvious and irrefutable fact that his peculiarly Jacintian life contained all the interests and facilities available in the nineteenth century to a man who was neither a genius nor a saint. This was true. Despite an appetite dulled by twelve years of Champagne and rich sauces, he preserved his pine-tree vigor; the bright flame of his intelligence neither flickered nor burned low; the good earth of Portugal and a few large companies kept him regularly supplied with money; in the inconstant and skeptical City of Paris he was surrounded by ever active and ever faithful friends; No. 202 was filled to bursting with comforts; no anguish of the heart tormented him, and yet still he was sad. Why? And from there he leaped, with dazzling certainty, to the conclusion that his sadness—that gray hairshirt in which his soul was shrouded—came not from him, from Jacinto, but from Life, from the regrettable, disastrous fact of being alive!

And thus the healthy, intelligent, wealthy, well-loved Jacinto slid into Pessimism.

It was an angry Pessimism too, for (as he himself said) he had been born to be as naturally optimistic as a sparrow or a cat. And up until he was twelve years old— thoroughly spoiled, with clothes on his back and his plate always full—he had never felt fatigue or melancholy or irritation or sadness, and to him tears were so incomprehensible as to seem immoral. Only when he grew up and went from animal nature to human nature, did he notice this leavening of sadness, which had remained undeveloped in the tumult of his initial excitement and curiosity, but had then spread and invaded everything, becoming consubstantial with him and with the blood in his veins. Suffering then was inseparable from Living, with different sufferings for different lives. In the mass of humanity it was the terrible struggle for bread, for a roof, for warmth; in a different social caste, troubled by higher needs, it was the bitterness of disappointments, the pain of a dissatisfied imagination or of pride bumping up against some obstacle; in Jacinto, who was possessed of every advantage, but had no desires, it was tedium. Bodily misery, spiritual torment and intellectual disgust—that was Life! And now, at thirty-three, his main occupations were yawning and running bored fingers over his face as if feeling and yearning for the skull beneath.

That was when my Prince immersed himself passionately in reading all the poets and theoreticians of Pessimism, from Ecclesiastes to Schopenhauer. As he read, he found comforting proof that his malaise was not purely and meanly "Jacintian," but the grandiose result of a Universal Law. Four thousand years ago, in far-off Jerusalem, Life, even at its most triumphant and delightful, had also been mere Illusion. Even that consummate Conqueror and Builder, the incomparable King Solomon, with all his divine knowledge, had yawned and grown bored despite the spoils of his conquests, the brand-new marble of his temples, his three thousand concubines, and the queens who traveled from the depths of Ethiopia so that he could impregnate them and plant a god in their wombs! No, there was nothing new under the Sun, and the eternal repetition of all things is the eternal repetition of evils. The more you know the more you suffer. The righteous and the unrighteous are born out of the dust and will to dust return. Everything turns to ephemeral dust, be it in Jerusalem or in Paris! And he, an obscure individual living in No. 202, suffered because he was a man and because he was alive, just as the magnificent son of David had suffered on his throne of gold, flanked by his four golden lions.

At the time, Jacinto was never to be seen without Ecclesiastes! He would travel around Paris with Solomon in the carriage with him, as a brother in sorrow, with whom he repeated the desolate cry that is the sum of all human truth—*Vanitas vanitatum!* All is vanity! At other times, I would find him early in the morning lying on the sofa in a silk dressing gown and imbibing Schopenhauer, while the pedicurist knelt before him on the carpet, respectfully and expertly buffing his toenails. Beside him lay a Saxe porcelain tea cup, full of that Mocha coffee sent by the emirs of the desert and which he never found strong enough or sufficiently aromatic. Now and then, he would rest the book on his chest and give the pedicurist a compassionate, appraising glance, as if wondering what particular pain might be torturing him, because each life has its sorrow—possibly the fact of having to be perpetually touching other people's feet. And when the pedicurist got up, Jacinto would give him a broad smile of confraternity, as if to say "Goodbye, my friend!" but meaning "Goodbye, my brother!"

This proved to be the most splendid and superbly diverting period of his tedium. Jacinto had at last found an agreeable occupation—cursing Life! And in order to curse it in all its forms, the most lavish, the most intellectual, the most pure, he loaded his own life with new luxuries, with new spiritual interests, even with humanitarian enthusiasms and supernatural speculations.

That Winter, No. 202 glowed magnificently. Jacinto, in imitation of Heliogabalus and the Banquets of Color described in the *Historia Augusta*, decided to offer his friends a sublime pink supper, in which everything was pink, the walls, the furniture, the lights, the dishes, the glasses, the ices, the Champagne, and even (thanks to the endless inventiveness of Haute Cuisine) the fish, meat and vegetables; even the footmen serving at table were dressed in pink uniforms and dusted with pink powder, while cool rose petals drifted down from a pink silk velarium suspended from the ceiling. The bedazzled City cried: "Bravo, Jacinto!" And at the end of this sparkling party, my Prince stood before me, hands on hips and declared triumphantly: "What a bore, eh?"

Then it was the turn of Humanitarianism. In a country house surrounded by gardens, he set up a hospice for homeless old men and another for sick children on the shores of the Mediterranean. Then along with Major Dorchas, Mayolle and Mayolle's Hindu friend, he investigated Theosophy, and set up extraordinary experiments to prove the mysterious phenomenon of "externalized motion." Then, desperately, he linked No. 202 up with the telegraphic wires of *The Times*, so that his study, like a heart, would pulsate with the whole Social Life of Europe.

And after each sally into elegant display, humanitarianism, sociability, and investigative intelligence, he would turn to me, arms gleefully outspread, and declare triumphantly: "You see, Zé Fernandes, it's all an utter bore!" Then he would snatch up his Ecclesiastes or his Schopenhauer and, reclining on the sofa, voluptuously savor the way in which Doctrine dovetailed so perfectly with Experience. He had a Faith—Pessimism; he was a rich and energetic apostle and lavished all his efforts on proving the truth of his Faith! Yes, that year, my unhappy Prince thoroughly enjoyed himself!

At the beginning of Winter, however, I noticed with concern that Jacinto was no longer reading Ecclesiastes and had begun to neglect Schopenhauer. Not even parties, theosophisms, hospices or wires connected directly to *The Times* seemed now to interest my friend, even as glorious proofs of his Beliefs. His sole, abominable occupation became once more to yawn and press lethargic fingers to his face, feeling the skull beneath the skin. One evening, in the melancholy twilight of the Library, before the lights flickered on, he alarmed me greatly by speaking in chilling tones of the swift, painless deaths brought on by a shock from a vast electric battery or by the compassionate violence of prussic acid. Good God! Pessimism, which had taken the form in my Prince's intelligence of an elegant conceit, had suddenly attacked his Will!

His every movement became that of an unconscious ox trudging onwards beneath the yoke and the goad. He no longer expected contentment from Life, he did not even regret that it brought him tedium and sadness. "It's a matter of the utmost indifference to me, Zé Fernandes!" And he would have gone to his window to receive an imperial crown from the people with as much indifference as he would have plumped himself down on a battered armchair in order to sit and say nothing. Since everything was in vain and led only to still greater disappointments, what did it matter whether one immersed oneself in the most brilliant of activities or in the most loathsome inertia? He had acquired the irritating habit of constantly shrugging his shoulders. Faced by a choice between two ideas, two paths, two dishes, he would merely shrug! What did it matter? He performed the slightest action, be it striking a match or unfolding a newspaper, with such disconsolate slowness that he seemed to be entirely bound and trammelled, from his fingers to his soul, by the tight bonds of some invisible piece of string.

I remember with great displeasure the day of his birthday on January 10th. Early in the morning, he had received from Madame de Trèves, along with a letter, a basket of camellias, azaleas, orchids, and lilies of the valley. It was this kind gesture that reminded him of the day's significance. He blew the smoke from his cigarette over the petals and murmured with a slyly mocking smile:

"So I've been caught up in this whole boring business for thirty-four years now!"

When I suggested telephoning his friends and inviting them to come to No. 202 to drink the birthday boy's Champagne, he angrily rejected the idea. Certainly not! He could imagine nothing worse! He even bawled an order at Cricket:

"I'm not in to anyone today. Tell them I've escaped to the country or to Marseilles. Tell them I've died!"

He continued in this same ironic vein until lunch, when he found himself faced by a mountain of notes, telegrams and letters on the ebony table, like an homage from the City. When more flowers were delivered, in beautiful baskets tied with beautiful ribbons, he compared them to the flowers one places on a grave. And his interest was only momentarily caught by a present from Efraim, an ingenious table that could be lowered to carpet level or raised up to the ceiling—though God knows why.

A gloomy rain set in after lunch, and so we did not budge from No. 202, but stayed at home, warming our feet by the fire in lazy silence. In the end, I drifted into a beatific sleep. I was woken by Cricket's hurrying footsteps. Jacinto, slumped in his armchair, was cutting out paper shapes with scissors! Never had I so pitied this friend of mine—he who had worn out his youth accumulating every idea formulated from Aristotle onward and gathering together every invention dreamed up since Theramenes created the wheel—as I did on that festive afternoon, when, surrounded by the maximum amount of Civilization in order to enjoy to the maximum the joy of living, he was reduced to sitting by the fireside cutting out paper shapes with a pair of scissors!

Cricket had brought him a present from the Grand Duke—a silver box lined with cedar and full of a precious tea, picked, flower by flower, in the fields of Kiang-Su by the pure hands of virgins and transported in caravans across Asia as if it were some venerable relic. To wake us from our torpor, I suggested that we drink some of this divine tea—an occupation in keeping with the sad afternoon, with the heavy rain drenching the windows and the bright flames dancing in the fireplace. Jacinto agreed, and a footman immediately carried in Efraim's new adjustable table so that we could enjoy its many uses for the first time. However, after raising it up, much to my horror, as far as the crystal chandeliers, my Prince, despite a hard and desperate battle with its springs, could not bring the table back down again to a domestic, human level. And the footman duly carried it away again, like a piece of fantastical scaffolding, of use only to the giant Adamastor. Then the box of tea was brought in, along with teapots, lamps, strainers, filters, and a whole array of silver plates, all of which lent the majesty of a ritual to the making of tea—a process, in my aunt's house, that was so simple and sweet. Forewarned by my friend of the sublime nature of that tea from Kiang-Su, I reverently raised the cup to my lips. It was a pale infusion that tasted of sweet mallow and ants. Jacinto took a sip, spat it out and swore. We did not take tea.

After another pensive silence, I said quietly, staring into the fire:

"What about the work being carried out in Tormes—the chapel? Will they have built the new chapel by now, do you think?"

Jacinto had resumed his paper cutting.

"I've no idea. Silvério hasn't written since. I don't even know where they will have put the bones. What a gruesome business!"

Then it was time for the lights to be lit and for dinner to be served. I had ordered Cricket to have our masterly cook make a large dish of rice pudding, with Jacinto's initials and the happy date written on it in cinnamon, in charming, homely Portuguese fashion. And my Prince, sitting at the table and perusing the ivory tablet on which, at No. 202, the menus were written in red ink, loudly praised this patriarchal invention:

"Rice pudding! They've spelled 'pudding' with one 'd,' but no matter, it's still an excellent idea! I haven't eaten rice pudding since Grandmama died."

But what a disappointment when the pudding was brought in! It was a monumental dish, a work of art! The thick rice had been molded into the shape of an Egyptian pyramid and was surrounded by a cherry sauce, covered from top to bottom with dried fruit, and crowned with a count's coronet made of chocolate and segments of candied tangerine! And the initials and the date—which always look so grave and pretty when traced in ingenuous cinnamon—had, instead, been written along the edge of the dish in crystallised violets. Dumb with horror, we rejected the vile thing. Raising his glass of Champagne, Jacinto muttered, as if at a pagan funeral:

"*Ad manes*, to our dead!"

We withdrew to the Library to drink our coffee by the cosy warmth of the fire. Outside, the wind was howling as if across a mountain wilderness, and the drenched windows trembled beneath the angry, lashing rain. What a wretched night for the ten thousand poor who would be wandering Paris with no home and no food to eat! Perhaps the same storm was roaring above my village, nestled between hill and valley. But there, at least, the poor, beneath the shelter of a roof, with a saucepan full of greens, can huddle in their blankets by a warm fire. And for those who have neither firewood nor greens, there is always João das Quintãs or Aunt Vicência or the parish priest, who know all the poor by name and who, whenever the cart goes to the wood for kindling and the bread is put in the oven, remember the poor as if they were their own. Ah, little mother Portugal, still so kind to her children!

I sighed, and Jacinto yawned and stretched. And we ended up

leafing languidly through the newspapers that the majordomo had brought in an eloquent pile on a silver salver—newspapers from Paris and from London, weeklies, magazines, reviews, illustrated quarterlies. Jacinto opened each one and threw each of them down; of the magazines, he read only the list of contents, which was quite enough; as for the illustrated magazines, he cut open the pages with one indifferent finger and yawned his way through the engravings. Slumping still lower in his chair before the fire, he exclaimed:

"Oh, it's all just too boring! There's not a thing worth reading."

Then rebelling against the oppressive gloom enslaving him, he suddenly leaped up from his armchair with the vigor of someone casting off his shackles and stood there erect, looking around him with flashing eyes, his gaze hard and urgent, as if challenging No. 202, so cram-packed with Civilization, to furnish his soul with some strong, brief enthusiasm or his life with some pleasure, however fleeting. But No. 202 remained impassive: no light glowed more brightly to cheer him; only the windows trembled beneath the growing onslaught of wind and rain.

Defeated, my Prince slouched into his study and did the rounds of all those machines intended to complete or facilitate Life—the Telegraph, the Telephone, the Phonograph, the Radiometer, the Graphophone, the Microphone, the Writing Machine, the Adding Machine, the Electric Press, the Magnetic Press, all his tools and tubes and wires, just as a supplicant does the rounds of the altars from which he hopes to receive succour. All that magnificent Machinery stood there stiff and still, glinting coldly, and not a wheel turned and not a blade vibrated in order to entertain its Master.

Only the monumental clock marking the time in all the capitals of the world and the positions of all the planets took pity on him by striking midnight and announcing to my friend that another day had departed, bearing its weight away with it and thus lightening the grim burden of Life beneath which he groaned and bent his back. The Prince of Great Good Fortune decided then to retreat to bed . . . with a book. And for a moment, he stood in the middle of the Library, considering his thirty thousand volumes, which sat there with all the pomp and majesty of Learned Men in Council, then turned his gaze on the tumultuous piles of new books that waited in corners on the carpet for the repose and recognition of the ebony shelves. Dully twirling his moustache, he made his way at last to the section devoted to the Historians: he scrutinised centuries and sniffed out nations; he was briefly drawn to the splendor of the Byzantine Empire; he peered into the French Revolution, but recoiled, disappointed; he ran an uncertain hand over all of vast Greece from the creation of Athens to the destruction of Corinth. Then he brusquely turned to the row of Poets, shining in their bright Morocco leather bindings, revealing in golden letters on their spines, in their bold or languid titles, the contents of their souls. However, he was not drawn to any of those six thousand souls either and withdrew, disconsolate, to the Biologists. So dense and tightly packed were the Biology shelves that my poor Jacinto took fright as if confronted by an inaccessible citadel. He rolled the ladder further along and escaped up to the heights of Astronomy; he selected stars, relocated worlds; a whole Solar System collapsed with a roar. Bewildered, he came down the ladder and started searching through the piles of new, as yet unbound works, in their light combat dress of paper. He picked them up, leafed through them and flung them down; in order to extricate one volume, he demolished a whole tower of doctrines; he leaped over Problems and trampled on Religions; and glancing at a line here, poring over an index there, he interrogated them all and found all wanting as he drifted aimlessly, tumbling from one great wave of tomes to the next, unable to stop, in his eagerness to find a book! Then he crouched down in the middle of that vast room, all courage gone, studying those book-lined walls, that book-laden floor, his thirty thousand volumes, and he did not even have to taste them to feel absolutely sated, stuffed, and nauseated by their oppressive abundance. After a while, he returned to the pile of crumpled newspapers, glumly picked up an old copy of *Diário de Notícias*, and with that under his arm, went up to his room to sleep and forget.

: VIII :

At the end of that dark, pessimistic Winter, as I lay idling in bed one morning, sensing a timid breath of Spring in the pale sunshine bathing the windows, Jacinto, dressed in light, lily-white flannels, peered around the door of my room. He came slowly over to my bedside and very gravely, as if about to announce either his marriage or his death, unleashed upon me this formidable declaration:

"Zé Fernandes, I'm leaving for Tormes."

I sat up so suddenly that Dom Galeão's sturdy blackwood bed shook.

"For Tormes? Oh, Jacinto, have you killed someone?"

Delighted by my reaction, the Prince of Great Good Fortune took a letter from his pocket and read me these lines, lines he had doubtless read and pondered many times:

" 'Sir, I have great pleasure in informing you that work on the new chapel should be completed this week—' "

"Is it from Silvério?" I exclaimed.

"It is. He goes on: '. . . The venerable remains of your excellent ancestors, for whom, naturally, I have the greatest respect, will soon be able to be transferred from the Church of São José, where they have been kept thanks to the kindness of our good parish priest, who asks me to send you his warmest regards. I dutifully await your orders regarding this sad but important ceremony.' "

I threw up my arms and cried:

"And you want to be there for the ceremony!"

Jacinto put the letter back in his pocket.

"That seems the right thing to do, don't you think, Zé Fernandes? Not because of those distant ancestors, whom I never knew and who are nothing but bare bones now, but because of my grandfather, Dom Galeão. I didn't know him either, but No. 202 is full of him. After all, you're lying in his bed, and I still use his watch. I can't leave it to Silvério and the housekeepers to install him in his new tomb. It's a question of decency, of moral elegance. Anyway, I've decided. I pressed my fists to my head and shouted: 'I'm going to Tormes!' And I am. And so are you!"

I had put on my slippers and was tying the belt of my dressing gown.

"You do know, my dear Jacinto, that the house at Tormes is uninhabitable."

He fixed terrified eyes on me:

"Ugly, eh?"

"No, no, it's not ugly at all. It's a beautiful house built of beautiful stone. But the housekeepers, who have lived there for thirty years now, sleep in truckle-beds, eat soup cooked over the fire and use the main rooms for drying the maize. If I remember rightly, the only bits of actual furniture in Tormes are a wardrobe and a Chinese lacquer spinet with one leg and all its keys missing."

My Prince sighed and made a resigned gesture as if abandoning himself to Fate.

"Ah well! *Alea jacta est!* But since we won't be leaving until April, there's plenty of time to have it painted, new floors put in and windows glazed. I'll send carpets and beds from here in Paris. An upholsterer from Lisbon can be brought in later to refurbish things and cover up any holes. We'll take books and a machine for making ice. It's about time I put one of my houses in Portugal into some kind of decent order, don't you think? Especially a house like that, a house dating back to 1410. Why, the Byzantine Empire was still in existence then!"

I was applying large dollops of foam to my face with my shaving brush. My Prince, deep in thought, lit a cigarette and remained there at the dressing table, observing my progress with a glum attentiveness that made me uneasy. Finally, as if ruminating some sentence I had imposed on him and wanting to make quite certain of its meaning and substance, he said:

"So you definitely feel I have a duty, an absolute duty, to go to Tormes?"

I turned to my Prince with a look of amused astonishment on my soapy face:

"But Jacinto, any idea of duty came from you and you alone! And it does you honor too. Don't give that honor away to someone else!"

He threw down his cigarette and, hands buried in his trouser pockets, wandered about the room, bumping into chairs, colliding with the posts on Dom Galeão's ancient bed, and rocking slightly, like a boat untied from its safe mooring and setting off with no fixed course across an uncertain sea. Then he came ashore on the table where, in serried ranks, I kept the gallery of my family, arranged according to their importance in my affections, from the daguerrotype of Papa to the photograph of Carocho, my pointer.

And never had my Prince (whom I was contemplating as I attached my braces) seemed so hunched and so diminished, as if worn down by a file that had been wearing away at him for a long time now. Undone by Civilization, this is what the robust line of Jacintos had come to, this scrawny, over-refined man with no muscles and no energy. Those hairy Jacintos who returned to their high lands in Tormes, back from defeating the Moor at Salado or the Spaniard at Valverde, did not even bother taking off their battered armor to tend their fields and to train their vines to the elms, building their kingdom with lance and spade, each as strong and rough-hewn as the other. And now here was this last Jacinto, this small, shriveled Jacinto, with his soft skin bathed in perfumes, his little soul entangled in philosophies, trapped and sighing over his pathetic indecision about whether or not to live.

"I say, Zé Fernandes, who's this strapping peasant girl?"

I craned my neck to see the photograph he was holding up, in its honest scarlet plush frame.

"A little respect, please, Dom Jacinto! A little respect, sir! That is my cousin Joaninha de Sandofim, from the Casa da Flor da Malva."

"Flor da Malva," muttered my Prince. "Isn't that the house of the Lord High Constable, Nun'Alvares?"

"No, that's the Casa da Flor da Rosa, man, in the Alentejo! Honestly, your ignorance of things Portuguese is positively embarrassing!"

My Prince let the photograph of my cousin slip from between his limp fingers and then raised them once more to his face in that morbid way he had of feeling for the skull beneath the skin. Then, suddenly, he made a brave effort, pulled himself up straight and said:

"Right. *Alea jacta est!* We will leave for the country! And there's to be no time for reflection or rest. To work and *en route!*"

He gripped the golden door handle as if it were the black bolt that opens the door to all our Destinies, and once out in the corridor, he shouted for Cricket in a loud and urgent tone I had never heard before; indeed, Jacinto reminded me of a commander at dawn, ordering camp to be struck and for the troops to set off with all their flags and baggage.

That same morning (with the frantic haste of someone who has just downed a dose of castor oil) he wrote to Silvério ordering that the house be whitewashed and floors and windows repaired. Then, after lunch, he came rushing into the Library to make a telephone call to the director of the Universal Transport Company, asking him to come at once in order to arrange the dispatch of furniture and other comforts.

The director was like an advertising poster for his own company: he wore a close-fitting, double-breasted, dark check overcoat, travelling gaiters over white boots, a morocco leather bag slung across one shoulder, and, in his buttonhole, as proof of the universality of the services his company provided, a multicolored rosette composed of the exotic honors he had received from Madagascar, Nicaragua, Persia and other lands. As soon as Jacinto mentioned "Tormes, in the Douro . . ." he gave a superior smile and held up his hand, fending off any further clarification, proud of his intimate knowledge of all regions.

"Ah, yes, Tormes, of course, of course!"

He scribbled a rapid note in the notebook resting on his knee, while I stood amazed at the vastness of his chorographic knowledge and at his familiarity with even the most hidden corners of that mountainous region of Portugal and its ancient houses and estates. He had already put his notebook back in his bag. All we dear gentlemen had to do was to pack our clothes, furniture and other precious things into crates; then he would send his carts to collect the crates on which he would write the address in large letters, in heavy ink.

"Yes, of course, Tormes. On the Spain-Medina-Salamanca Line. Of course. Tormes. So picturesque, so ancient, so historic! Of course, of course!"

He gave the lowest and most dislocating of bows and left the Library taking long strides that seemed to devour whole leagues and spoke volumes for the speed of his Transport Company.

"You see," muttered Jacinto gravely. "Such promptness, such efficiency! In Portugal, it would be a disaster. Ah, there's nowhere like Paris!"

In No. 202 the colossal task began of packing up all the comforts my Prince would need for a month's stay in the rugged countryside—feather beds, tin baths, Carcel oil-lamps, large divans, curtains to conceal any large cracks and carpets to soften the rough floors. He ransacked the attics in which Dom Galeão's heavy furniture was stored, on the premise that a medieval mansion built in 1410 would be the perfect setting for vast romantic pier glasses made in 1830. Each morning, from every shop in Paris, there arrived packages and boxes and terrifying parcels, which were immediately unwrapped by the packers, leaving the corridors strewn with piles of straw and brown paper in which our hurrying feet became entangled. The cook breathlessly arranged the shipment of ovens, ice-boxes, jars of truffles, tins of conserves, and flagons of mineral water. Jacinto, fearing thunderstorms, bought a huge lightning rod. From dawn onwards, from the courtyards and the garden, came the sound of hammering and nailing, as if a whole city were being built. And the parade of luggage going out through the front door was reminiscent of Herodotus' description of the march of the Persians.

Jacinto pointed triumphantly from the window, savoring all this activity and discipline.

"You see, Zé Fernandes, such efficiency! We leave No. 202, arrive in the country and find No. 202 again! Ah, there's nowhere like Paris!"

My Prince's love affair with the City was rekindled as he prepared for his exodus. Having spent all morning harrying the packers, discovering new comforts for the abandoned house, telephoning long lists of merchandise through to every shop in Paris, he would step into the victoria or spring onto the seat of the phaeton and drive off to the Bois, where he would wave to Efraim's Talmudic beard, Madame Verghane's furiously black locks, to the psychologist in his fiacre and the Countess de Trèves in her new eight-spring caleche purchased with the combined proceeds of the Bourse and the Bedroom. Then he would round up friends for surprise parties at Voisin's or Bignon's, where he would unfurl his napkin with the impatience brought on by an excellent appetite, keeping a stringent eye on the wines to ensure that the Bordeaux was warm enough and the Champagnes cold enough. And at the Théâtre des Nouveautés, at the Palais Royal or the Théâtre des Bouffes, he would laugh and slap his thigh at tired old jokes in tired old farces, at hoary old bits of business performed by hoary old actors, just as he used to laugh when he was a child, before the war, in the days of the second Napoleon!

Within two weeks, his diary was once more filled to bursting. He dazzled everyone by the magnificence of his costume as Frederick II, Duke of Swabia, at the masked ball held by the Princess de Cravon-Rogan (to which I was also invited, as a Portuguese *toureiro*). And at the Association for the Promotion of Esoteric Religions he debated and argued bravely for the erection of a Buddhist temple in Montmartre!

To my horror, he also began speaking, as he used to at the *Grande école*, of "the maximum amount of Civilization possible." He ordered his old telescope to be packed up for him to use in Tormes. I even feared that an idea was germinating in his brain to create, up in the mountains, a City—with all its organs. My Jacinto also clearly didn't intend to allow his limitless accumulation of ideas to be interrupted by the weeks we were to spend in wild Tormes, for he burst into my room one morning in great distress, declaring that among all the many comforts and forms of Civilization, we had completely forgotten about books! It was true—how shameful of our Intellectual Selves! But which books to choose from the eloquent millions beneath whose weight No. 202 groaned? My Prince decided there and then to devote his mountain sojourn to the study of Natural History and, as ballast, we immediately filled the bottom of a vast crate with Pliny's twenty-five volumes. We then hurled in, by the armful, books on Geology, Mineralogy and Botany, topping them off with a sprinkle of airy Astronomy. And to hold these oscillating Sciences steady, we wedged them in place with a little Metaphysics.

However, when the very last crate, nailed down and bound in iron, left No. 202 on the very last cart sent by the Universal Transport Company, all of Jacinto's excitement vanished like the bubbles in a glass of Champagne. It was mid-March by then, and the weather was growing warmer. And once again, No. 202 echoed to the disagreeable sound of his yawns, and all the sofas creaked beneath the weight of his body when, mortally wounded by surfeit and tedium, he flung himself down on them, longing for eternal rest, surrounded by solitude and silence. I despaired. Would I have to put up yet again with the sight of my Prince bitterly feeling for the skull beneath the skin and, as twilight filled the Library with sad light, with listening to him speaking in hoarse tones of the sweetness of the swift death brought about by the compassionate violence of prussic acid? Please, no! And so one evening, when I found him stretched out on the divan, his arms folded on his chest, as if he were the marble statue on his own granite tomb, I almost yelled at him:

"Wake up, man! It's time we left for Tormes! The house must be all new and shiny and ready by now, and jam-full of *things*. The bones of your ancestors are begging to be laid to rest in their graves! Come on, we've got to bury the dead and make sure that we, the living, live! It's April 5th! The weather in the mountains will be perfect!"

My Prince gradually emerged from his stone-like inertia.

"Silvério hasn't written back to me yet, but you're right, everything must be ready by now. There'll be servants, I should think, and the cook from Lisbon will be arriving. I'm only taking Cricket, oh, and Anatole who polishes my shoes so well and is a pretty good pedicurist too. Today is Sunday."

He put his feet on the ground and cried out heroically:

"All right, we'll leave on Saturday! You write to Silvério!"

Then began the laborious, thoughtful poring over timetables,

with Jacinto's lean finger going back and forth on the map between Paris and Tormes. In order to choose the carriage in which
we would spend the dread journey, we twice waded through the
mud to the station master's office at Gare d'Orléans where we
drove him mad with our demands. My Prince declined one compartment because of the gloomy upholstery, then rejected another
because the bathroom was so horribly small! One of his concerns
was how to take a bath on those mornings when the train would
actually be moving. I suggested using a rubber one. Still uncertain, Jacinto sighed. But nothing terrified him as much as changing trains in Medina del Campo, at night, in the pitch dark of Old
Castile. The Rail Company of Northern Spain & Salamanca tried
in vain to reassure him by letter and by telegram, stating that
when he arrived by train at Irún, another identical compartment,
well-heated and well-lit, would be awaiting him on the train to
Portugal, with a supper laid on especially by one of the direc-
tors, Don Esteban Castillo, who had long been a rowdy, rubicund
friend of No. 202! Jacinto ran his hands anxiously over his face:
"And who will transport the bags and fur coats and books from
the compartment in Irún to the compartment on the Salamanca
train?" Desperate now, I insisted that the porters of Medina del
Campo were the fastest and most skilful in all of Europe! He muttered: "That's all very well, but . . . in Spain . . . and at night . . ."
The night, far from the City, with no telephone, no electric light,
no police stations, seemed to my Prince a place bristling with un-
pleasant surprises and assailants. He only calmed down when he
had ascertained from the Astronomical Observatory, under the
guarantee of wise Professor Bertrand, that there would be a full
moon on the night of our journey!

Finally, on Friday, we completed the vast amount of organization involved in this historic journey! Saturday dawned full of generous sun and caressing warmth. And I was just packing away, carefully wrapped in brown paper, the photographs of the sweet creatures who, during those last twenty-seven months in Paris, had called me *mon petit chou! mon rat chéri!*, when Jacinto burst into the room, looking pale and nervous and wearing a superb orchid in his buttonhole.

"Let's go to the Bois—just to say goodbye!"

We set off to make our grand farewell! And what a delight it was! I was aware at once of the comfort and elasticity of our carriage's cushions and springs. As we drove along the Avenue du Bois de Boulogne, I almost regretted that I could not forever roll along to the rhythmic trot of those two perfect mares, surrounded by the glitter and glint of metal and leather, on that tarmac surface as smooth as marble, edged by well-watered flowerbeds and temptingly cool lawns, passing the very cream of elegant Humanity, who had all just breakfasted on hot chocolate served in Sèvres or Minton porcelain cups, having emerged from among silks and tapestries worth three thousand francs, and who, with light hearts, were slowly, delicately, breathing in the beauty of April. The Bois glowed in a harmony of greens, blues and golds. No potholes or loose earth sullied the smooth paths that curved artfully through the woods; no unkempt branches spoiled the soft undulating foliage that the State keeps washed and brushed. The trilling of the birds was just loud enough to suggest the presence of a little avian grace; indeed, it seemed more natural in these sociable groves to hear the creaking of new saddles upon which swayed Amazons corseted by Redfern. By the Pavillon d'Armenonville we passed

Madame de Trèves, who enfolded us both in the caress of her smiling face, all the brighter at that hour because her rouge was still wet. Immediately behind her, riding along in a jingling phaeton, came Efraim's Talmudic beard, black and glossy, fresh from that morning's application of brilliantine. Other friends of Jacinto were walking along the Avenue des Acacias, and the hands that waved to him, slowly and affably, wore gloves the color of straw and pearl and lilac. Antoine de Todelle shot past us on a large bicycle. Dornan was sitting plumply on a wrought-iron chair beneath a flowering blackthorn and puffing on a huge cigar, as if immersed in the search for fine, sensual rhymes. We passed the psychologist—although he did not see us—engaged in a glumly flirtatious conversation with an invisible someone seated in a coupé that had a distinct air of the boudoir about it and to which only its plump driver lent dignity and decency. We were still driving along when the Duke de Marizac, on horseback, raised his stick and stopped our carriage to ask if Jacinto would be at the Verghanes' house that night for the tableaux vivants. My Prince mumbled "No, I'm leaving for the South," words that could scarcely get past his limp moustache. Marizac said how sorry he was, because it was sure to be a wonderful occasion. There would be tableaux vivants from the Bible and from Roman History! Madame Verghane was to be Mary Magdalene, with bare arms, bare breasts, bare legs, washing Christ's feet with her hair! And as for Christ, a strapping young man—a relative of the Trèves, who worked at the Ministry of War—would be bound, moaning and prostrate, to a cardboard cross! Then there was Lucretia in bed and Tarquin beside her, holding a knife and drawing back the sheets! And afterward there would be supper, at separate tables, with everyone in historical costumes. He had already paired up with Madame de Malbe, who was playing Agrippina! Now *there* was a wonderful tableau, with Agrippina dead and Nero coming to study her body, admiring some parts and scorning others as imperfect. It had been agreed, however, out of politeness, that Nero would unreservedly admire *all* of Madame de Malbe's parts. In short, it looked set to be a superb evening—and terribly educational too!

We waved a long farewell to the merry Duke. And as we drove home, Jacinto remained plunged in a frowning silence, his arms stiffly folded, as if pondering weighty, important matters. Finally, as we passed the Arc de Triomphe, he muttered:

"It's a very grave thing, leaving Europe!"

At last, we set off! We left No. 202 in the sweet, misty twilight. Cricket and Anatole followed in a fiacre piled high with books, cases, overcoats, raincoats, pillows, mineral water, leather bags and blankets, and behind them came a cart groaning under the weight of twenty-three trunks. At the station, Jacinto bought all the newspapers, all the illustrated reviews, more timetables, more books and a very complicated and unfriendly-looking corkscrew. Guided by the station master and by the secretary of the Rail Company, we filled our compartment with these things. I put on my silk cap and my slippers. A whistle pierced the night. Paris flickered and glowed in a last flaring of lights. In order to drink it in, Jacinto rushed to look out of the carriage window, but we were already rolling through the darkness of the provinces. My Prince fell back onto his seat.

"What an adventure, Zé Fernandes!"

As far as Chartres, we sat leafing through the magazines in silence. In Orléans, the guard arrived and very respectfully made our beds. Exhausted by my fourteen months of Civilization, I fell asleep and only woke up in Bordeaux when Cricket hurried in with our hot chocolate. Outside, a fine rain was falling softly from a heavy sky the color of grubby cotton-wool. Jacinto hadn't slept at all, fearing that the sheets might prove rough and damp. Sitting in a white flannel dressing-gown, his face pinched and tired, he dipped a cake in his hot chocolate and grumbled darkly:

"This is terrible! And now, on top of everything, it's raining!"

In Biarritz, we both said with indolent certainty:

"It's Biarritz."

Then Jacinto, who was peering out of the misted window, recognized the slow, lanky gait, the sad, pointed nose of the historian Danjon. For it was he, that eloquent man, dressed in a check suit, beside a chubby lady accompanied by a small, hairy dog on a lead. In his eagerness to enjoy some vicarious contact with the City and with No. 202, Jacinto flung down the window and called to the historian, but the train had already plunged off into the rain and mist.

As we crossed the bridge over the Bidassoa, Jacinto—clearly sensing an end to his life of ease and foreseeing the thornier world of UnCivilization—said with a glum sigh:

"Goodbye France! This is where Spain begins!"

Outraged, I—scenting the generous air of that blessed land—leaped up in front of my Prince, and giving a spirited wiggle of my hips and snapping my fingers like castanets, I intoned an Andalusian song:

> *A la puerta de mi casa*
> *¡Ay Soledad, Soleda . . . á . . . á . . . á!*

He held out supplicant arms to me.

"Please, Zé Fernandes, have pity on the infirm and the sad!"

"Irún! Irún!"

In Irún we enjoyed a lavish lunch laid on by the Rail Company, who were watching over us like an omnipresent goddess. Then the *jefe de la aduana* and the *jefe de la estación* carefully installed us in our next compartment, furbished in olive-green satins, but so small that many of our comforts, in the form of blankets, books, bags and raincoats, had to be transferred to the sleeping compartment in which Cricket and Anatole, both in tartan caps, were relaxing and smoking large cigars. *¡Buen viaje! ¡Gracias! ¡Servidores!* And off we went, with a whistle, through the Pyrenees.

Under the influence of that dulling rain, of that endless succession of identical mountains that seemed to shiver and dissolve in the mist, I slipped into a sweet sleep, and when I opened my eyes, I found Jacinto, sitting in one corner, his book closed on his lap and his lean fingers resting on the book, as he regarded the mountains and valleys with the melancholy of someone entering the land of his exile. At one point, he threw down the book, pulled his soft hat more firmly down on his head and sprang to his feet with such resolve that I feared he might stop the train, jump out and run all the way back through the Basque Country and Navarre to No. 202. Shaking off my torpor, I cried: "No, my friend, no!" However, my poor companion was merely changing positions in order to continue his tedium in another corner, on another cushion, with another closed book. And as the dark of evening came on, and with it a storm of wind and rain, a more deep-rooted terror took hold of my Prince, thus torn from Civilization and carried off into the Nature that was even now encircling him with such savage brutality. He kept interrogating me about Tormes.

"I imagine the nights there must be dreadful, eh, Zé Fernandes? Pitch-black and terribly lonely. And is there a doctor anywhere near?"

Suddenly, the train stopped. The rain beat on the windows harder and more loudly. We were in the middle of nowhere, in utter darkness, with a great, wild wind rolling and gusting around us. The train whistled anxiously. A lantern flashed and came running toward us. Jacinto was nervously tapping his foot. "Oh, this is ghastly, ghastly!" I opened the door a crack. Heads craned out of dimly lit windows, saying in frightened voices: *¿Qué hay?¿ Qué hay?* Soaked by a sudden gust of rain, I drew back; the minutes passed slowly and silently as we desperately wiped the fogged windows in an attempt to peer into the darkness. Then, with perfect serenity, the train started to move again.

Soon the dim lights of a ramshackle station appeared. A ticket-collector, his oilskin jacket dripping, came into the compartment, and we learned from him, as he hurriedly stamped our tickets, that the train, much delayed, might not reach Medina in time to make the connection with the Salamanca train!

"But what will happen then?"

The oilskin jacket, however, had slipped out through the door and vanished into the night, leaving behind a smell of oily dampness. We were plunged into a new torment. What if the Salamanca train had left? The compartment would be uncoupled at Medina, and our precious bodies and our precious souls would be tipped out into the mud along with our twenty-three trunks, in a right royal Spanish confusion and beneath a storm of wind and rain!

"Oh, Zé Fernandes, imagine having to spend the night in Medina!"

This seemed to my Prince a supreme misfortune: a night spent in Medina, in some sordid inn that stank of garlic and had whole armies of bedbugs trooping across the yellowing sheets. I kept glancing anxiously at the hands on my watch, while Jacinto, leaning out of the window with the clamorous rain beating on his face, peered into the dark, hoping to see the lights of Medina and a train patiently waiting. Then he fell back on the seat, dried his moustache and face, and roundly cursed Spain. The train was racing along now, pushing through the vast wind of that desolate plain. Every whistle was a new cause for anxiety and excitement. Could it be Medina? No. it was just some obscure halt, where the train lingered, huffing and puffing, while sleepy, hooded figures, swathed in blankets, prowled around under the shelter, figures made more lugubrious still by the dim light from their lanterns. Jacinto thumped his knee: "But why stop this wretched train? There *are* no other trains, not even any passengers! But then that's Spain for you!" The bell rang faintly, and once more we were cutting through the night and the storm.

Resignedly, I started reading an old *Journal du Commerce* I had brought with me from Paris. Jacinto stamped rancorously up and down the thick carpet, growling like a wild beast. Another seemingly eternal hour slipped by. One toot on the whistle, then another! Far off, some brighter lights blinked in the mist. The wheels screeched and jolted to a halt, the carriages bumping. At last, Medina! The grubby wall of a shed gleamed palely, and suddenly the door was flung open, and a bearded gentleman in a Spanish cape was calling for Señor Don Jacinto: "Quick! Quick! The Salamanca train is about to leave!"

"*¡Que no hay un momento, caballeros! ¡Que no hay un momento!*"

I dazedly grabbed my overcoat and the *Journal du Commerce.* We leaped from the compartment and ran down the platform, across the tracks, through the puddles, stumbling over bundles, propelled along by the wind and by the man in the Spanish cape. Then we slipped, panting, in through another door, which slammed shut with a tremendous crash. We were in a compartment whose walls were lined with a dark green cloth that absorbed what little light there was. And I was just about to reach out to receive from the harassed porters our bags, books and blankets when, in silence, without a sound, the train started moving. We both raced to the window, shouting angrily:

"Stop! Our bags, our blankets! Over here. Cricket! Cricket!"

Our shouts were carried away on a great gust of wind. Once more there was only the dark plain and the hurling rain. Jacinto raised his fists and spluttered furiously:

"What a service! The wretches! Only in Spain! And now what? We've lost our bags! I don't have a clean shirt or even a hairbrush!"

I calmed my unhappy friend:

"Listen! I spotted two porters gathering our things together. Cricket is sure to have it all under control. But, naturally, what with the rush, he'll have put everything in his own compartment. It was a mistake, really, not to keep him with us. We could even have had a game of cards!"

Otherwise, the solicitude of the Company, that omnipresent

goddess, continued to watch over us, for outside the washroom was the basket containing our supper and on the lid a pencilled note from Don Esteban, bearing these friendly words: "For Don Jacinto and his illustrious friend. Enjoy your meal!" I could smell partridge. And a little tranquility entered our hearts along with a sense that our bags must also be under the protection of that same omnipresent goddess.

"Are you hungry, Jacinto?"

"No, I'm not. I'm horrified, furious, fuming . . . and sleepy."

And so it was. After such conflicting emotions, all we wanted were the beds that awaited us, soft and ready. By the time I had removed tie and clothes and laid my head upon the pillow, my Prince—who had not even bothered to undress, apart from wrapping his feet in *my* overcoat, which was all that remained of our luggage—was snoring majestically.

Then, many hours and miles later, I noticed standing by my bed, in the pale morning light sifting in through the green curtains, a uniform and a cap, which murmured very softly and very sweetly in Portuguese:

"Do you have anything to declare, gentlemen? Any personal baggage?"

We were in Portugal! And equally softly and sweetly I murmured:

"No, we have nothing here. Ask for Cricket, our servant. He's in another compartment back there. He has the keys, he has everything. Yes, ask Cricket."

The uniform noiselessly disappeared, like a beneficent shadow. And I fell asleep again, thinking about Guiães, where Aunt Vicência, her white shawl fastened across her breast, would be bustling about and doubtless already preparing the suckling pig.

I awoke wrapped in a long, sweet silence. We were standing at a very quiet, very clean station, where white roses climbed the walls and more roses grew in clumps in a garden, in which a little pond covered in algae was quietly sleeping beneath two mimosa trees whose flowers gave off the most wonderful scent. A pale young man, in a honey-colored overcoat, was pensively studying the train, flexing his walking stick on the ground. Crouched right by the garden gate, an old lady, next to her basket of eggs, was counting copper coins into her lap. Gourds were drying on the roof. Up above glowed a deep, rich, soft blue that made my eyes fill with tears.

I shook Jacinto awake.

"Wake up, man, you're in your own country!"

He untangled his feet from my overcoat, smoothed his moustache and unhurriedly joined me at the open window in order to take a look at *his* country.

"So this is Portugal, eh? Hm, it smells good."

"Of course it smells good, you fool!"

The bell tinkled languidly, and the train slid smoothly away, as if it were just out for a pleasant little trip on those two ribbons of steel, whistling to itself and enjoying the beauties of land and sky.

My Prince made a gesture of despair:

"And without a shirt or a brush or a drop of eau-de-cologne! Here I am entering Portugal and I'm filthy!"

"There's a stop in Régua, and we'll have time then to find Cricket and re-acquaint ourselves with all our comforts. Look, there's the river!"

We were travelling along the side of a rocky mountain, above terraces planted with vines. Beyond, we could see a fine house, a place of opulent repose, with a little whitewashed chapel set in a grove of orange trees full of ripe fruit. On the river, where the dark, desultory waters did not even break against the rocks, a boat in full sail and laden with barrels was making its slow way downstream. Farther off, where olive trees were dwarfed by vast mountains, other fields—the pale green of mignonette—rose up to meet bare, sun-baked rocks drinking in the fine abundance of blue. Jacinto was still stroking his moustache.

"The Douro, eh? Very interesting. It does have a certain grandeur. But now, Zé Fernandes, I really am hungry!"

"Me too!"

We removed the lid of Don Esteban's basket and found therein a veritable feast of ham, lamb, partridges and other cold meats, all warmed by the Andalusian sun of two noble golden bottles of Amontillado and two bottles of Rioja. As he ate the ham, Jacinto contritely bemoaned the error of his ways. Fancy leaving Tormes, that historic house, abandoned and empty! How delightful it would be, on that warm, glowing morning, to travel into the mountains and find his house well-equipped and thoroughly civilized. To encourage him further, I reminded him that what with the work carried out by Silvério and all those "civilized" crates sent from Paris, Tormes would be comfortable enough even for Epicurus. Ah, but Jacinto intended it to be a perfect palace, a No. 202 in the wilderness! And as we talked, we attacked the partridges. I was just uncorking a bottle of Amontillado, when the train slid very quietly into a station. It was Régua. And my Prince immediately lay down his knife in order to summon Cricket and demand the cases that contained all we would need to wash our bodies.

"Wait, Jacinto! We've got plenty of time. The train stops here for an hour. Enjoy your food in peace. Let's not spoil our meal worrying over our baggage. Cricket will be here soon enough."

And I even drew the curtain because, outside, a very tall priest, with a cigarette stuck to his lip, had stopped to peer indiscreetly in at our feast. However, once we had devoured the partridges and Jacinto was confidently unwrapping some Manchego cheese, and still neither Cricket nor Anatole had appeared, I began to feel uneasy and ran to the door to chivvy those laggardly servants along. And at that precise moment, the train slipped out of the station with the same silent stealth. My Prince was most displeased:

"Still no comb and brush! And I so wanted to change my shirt. It's all your fault, Zé Fernandes!"

"I can't understand it. The train always stops here for ages. But today it's off like a shot. Be patient, Jacinto. In two hours' time we'll be at Tormes station. Besides, there's no point in changing your shirt right before climbing a hill. When we arrive, we can take a bath before dinner. They must have installed the bath by now."

We consoled ourselves with a couple of glasses of a divine brandy from Chinchón. Then, reclining on the sofas, savoring our two remaining cigars, with the windows open to the adorable air, we talked about Tormes. Silvério would doubtless be waiting for us with the horses.

"How long does the ride take?" asked Jacinto.

An hour, I told him. And once we had bathed, there would be plenty of time for a stroll around the estate with the caretaker, the excellent Melchior, so that the lord of Tormes could solemnly take possession of his domain. And that night we would enjoy our first country banquet, with all of old Portugal's usual delicacies!

Jacinto smiled, seduced by my description.

"I wonder what kind of a cook Silvério has found for me. I recommended that he find me a superb, classic Portuguese cook, but one who knew how to truffle a turkey and how to cook beef in a gizzard broth and other such simple French dishes. It's a shame you can't stay at Tormes, but have to go straight to Guiães."

"Sorry, old man, but it's Aunt Vicência's birthday on Saturday. A sacred day! But I'll be back. In two weeks' time I'll be in Tormes again so that we can plunge together into bucolic life and, of course, attend the reinterment."

Jacinto pointed at something.

"What house is that over there, beyond the hill, with the tower?"

I didn't know. The estate of some great Douro nobleman. Tormes was similarly stocky and sturdy. A centuries-old house built to last for centuries—but without a tower.

"And can you see Tormes from the station?"

"No, it's high up in a fold in the hills, among the trees."

My Prince was obviously beginning to feel the stirrings of curiosity about his rough ancestral home. He kept looking impatiently at his watch. Another thirty minutes! Then, breathing in the air and the light and feeling the first enchantment of the initiate, he said:

"What sweetness! What peace!"

"It's half past three, Jacinto. We should be nearly there."

I stuffed my old copy of the *Journal du Commerce* in the pocket of my overcoat, which I then draped over my arm, and we both stood at the window, excitedly waiting for the tiny station of Tormes, the happy end of all our trials. The station appeared at last, bright and simple, by the river, among the rocks, with large sunflowers filling its little garden, two tall fig trees shading the courtyard and behind it the mountains clothed in dense, ancient forests. As we drew into the station, I was pleased to see the vast paunch, chubby childish cheeks, and fair hair of the station master, Pimenta, my classmate in Rhetoric at school in Braga. The horses were doubtless waiting in the shade of the fig trees.

As soon as the train stopped, we jumped gaily down. The friendly, big-bellied figure of Pimenta came rolling over to me.

"Greetings, Zé Fernandes!"

I introduced the lord of Tormes, and then asked:

"Listen, Pimenta, isn't Silvério here to meet us?"

"No. Silvério's been in Castelo de Vide for nearly two months now, looking after his mother who got gored by an ox!"

I looked anxiously at Jacinto.

"Oh, no! And what about Melchior, the caretaker? Has no one brought the horses to take us up to the house?"

The worthy station master raised astonished golden eyebrows.

"No. There's no Melchior and no horses. I haven't seen Melchior for I don't know how long!"

The porter was slowly ringing the bell for the train to leave. We looked around and seeing no sign of servants or trunks on the smooth, empty platform, my Prince and I let out the same anxious cry:

"What about Cricket? What about the baggage?"

Thinking that perhaps he and Anatole were both deep asleep, we climbed onto the running-board and peered into the compartments, startling the people sitting peacefully inside with the same resounding bellow: "Cricket, are you there, Cricket?" In a third-class compartment, where someone was strumming a guitar, some joker was wailing: "Has anyone seen a cricket around here? Some gentlemen here are asking for a cricket!" But there was no Anatole and no Cricket!

The bell tinkled again.

"Wait, Pimenta, you can't let the train leave! What about our baggage?"

And in my distress, I propelled the enormous station master in the direction of the baggage compartment so that he could help us find our twenty-three trunks! We found only barrels, wicker baskets, tins of oil, and a trunk tied up with rope. Jacinto, deathly pale, was biting his lip. And a wild-eyed Pimenta was saying:

"I'm sorry, my friends, but I can't hold the train up any longer!"

The bell rang, and in a fine puff of pale smoke, the train disappeared behind the high hills. Everything around seemed even more silent and deserted. There we were, lost and alone in the mountains, with no Cricket, no administrator, no caretaker, no horses and no baggage! I still had my pale overcoat, from the pocket of which still protruded that old copy of the *Journal du Commerce*, and Jacinto had his walking stick. And they were all our possessions!

Pimenta was gazing at us with wide, pitying, puffy eyes. I told him about the bewildering change of trains at Medina in the middle of a storm and how Cricket had got left behind, and was still stuck there with twenty-three trunks or had perhaps headed off to Madrid leaving us without so much as a handkerchief.

"No, not even a handkerchief. This copy of the *Journal du Commerce* is the nearest thing I have to clean white underwear."

"Dreadful!" muttered Pimenta, impressed. "And what now?"

"Now," I exclaimed, "we have to climb up to the house on foot. Unless there are a couple of mules we can borrow."

Then the porter remembered that nearby, in Casal da Giesta, which was part of the Tormes estate, his friend the caretaker had a good mare and a donkey. And the excellent fellow set off at a run, while my Prince and I sank down on a bench, as weary and dejected as shipwreck victims. The vast Pimenta, with his hands in his pockets, kept staring at us and muttering: "Dreadful!" Below us, the river, as if lulled to sleep by the already heavy heat of May, flowed lazily onward, silently embracing a large rocky island that glittered in the sun. Beyond, the mountains formed gentle humps, and in one deep fold, as if forgotten by the world, nestled a small, compact, white village. An immense silence filled that immense space. In those wildernesses of hill and rock, the bustling sparrows on the roof seemed like quite sizeable birds, and the rotund, rubicund figure of Pimenta dominated and filled the whole region.

"It's all arranged, sir! The mare and the donkey are coming now! All that's missing is a saddle for the donkey!"

It was the porter, excellent man, returning from Giesta, brandishing two rusty spurs, neither of which made a pair. And it was not long before down the lane came a chestnut mare, a donkey with a packsaddle, a boy and a setter, all ready to take us up to Tormes. We shook Pimenta's sweaty, friendly hand. I let the lord of Tormes take the mare. And we set off up the path, which had not been smoothed or cleared since the days when it was first trodden by fourteenth-century Jacintos in their rough hobnail boots, as they cut across country from the river to the mountains. After we had crossed a rickety wooden bridge over a stream flowing fast over a pebble bed, my Prince—his owner's eye grown suddenly acute—noticed the sturdy, heavily laden olive trees. And soon, in the face of the incomparable beauty of that blessed land, all our ills were forgotten!

With what brilliant and bounteous inspiration did the Divine Artist of the mountains create, tend and embellish this, his beloved Portugal! Its grandeur was equalled only by its grace. Troops of trees clothed the deep valley sides, their rounded tops of a green so fresh that they resembled a covering of invitingly soft moss. From the slopes, overhanging the rocky path, long branches offered a sweet awning, their fragrance shaken free by the light flutterings of birds. From the ancient ivy-grown walls bordering the fields snaked the fat roots of trees around which still more ivy grew. Out of every crack wild flowers sprang. The white rocks of the hillsides revealed bare hard breasts polished by wind and sun; others, covered in lichen and flowering brambles, protruded like the decorated prows of galleys; and among the rocks clustering together on the peaks perched the occasional hut, all battered and crooked, peering out through black windows from beneath the disheveled mop of greenery that the wind had sown on its roof tiles. Everywhere there was the whisper of life-bringing water. Bright little brooks fled, laughing, over the pebbles, between the hooves of the mare and the donkey; broad streams went roaring helter-skelter from rock to rock; straight, shining threads of water like silver strings fell trembling and glittering from the heights to the depths; and many a spring, placed by the side of the path, poured beneficently forth, waiting for man or beast to drink from them. Sometimes the whole of a hillside formed one great field, dominated by a single vast, ancestral oak tree, as if it were both lord and guardian. Down below grew the dark green of sweet-smelling orange trees. Paths made from loose slabs of stone encircled lush meadows in which sheep and cows grazed or, narrower still and flanked by walls, disappeared beneath dense vine-trellises, all shade and repose and coolness. We climbed the narrow street of a hamlet consisting of only ten or twelve cottages surrounded by fig trees and from which there rose, escaping the hearth through the thin-skinned roof, a white skein of smoke that smelled of pine-wood. On the distant hills, in the midst of the pensive dark green of the pine forests, we could see the occasional small white chapel. The fine, pure air entered the soul and spread joy and strength. A faint tinkle of cowbells faded away on the hillsides.

Ahead of me on his mare, Jacinto was murmuring:

"How beautiful!"

And behind him astride Sancho's mule, I, too, murmured:

"Yes, how beautiful!"

Cool branches brushed our shoulders, familiar and affectionate. Behind the brambles, heavy with the berries to come, the many apple trees, having nothing ripe to offer, instead held out to us their hard green fruits. The windows of an old house with a cross on top glinted hospitably as we passed. For a long time a blackbird followed us, from holm oak to elm, whistling our praises! Thank you, brother blackbird! Thank you, apple trees! Here we are! Here we are! And may we stay here with you always, you welcoming, fertile, peaceful mountains, most blessed of all mountains!

And so, in leisurely fashion, marveling as we went, we reached that avenue of beech trees whose grave nobility I had always found so charming. Flicking the donkey and the mare with a switch, our boy, his setter at his heels, cried: "Here we are, my masters!" And indeed, at the end of the avenue we could see the gateway to Tormes with its coat of arms carved in age-old granite, adorned and aged still further by a pelt of moss. Inside, the dogs were already furiously barking. And when Jacinto, on his sweating mare, and I behind him, on Sancho's mule, crossed the manorial threshold, a plump man, shaven-headed like a priest, with no waistcoat and no jacket on, came hurrying down the worn stone steps of the porch to call off the dogs—who seemed to have taken particular exception to my Prince. It was Melchior the caretaker. As soon as he recognized me, his mouth spread into a wide, hospitable, toothless grin; but when I revealed to him that the gentleman with the fair moustaches who was just climbing down from the mare and rubbing his haunches was none other than the lord of Tormes, good Melchior shrank back in horror and terror as if he had seen a ghost.

"No! Well, in the name of all that's holy . . ."

And between growls from the dogs and his own many despairing gestures, he stammered out a story which in turn horrified Jacinto, as if the black wall of the house were collapsing on top of him there and then. Melchior was not expecting His Excellency. No one was expecting His Excellency (or as he said "His Incellency"). Senhor Silvério had been in Castelo de Vide since March with his mother, who had been gored in the groin. There had clearly been some misunderstanding! Letters must have gone astray, because Senhor Silvério was only expecting His Incellency in September, for the harvest! Work on the house was continuing slowly, very slowly. The roof, on the south side, was as yet untiled;

many of the windows still lacked glass; and as for staying there, not a single bed was made up!

Jacinto crossed his arms trying to restrain the tumultuous rage building inside him. Finally, he roared:

"But what about the crates? We sent the crates from Paris in February, a whole four months ago!"

Poor Melchior stared at him with his little eyes, now filling with tears. What crates?! Nothing had arrived, nothing had come! And in his distress, he looked across at the courtyard arches and felt in his trouser pockets. Crates? No, he had no crates!

"And now what do we do, Zé Fernandes?"

I shrugged.

"Well, my friend, all you can do now is come with me to Guiães . . . except that it's a good two hours' ride from here. And we have no horses! The best thing would be to have a look at the house, eat the plump chicken that our friend Melchior here will roast on a spit for us, sleep on a simple pallet bed and tomorrow, bright and early, before it gets too hot, we'll trot off to Aunt Vicência's."

Jacinto retorted furiously:

"The only trotting I'm doing tomorrow is back down to the station and then straight to Lisbon!"

And he stormed angrily up the worn steps of his house. A long verandah of black beams and granite pillars ran around the front of the building and was adorned with wooden containers full of carnations in bloom. I picked a yellow flower and followed Jacinto into the main rooms, only to hear his suppressed cry of horror. As vast and echoing as a chapter house, their thick walls blackened by time and neglect, they were icy cold and depressingly bare, apart from the odd pile of baskets or a hoe and some planks abandoned in one corner. Through the cracks in the high oak-panelled ceilings, one could see patches of sky. The windows, bereft of glass, still had their thick shutters complete with bolts and bars, and these, when closed, guaranteed total darkness. Here and there, the occasional rotten creaking floorboard gave way beneath our feet.

"It's completely uninhabitable!" said Jacinto under his breath. "It's ghastly! Hideous!"

In other rooms, though, the floors had been patched with new boards. More signs of repair work in the form of paler wood flecked the ancient ceilings made of rich, somber oak. Some walls dazzled us with the crude brightness of fresh whitewash, but the sun could barely penetrate the new panes of glass, which were fogged and greasy with putty and with the glaziers' fingerprints.

Finally, we went into the last and largest of the rooms with its six windows; it was furnished only with a wardrobe and, in one corner, a small, grubby pallet. We stopped right there and gloomily deposited on it what remained of the contents of the twenty-three trunks—my white overcoat, Jacinto's walking stick, and, our joint property, the copy of the *Journal du Commerce*. Through the gaping glassless windows, the generous mountain air blew in as if over a threshing-floor, bringing with it the fresh smell of watered gardens. But what we saw from where we were standing was a pine wood covering the hillside and marching down the gentle slope, like an army with pine trees in the vanguard, tall and erect and plumed in black; further off, beyond the river, we could see the mountains, of a delicate shade of violet, and above, the smooth perfection, the divine majesty of the cloudless sky. From the valleys below came the voice of a shepherd singing, heartfelt and melancholy.

Jacinto walked slowly over to one of the window seats, where he collapsed, overwhelmed by the disaster that had befallen him, helpless before the abrupt disappearance of all Civilization! I prodded the straw bed, which was as hard and cold as granite in Winter. And remembering the luxurious spring beds with feather mattresses, so lovingly packed at No. 202, I, too, gave vent to my indignation:

"But where are the crates, damn it? How could anyone lose thirty or more enormous crates?"

Jacinto gave a bitter shrug.

"They must be stuck in a shed somewhere. In Medina, perhaps, at that ghastly station. Indifference on the part of the Transport Company, inertia on Silvério's part. Well, what can one expect of a barbarous place like the Iberian Peninsula?"

I went and knelt down on the other window seat, taking consolation in the sky and the hills.

"But then it is *so* beautiful!"

And after a grave silence, my Prince rested his cheek on his hand and murmured:

"Yes, it is lovely . . . and so peaceful!"

Underneath the window grew a lush vegetable plot full of cabbages, beans, rows of lettuces, and the large trailing leaves of pumpkins. An old, neglected threshing-floor looked out over the valley where a faint, tenuous mist was already rising up from some deep-set stream. The whole of that side of the house was surrounded by orange-trees, and from a rustic fountain, half-choked by tremulous roses, flowed a long glittering thread of water.

"I could really do with some of that water!" declared Jacinto, grave-faced.

"So could I. Let's go down into the garden, shall we? And we can call in at the kitchen on the way, to ask about that chicken."

We returned to the verandah. My Prince, more reconciled now to cruel destiny, plucked a red carnation. And through another low sturdy door we entered another room, strewn with rubble, with no ceiling and covered only by thick beams from which flew a flock of sparrows.

"Look at this!" muttered Jacinto with a horrified shudder.

Then we went down some dark steps, worthy of a castle, and felt our way along a gloomy, roughly paved corridor lined with deep chests, large enough to store the grain of a whole province. At the end was the enormous kitchen, a mass of black shapes: black wood, black stone, dense black stains from centuries of soot. And on the black floor, in the midst of all that blackness, glowed the red fire, licking at iron pots and pans and giving off a cloud of smoke that disappeared through the open grate in the wall and into the leaves of the lemon trees outside. The vast fireplace, where the Jacintos of the Middle Ages used to cook and roast whole sides of pork and beef, had been abandoned by the frugal caretaker and his wife, and all that it held was a black, dusty pile of baskets and tools. The only light came from an open door, which gave onto a rustic little vegetable patch where red cabbages rubbed shoulders with exquisite jonquils. Around the fire, a group of women were hurriedly plucking chickens, stirring pots, chopping onions, and talking feverishly. All fell silent when we appeared, and poor harried Melchior, the blood rushing to his plump priestly face, sprang up from among them and ran to assure us: "Your Incellencies' dinner won't take an instant to prepare."

"And what about beds, friend Melchior?"

The worthy man mumbled an embarrassed apology about only being able to offer us straw mattresses on the floor.

"That will be fine," I said to console him. "It's just for one night and you've got fresh sheets I'm sure."

"Oh, don't worry, we have plenty of fresh sheets. But I feel dreadful, sir. Caught without a good wool mattress to offer you or a nice loin of beef. In fact, as I was saying to my missus, Your Incellencies could always sleep at Silvério's house. They have proper iron bedsteads there and washstands. Of course, it is over a league away along a bad road, but—"

Jacinto kindly interrupted him:

"No, don't worry, everything will be fine, Melchior. It's only for a night. Besides, I like the idea of sleeping in Tormes—in my house in the mountains!"

We went outside into a scrap of garden closed off by large rocks overgrown with greenery and bordering the terraces where fields of golden rye were growing. My Prince placed his lips to the spout of the fountain there and greedily gulped down some of the bright icy water; he admired the round crisp lettuces and jumped up to grab the high branches of a leafy cherry tree, heavy with fruit. Then, walking around the old press, its roof almost white with doves, we reached a path cut into the side of the hill. And as we walked quietly along, my Prince expressed his astonishment at the cornfields, at the ancient oak trees planted by ancient Jacintos, at the cottages scattered over the hillsides along the dark edge of the pine woods.

Again we walked down the avenue of beeches and through the manorial gate where we were again greeted by the barking of the dogs, although they were more restrained this time, sensing the presence of their Master. Jacinto agreed that there was indeed something "rather noble" about the façade of his house, but what he particularly liked was that long avenue, so broad and straight, as if designed to receive a cavalcade of gentlemen wearing plumed hats and accompanied by pages. Then, from the verandah, noticing the new roof on the chapel, he praised that "idler" Silvério for at least taking care of God's dwelling-place.

"And this verandah is very pleasant too," he said, burying his face in the carnations to breathe in their scent. "What's needed, though, are some big armchairs and a couple of large wicker divans . . ."

Inside, in "our drawing-room," we both sat down on the window seats, contemplating the gentle twilight peace slowly descending on valley and mountain. High up, one small star twinkled, diamond-bright Venus, the languid herald of night and its contentments. Jacinto had never before taken a long look at that amorously brilliant star, which perpetuates in our Catholic sky the memory of the incomparable goddess, nor had he ever contemplated, with attentive soul, the majestic way in which Nature falls asleep. The darkening of the hills as they drew the shadows up about them; the trees falling silent, grown weary of whispering; the bright whiteness of the houses softly growing dim; the blanket of mist, in which the coldness of the valleys huddles for warmth; the sleepy clanging of a bell rolling over the hillsides; the secretive murmur of water and of dark grasses—for him, each was an initiation. From that window, open onto the mountains, he could glimpse another life, one not filled up by Man and his tumultuous doings. And I heard my friend utter a sigh like that of someone who can at last rest.

We were torn from this enchanted state by Melchior, softly informing "His Incellencies" that dinner was ready. It was served in another even barer and more neglected room, and my super-civilized Prince stopped short at the door, horrified by the discomfort, meagerness and roughness of things. On the table, on a cotton cloth, against the blackened wall stained by the smoke from oil-lamps, two tallow candles in tin candleholders lit large yellow earthenware plates, flanked by tin spoons and iron forks. The very thick glasses retained the purple shadow of the wine poured into them over many plentiful years of plentiful harvests. The earthenware bowl, filled with black olives, would have pleased Diogenes himself. Impaled in the crust of a huge loaf of bread was an equally huge knife. And on the manorial chair reserved for my Prince—the last remnant of the Jacintos of old, with its stiff back and its worm-eaten wood—the horsehair stuffing was escaping by the handful through the torn leather of the worn seat.

A formidable young woman, with enormous breasts that jiggled about inside the sprigged fabric of her shawl, and still sweating and red-faced from the heat of the fire, came lumbering in, bearing a steaming tureen. And Melchior, who followed with the pitcher of wine, hoped that "His Incellencies" would forgive him but there hadn't been time for the soup to clarify. Jacinto occupied his ancestral seat, and for several moments (moments of wide-eyed anxiety for the excellent Melchior) used one corner of the table cloth to rub energetically at the black fork and the dull tin spoon. Then, very cautiously, he tried the chicken soup, which smelled divine. He tasted it and with surprised shining eyes looked up at me, his comrade in misery. He took another more considered sip from a fuller spoon this time, then smiled in amazement: "It's good!"

It was delicious, made from chicken liver and giblets; the smell of it touched one's heart; I served myself three whole bowlfuls of the stuff.

"I'll have some more too," exclaimed Jacinto with great conviction. "I'm so hungry. Good God, I haven't been this hungry in years."

He was the one to scrape out the tureen and then turn to watch the door, waiting for the strapping young woman with the quivering breasts to bring in the next delicacy. Making the floor tremble and with her face still redder, she duly returned and placed on the table a dish overflowing with rice and broad beans. What a disappointment! In Paris, Jacinto had always hated broad beans. Nevertheless, he tried a timid forkful, and again his eyes, dimmed by pessimism, lit up and again he looked at me. He took another larger forkful, concentrating this time and eating as slowly as a friar, savoring every mouthful. Then he cried:

"Excellent! Now these beans I like. What a bean! So delicious!"

And overcome by blessed gluttony, he praised the mountains, praised the perfect art of those talkative women busily stirring saucepans in the kitchen, and praised Melchior who was presiding over the banquet.

"You wouldn't get rice and beans like this even in Paris, Melchior, my friend!"

The excellent man smiled, all his anxieties dissipated.

"Well, it's what we give to the farmhands, sir! And by the plateful too! It would make Your Incellencies laugh! I can see Dom Jacinto is going to get fat and strong living here!"

The good man genuinely believed that, lost in the distant Parises of the world, the lord of Tormes—far from the plenty of Tormes—had been starving and growing thin. And my Prince really did seem to be satisfying an ancient hunger and a long nostalgia for such abundance, lavishing ever more praise on each dish that appeared. Faced by the golden chicken roasted on the spit and by the lettuce he had so admired in the garden, now drizzled with a little mountain olive oil worthy of the lips of Plato, he finally roared: "It's utterly divine!" But this was as nothing to the enthusiasm he expressed for the wine of Tormes, poured from on high from the plump green pitcher, a cool, lively, succulent wine with more soul and more soul-enhancing qualities than many a poem or holy book. By the light of the candle, gazing at his thick glass edged now with rosy foam, my Prince, an optimistic glow on his face, quoted Virgil:

"Quo te carmina dicam, Rethica? Who can best sing thy praises, O lovely wine of the mountains?"

And I, not wanting to be bested when it came to a knowledge of the classics, unleashed my own line from Virgil, praising the sweetness of rural life:

"Hanc olim veteres vitam coluere Sabini. Thus lived the old Sabines. Thus Romulus and Remus. Thus valiant Etruria grew strong. Thus Rome became the wonder of the world!"

And motionless, still holding the pitcher, Melchior stared at us in infinite amazement and religious reverence.

Yes, beneath the auspices of Melchior, we dined deliciously and, afterward, ever provident and tutelary, he furnished us with tobacco. And, with a long country night ahead of us, we returned to the glassless windows in the vast hall to contemplate the sumptuous Summer sky. We philosophized phlegmatically and eloquently.

In the City (as Jacinto remarked) no one ever looks at or even thinks about the stars because the gas lamps and the electric lights block them out. That is why (as I remarked) no one ever enters into that communion with the Universe which is the sole glory and sole consolation of Life. In the mountains, though, with no hideous six-storey buildings, with no smoke to conceal God, with none of the worries which, like pieces of lead, drag the soul down to the lowliest dust, a Jacinto and a Zé Fernandes, sitting together at a window, at ease after a good dinner, can look at the stars and the stars can look back at them. Some stars, it is true, do so with eyes of sublime immobility or sublime indifference, but others do so curiously, yearningly, with a light that beckons, a light that calls, as if trying, from far far away, to reveal their secrets or, from far far away, to understand ours.

"What star is that, Jacinto, that really bright one, just above the eaves?"

"I don't know. And that one over there, Zé Fernandes, above the pine woods?"

"I don't know."

We didn't know. I because of the thick crust of ignorance with which I had left the womb of my Spiritual Mother, Coimbra University. He because in his Library he had three hundred and eight treatises about Astronomy, and when Knowledge accumulates like that, it forms a mountain that can neither be moved nor even chipped away at. But what did it matter to us if a star over there was called Sirius and another star Aldebaran? What did it matter to them if one of us was called Jacinto and the other Zé Fernandes? They are so immense and we so tiny, and yet we are the work of the same Will. And all of them, Neptunes and Zé Fernandeses, constitute different forms of a unique Being, and our various differences add up to the same compact Unity—molecules of the same Whole, governed by the same Law, travelling toward the same End. From star to man, from man to clover, from clover to the loud sea, it's all the same Body, in which the same God circulates like blood. And the slightest tremor of life, however small, that passes through a single fiber of that sublime Body affects all the other fibers, even the most humble, even those which seem inert and lifeless. When a Sun I have never seen and never will see dies of inanition somewhere in the depths of the Universe, the slender branch of that lemon tree down in the garden feels a secret shudder of death, and when I stamp on the floor here in Tormes, monstrous Saturn trembles, and that tremor shakes the whole Universe! Jacinto slammed his hand down hard on the window ledge and I cried out:

"Believe me, the Sun trembled!"

And then (as I remarked) we must also consider that on each of those grains of luminous dust there exists a creation which is constantly being born and dying and being reborn. At this very moment, other Jacintos and other Zé Fernandeses, sitting at the windows of other Tormeses, are contemplating the night sky and the tiny point of light that is our own mighty Earth and which we so exalt. They will not all have the same fragile, awkward form as we do (with the exception of the Apollo in the Vatican or the Venus de Milo or perhaps the Princess de Carman), so singularly ugly and absurd. But whether they be hideous or ineffably beautiful, colossal and made of granite-hard flesh or light as gauze and floating in the light, they are all thinking beings with full consciousness of Life—because each of those Worlds doubtless has its Descartes, or else our Descartes has already spread his Method to them all, his dark protective cape, his elegant perception, formulating the one possibly certain certainty, the great *I think therefore I am.* Thus all we Inhabitants of the Worlds, at the windows of our mansions, whether over there on Saturn or here on our little Earth, are constantly performing a sacrosanct act that penetrates and fuses us into one—namely, experiencing in thought the common nucleus of our individual ways of being and thus understanding for a moment, in our consciousness, the Oneness of the Universe.

"What do you think, Jacinto?"

My friend grunted:

"Hmm . . . maybe. Goodness, I'm sleepy."

"Me too. 'We have come a long way, my dear sir!' as Pestaninha used to say in Coimbra. But what could be more beautiful or more futile than a conversation high in the mountains, looking up at the stars! Do you still intend leaving tomorrow?"

"I certainly do, Zé Fernandes! I can say with the certainty of a Descartes: 'I think therefore I flee!' What do you expect me to do in this old ruin, without a bed, without a mattress, without a book? Man cannot live on beans and rice alone! But I'll stay in Lisbon to talk to Sesimbra, my administrator there, and wait until this work is finished, until the crates reappear and I can return in decent fashion, with some clean clothes, for the re-interment."

"Oh, of course, the bones!"

"And then there's that fool Cricket! Where the devil can he have got to?"

Walking slowly up and down in the vast room, where the tallow candle had melted down in its tin candleholder until it was about as bright as a cigarette end in the middle of an open field, we pondered Cricket's fate. The dear man had either been ejected, screaming, from the train into the mud of Medina, along with the twenty-seven trunks or else, blissfully sleeping, had traveled on with Anatole in the train to Madrid. To my Prince both these possibilities spelled disaster for his personal comfort.

"No, listen, Jacinto. What if Cricket got stuck in Medina, spent the night at an inn killing bedbugs, and set off this morning for Tormes? When you go down to the station tomorrow at four o'clock, you'll find your precious servant and all your precious trunks in the train that will take you to Oporto and then on to Lisbon."

Like someone caught in a net, Jacinto frantically waved his arms about:

"But what if he continued on to Madrid?"

"Then some time this week, he'll turn up in Tormes, where he'll find orders to go back to Lisbon and rejoin your entourage. There's still the interesting matter of my baggage, too. If you do find Cricket at the station tomorrow, separate out my black case and the canvas bag and the hatbox. Cricket knows which ones are mine. And ask that fat fellow, Pimenta, to send word to me in Guiães. If Cricket finally fetches up in Tormes, hotfoot from Madrid, with all that baggage, then tell him to leave my things here with Melchior. I'll speak to Melchior tomorrow."

Jacinto tugged furiously at his collar:

"But how can I leave for Lisbon tomorrow wearing a shirt I've been wearing for two days now and which is already itching like mad? And without so much as a handkerchief or a toothbrush!"

Ever fertile in ideas, I spread my hands in a gesture of grand beneficence.

"It can all be sorted out, Jacinto. If I leave here early, at six o'clock, I can be in Guiães by ten before it gets too hot. And before I even sit down for some lunch and a chat with Aunt Vicência, I will immediately despatch a boy to bring you a bag of clean clothes. My shirts and my underwear might be a little on the large side, but a beggar like you has no right to look elegant and wear well-cut clothes. If the boy rides hard, he should be here by two o'clock, just in time for you to change and go down to the station. I can even put a toothbrush in the bag too."

"Would you, Zé Fernandes? Then pack a sponge as well . . . and a bottle of eau-de-cologne!"

"Lavender water—just the thing—made by Aunt Vicência."

My Prince sighed, suddenly overwhelmed by his miserable, squalid state and by my promised gift of clothes.

"Let's go to sleep then, I'm worn out with emotion and with the stars."

Just then, Melchior tentatively pushed open the heavy door to tell us that our beds were ready. And when we followed the good man, what did we see, my Prince and I, we who, only a short time before, had been brothers to the stars? Two straw pallets lay on the floor of two small rooms that were separated by a gloomy stone arch. At the head of the larger bed, destined for the lord of Tormes, a tin candlestick on an upturned pannier, and, at the foot, by way of a washstand, a glazed bowl on a three-legged stool. I, being from those parts, had neither bowl nor pannier.

My super-civilized friend cautiously prodded the straw mattress with one foot. It must have seemed to him intransigently hard, because he remained standing by it, drawing his fingers over his pale face.

"And the mattress isn't the worst of it either," he said at last with sigh. "I don't even have a nightshirt to wear or any slippers! And I can't go to bed in a starched shirt."

At my suggestion, we consulted Melchior. Again, the worthy man found a solution, bringing Jacinto a pair of clogs to comfort his feet and, to clothe his body, a nightdress belonging to Melchior's wife, an enormous burlap affair, as rough as a penitent's serge tunic, with frills and flounces as crisp and hard as carved wood. To console my Prince I reminded him that when Plato was writing his *Symposium on Love* and when Vasco da Gama was rounding the Cape, they'd had no better beds to sleep in! Hard mattresses make strong souls, I told him. And it is only in a rough serge tunic that one can enter Paradise!

"You don't happen to have anything I can read, do you?" asked my friend tartly. "I can't go to sleep without a book."

Me? A book? All I had was the old copy of the *Journal du Commerce* that had escaped the dispersal of our goods. I tore the newspaper in half and, in brotherly fashion, shared it with Jacinto. He took his half, which happened to be the pages containing the advertisements. Only someone who has seen Jacinto, lord of Tormes, sitting crouched on the edge of the mattress, his feet buried in a pair of wooden clogs and his body swathed in the coarse folds and stiff frills of a rustic nightdress, as he perused the departure times of steamships on that scrap of old newspaper by the light of a tallow candle slowly melting onto a rough wicker pannier—only he can have a true image of total and utter Despair.

I was standing in my own spartan bedroom, unbuttoning my

waistcoat and feeling deliciously tired, when my Prince called to me:

"Zé Fernandes . . ."

"Yes."

"Can you put a buttonhook for my boots in the bag as well?"

Stretched out comfortably on the hard mattress, I murmured as I always do as I slide into Sleep, which is a cousin to Death: "God be praised!" Then I picked up my half of the *Journal du Commerce*.

"Zé Fernandes . . ."

"What is it?"

"Could you also put some tooth-powder in the bag . . . and a nail file . . . Oh, and a novel!"

The half-newspaper was already slipping from my sleeping hands, but from his bedroom, after blowing out the candle, came these words, half-spoken, half-yawned:

"Zé Fernandes . . ."

"Hmm?"

"Write to me in Lisbon, at the Hotel Bragança. At least the sheets here are clean, and they smell nice and wholesome too!"

: IX :

I SET OFF FOR GUIÃES early the next morning, taking care
not to wake Jacinto, who was sleeping beatifically on his bed of
granite, hands folded on his chest.

A week later, as I was returning one morning for lunch, I found
in the corridor my much-missed luggage, which a boy from Casal
da Giesta had brought up in a cart "with regards from Senhor
Pimenta." My thoughts immediately leaped to my Prince and I
despatched a telegram to the Hotel Bragança in Lisbon with this
merry cry: "Are you there? Cricket and Civilization restored I
hear! Hurrah! Fond regards!" I only noticed Jacinto's silence
after another week—a week taken up with the delicate business of
picking the asparagus with which I had previously "civilized" Aunt
Vicência's garden. On a postcard I sent the same hearty greeting:
"Are you there? Is it the pleasures of Lisbon that have made you so
distracted and silent? As for me, I'm full of asparagus! Write soon
and tell me when you'll be arriving. Wonderful weather here. 73
in the shade. What's happened to the bones?" Then it was time
for the festival of Our Lady of Roqueirinha, and during the period
of the new moon, I was out clearing undergrowth on my estate in
Corcas. Then Aunt Vicência suffered a stomach upset after eating

some black pudding. And my Prince's ungrateful, intransigent silence continued.

Then, one afternoon, returning from Flor da Malva, from my cousin Joaninha's house, I stopped in Sandofim, at Manuel Rico's store in order to drink a certain white wine which my soul knows and for which it always yearns.

Opposite, outside the blacksmith's, Severo—Melchior's nephew and the best horse-doctor and farrier in the region—was sitting astride a bench, shredding some tobacco. I called for another glass of wine, and he stroked the neck of my mare whom he had recently cured of a chill; and when I asked after Melchior, Severo said that he had dined with him only yesterday in Tormes and had seen the Master too.

"Really! So Senhor Dom Jacinto is at Tormes?"

Severo was most amused.

"Didn't you know, sir? That's where he is and has been for the last five weeks, and he shows no sign of leaving either. It looks like he'll be staying for the grape-harvest. Oh, it's all very grand there now!"

Good heavens! The next day, after Sunday mass and despite the sweltering heat, I hurriedly trotted off to Tormes. When Melchior's wife heard the guard-dogs barking as I entered the gate, she came running from the courtyard, a basket of laundry under her arm. "Where's Senhor Dom Jacinto?" I asked. He was, she replied, with Silvério and Melchior in the fields near Freixomil.

"And what about Senhor Cricket, the black man?"

"I saw him just now in the orchard, with the French gentleman, picking lemons."

All the windows shone with bright new glass panes. In one corner of the courtyard, I noticed buckets of whitewash and pots of paint. On that Holy Day, a stonemason's ladder was resting against the roof. And by the chapel wall, two cats were sleeping on piles of straw evidently unpacked from large crates.

"So," I thought, "Civilization has arrived."

I tethered my horse and ran up the steps. On the verandah, on a pile of laths, a zinc bath glinted in the sun. Inside the house, I found all the floors mended and swept clean. The bare, freshly white-washed walls were as cooling as the walls of a convent. One room, to which I was led by three doors flung wide in frank country fashion, was clearly Jacinto's; his clothes hung from wooden hangers; the iron bedstead, with its fustian bedspread, seemed to shrink, like a shy virgin, into a corner between the wall and the little bench where a bright brass candlestick sat upon a volume of *Don Quixote*. In the yellow-painted washroom, the color of bamboo, there was only room for a jug, a bowl and a large slab of soap; and tidily stowed on one small shelf were brush, scissors, comb, a mirror of the kind you can buy at fairs, and the lavender water I had sent him from Guiães. The three curtainless windows gazed out at the beauty of the mountains, breathing in the soft delicate air, perfumed with the resins from the pine woods and the roses from the garden. Across the corridor, another room was furnished with the same simplicity. My Prince, with his usual foresight, had clearly intended it for me, Zé Fernandes. I immediately hung up my lustrine dust-coat there.

In the vast drawing room, where we had philosophized as we pondered the stars, Jacinto had created a place of repose and study; this was clearly the "grandness" that had so impressed Severo. The ample wicker armchairs from Madeira were comfortably upholstered with chintz cushions. On the enormous whitewood table, made in Tormes, I was surprised to find a three-branched metal candlestick, a friar's inkpot with duck quills in it, and a simple chapel-vase overflowing with carnations. Between two of the windows stood an old chest of drawers inlaid with wrought-iron work, with, on its rosy marble top, the devout weight of a crèche in which the Magi, shepherds carrying splendid bags, and lambs with fluffy wool, were all hurrying through the rocks to the Child, who was wearing an enormous royal crown and lying in the creche, arms open to greet them. A row of wooden shelves filled another stretch of wall, between two dark portraits framed in black; on one shelf rested two shotguns; on the others a few noble books stood in scattered groups, like learned men on the benches of a council meeting: a Plutarch, a Virgil, an *Odyssey*, *The Enchiridion of Epictetus*, and *Froissart's Chronicle*. Elsewhere, caned chairs, very new and freshly varnished, formed neat rows. And in one corner stood a bundle of beanpoles.

Everything glowed with cleanliness and order. The closed shutters sheltered the room from the sun beating fiercely on that side of the house, scalding the stone window ledges. In the soft darkness, the floor, freshly sprinkled with water, exuded coolness and the carnations their sweet perfume. Not a sound came from the fields or from the house. Tormes slept in the splendor of that holy morning. And touched by that consoling country-convent stillness, I finally sat down in one of the wicker armchairs by the table, languidly opened a volume of Virgil, and read out loud:

> *Fortunate Jacinthe! Hic, inter arva nota*
> *Et fontes sacros, frigus captabis opacum . . .*

Fortunate Jacinto indeed! Now amid these fields which are yours and these waters that are sacred to you, you can enjoy at last your harvest of shade and peace!

I read on. And weary after the two-hour ride from Guiães through the heat, I was irreverently dropping asleep over the divine Bucolic, when a friendly cry awoke me! It was my Prince. And once I had extricated myself from his firm embrace, I forthrightly compared him to an etiolated plant that had been shrivelling up in the darkness, among rugs and silks, but which, once placed outside in the wind and the sun and watered profusely, grows green again, bursts into flower and does honor to Mother Nature! Jacinto no longer walked with a slight stoop. The mountain air, or perhaps simply a more authentic way of life, had overlaid the glum pallor of that super-civilized man with the warm brown glow of blood renewed, leaving him looking magnificently reinvigorated. In the City, his eyes had grown crepuscular, as if averted from the World; now, though, there danced in them a noon-tide light, resolute and generous, content to drink in the beauty of things. Even his moustache had grown curly. And he no longer drew his hand disconsolately across his face, but triumphantly slapped his thigh. What can I say? This was a brand-new Jacinto! And I felt almost frightened because I would have to learn and understand this new Prince's new ideas and manners.

"So how are you, Jacinto?"

He jovially shrugged his newly broad shoulders. And as he strode regally up and down the refurbished floorboards in his white shoes covered in dust, all he could say was that when he woke up in Tormes after that first night and after taking a bath in a tub intended for treading grapes, he had suddenly felt clearer—

freer! He had lunched on a sublime plateful of eggs and *chouriço* sausage. Then, filled by light thoughts of liberty and peace, he had tramped the whole of those magnificent mountains. He had sent to Oporto for a bed and some hangers for his clothes . . . and there he was.

"And you're staying all Summer?"

"No! Only a month . . . or possibly two! As long as there's plenty of *chouriço* sausage and as long as the water from the fountain, scooped up with an old roof-tile or a cabbage leaf, continues to taste like nectar!"

I plumped myself down again in the wicker armchair and gazed—no, stared—outright at my Prince! He was rolling a cigarette with some thick tobacco taken from a glass bowl. He exclaimed:

"I'm up and about from daybreak on! Today I caught four magnificent trout down there in Naves, in a little stream that flows along the Seranda valley. We'll have them for supper!"

However, eager for the story of his resurrection, I asked:

"So you didn't go to Lisbon, then? I sent you a telegram."

"Telegram? Lisbon? No, I was up by the fountain of Lira, in the shade of a great tree, *sub tegmine* something or other, reading that adorable man Virgil. As well as sorting out my palace, of course! What do you think of it, Zé Fernandes? In just three weeks, I've had new floors put in *and* new windows, and I've had it white-washed and furnished with chairs! The whole parish worked on it! Even I helped with some of the painting, using the most enormous brush! Have you seen the dining-room yet?"

"No, I haven't."

"Then come and admire the sheer beauty of simplicity, you barbarian!"

It was the same room where we had heaped praises on that dish of rice and beans, but now it was scrubbed and whitewashed, with a baseboard painted in a strident blue, in which I sensed my Prince's hand. A linen cloth from Guimarães covered the table, with its fringed edges touching the floor. The bottom of the sturdy earthenware dishes was emblazoned with a yellow cockerel. It was the same cockerel and the same crockery that we used in Guiães to serve the farmhands their bean stew.

Out in the courtyard the dogs started barking, and Jacinto ran to the verandah with a curious lightness that delighted me. How completely he had torn himself free from the net in which he had once, all unknowing, been so entangled! At that moment, Cricket appeared, wearing a linen jacket and holding a bottle of white wine in each hand. He was thrilled to see me there, but his venerable face no longer glowed as it had in Paris with its usual blithe ebony serenity. It even seemed to me that he walked with a slight stoop. When I asked him about his change of abode, he pensively stuck out his plump lower lip, and answered:

"The master likes it, so I like it too. And the air here is very good, Senhor Fernandes, very good!"

Then, more quietly, casting a desolate eye over the Barcelos crockery, the bone-handled knives and the wooden dishes more suited to a Franciscan refectory, he added:

"But everything's so mean here, so meager!"

Jacinto returned with a roll of newspapers tied with string:

"It was the postman. As you see, I haven't entirely turned my back on Civilization. Here's the press, for example, but no *Figaro*, no ghastly *Deux Mondes*! Just newspapers about agriculture! So I can learn how to get the best yield, and find out in which month I should marry the vine to the elm and how to take care of the provident bee. *Quid faciat laetas segetes* . . . Otherwise, I had already gleaned enough from *The Georgics*, which, of course, you don't know!"

I laughed.

"Now stop right there: *Nos quoque gens sumus et nostrum Virgilium sabemus!*"

But my brand-new friend was leaning out of the window and clapping his hands, the way Cato would have summoned the serfs in the simple Rome of his day. And he called out:

"Ana Vaqueira! A nice clean glass of water from the old fountain!"

I started back, vastly amused:

"Jacinto! What about the carbonated water and the phosphated water and the sterilised water and the soda water?"

My Prince gave a proudly scornful shrug. A beautiful girl then appeared, bearing on a tray a large glass of water, the glass all frosted from the snowy coolness of its glittering contents. I particularly admired the girl. What eyes! Of such a liquid, serious black! And the way she walked, swaying her hips—the harmony and grace of a Latin nymph!

And no sooner had this splendid vision disappeared through the door than I declared:

"I say, Jacinto, I want a glass of water too! And if she's the one charged with bringing me things, then I'll call for something every five minutes! What eyes! What a body! The living poetry of the mountains!"

My Prince smiled and said gravely:

"Now let's not delude ourselves, Zé Fernandes, nor imagine that we're in Arcadia here. She may be a beautiful girl, but she's also very stupid. She contains no more poetry, no more sensibil-

ity, indeed no more beauty than a fine Friesian cow. Not for nothing is she called Ana Vaqueira—Ana the Cowherd. She works hard,
eats well, conceives easily. That's why Nature made her so strong
and healthy; and she does her duty. Her husband doesn't seem too
happy though, because he beats her. No, my friend, the countryside is a wonderful thing and I'm very grateful to it, but what you
get here is the female in all her animality and the male in all his
egotism. But they're utterly authentic, utterly real. And I find that
authenticity very restful, Zé Fernandes."

Savoring the coolness, silence and freedom of the vast house,
we slowly made our way to the room Jacinto had designated the
"Reading Room." And suddenly, when I spotted in one corner a
crate, its lid half open, such intense curiosity assailed me that I
almost choked.

"What happened to the crates, Jacinto, all those crates that we
sent, crammed with Civilization? Did you ever find out? Did they
ever turn up?"

My Prince gaily slapped his thigh:

"Oh, it's sublime! Do you remember that little man with the
shoulder bag, whom we so admired for his sagacity and his knowledge of geography? Do you remember how as soon as I mentioned
Tormes, he cried out: 'Oh, yes, Tormes, of course, very ancient,
very interesting' and scribbled down the name, saying that was all
he needed to know. Well, he sent everything to Alba de Tormes
in Spain! Everything's in Spain!"

I rubbed my chin sadly.

"And he seemed such an intelligent, expeditious man, who did
honor to the name of Progress! So he sent it all to Spain! Have you
asked for the crates to be forwarded to you here?"

"No, not yet. Perhaps later. At the moment, Zé Fernandes, I'm just enjoying the delight of getting up in the morning and having only one brush for brushing my hair."

I looked at my friend, thinking back to the past.

"You used to have about nine, didn't you?"

"Nine? I had twenty, possibly thirty! And it was a real nuisance, because they still weren't enough! I never looked really well groomed when I was in Paris. It was the same with my thirty thousand volumes. There were so many that I never read a single one of them. Indeed, it was the same with everything. I was so overwhelmed by things to do that I never did anything useful!"

Later on, when the heat had passed, we wandered along the winding paths of that magnificent estate which covers two undulating leagues of hill and vale. I had not been in Nature with Jacinto since that far-off farcical day when he had suffered so in the busy, safely policed forest of Montmorency. Now, though, with what confidence and idyllic love he strode through that same Nature from which he had been estranged for so many years by theory and habit! He was no longer afraid of the mortal dampness of the grass; nor did he fend off the impertinent touch of branches; nor did he find the silence of the heights as troubling as a depopulated Universe. But with real delight, with a consoling sense of stability restored, he strode in his large boots across the soft ground, as if it were his natural, paternal element: for no reason, he would leave the easier tracks in order to plunge into thick undergrowth and receive on his cheek the caress of the tender leaves; he would stand motionless on the top of hills, begging me not to speak, almost not to breathe, the better to drink in the silence and the peace; and twice I came across him beside a particularly talkative brook, listening and smiling, as if the water were confiding in him.

Then he would philosophize endlessly, with the enthusiasm of the converted eager to convert others:

"It's extraordinary how here one's intelligence is set free and how everything is filled with strong, deep life! I challenge you to say now that the countryside's no place for thought—"

"Me?! I never said anything of the sort, Jacinto—"

"Because that's a very crass and narrow-minded way of thinking—"

"But I—"

"No, no, you don't understand. Life isn't just about thinking, my dear doctor —"

"But I'm not a doctor!"

"Life is essentially Will and Movement, and in that piece of land planted with maize is a whole world of impulses and forces that achieve their supreme expression in Form. No, no, your philosophy is utterly crass—"

"*My* philosophy!"

"And then, my friend, there's the inexhaustible, miraculous diversity of forms, each one of which is beautiful!"

He grabbed my arm and demanded my reverent attention. I would never find in Nature an ugly or a repeated shape! No two leaves of ivy, as regards color or form, were ever the same! In the City, on the other hand, each house slavishly repeats the other houses; every face reproduces the same indifference or the same disquiet; ideas all have the same value, the same stamp, the same form, like coins; and even something as personal and private as an illusion is identical in everyone, and everyone breathes the same vain hope—all lost in it as if in the same mist. Sameness, that's what's so dreadful about Cities!

"But here! I mean take that chestnut tree for example. I've seen it every morning for the last three weeks, and it looks different every time. Its expression is always new and diverse, always interesting, thanks to the constantly changing effects of shadow, sun, clouds and rain. I could never grow tired of its company."

"It's a shame it can't talk," I muttered.

My Prince drew back, eyes flashing with apostolic zeal.

"What do you mean 'it can't talk'? Why, it's a wonderful conversationalist! Obviously it doesn't come out with sayings or invent theories *ore rotundo*, but I never walk by without it suggesting some thought to me or revealing some truth. Even today, when I was coming back from my trout-fishing, I paused beneath it and the tree immediately made me realize how free its whole vegetable life is from the labor, anxiety and effort that human life imposes; it doesn't have to worry about food or clothes or shelter; since the tree is God's beloved child, it never has to concern itself with looking for nourishment, because God will nourish it. And it's that certainty which gives it such grace and majesty. Don't you agree?"

I smiled and nodded. However récherché and specious these ideas might be, what did it matter if the metaphors were slightly overblown and the metaphysics somewhat under-ripe, plucked in haste from the branches of a chestnut tree? Underneath that ideology lay an excellent reality, the reconciliation of my Prince with Life. After all those years in the tomb—a soft, comfortable tomb in which he had lain wrapped like a mummy in the linen bandages of Pessimism—his Resurrection was guaranteed!

My Prince really wore me out that afternoon! With insatiable curiosity, he sniffed his way into every corner of the mountains! He sprinted up hills as if hoping to find there the never-before-seen splendors of a never-before-seen world. And his one torment was not knowing the names of the trees or of the humblest flower growing on some rocky ledge. He kept leafing through me as if I were a Botanical Dictionary.

"I've studied all kinds of things, been taught by the most illustrious teachers in Europe, I own thirty thousand books, and yet I don't know if that gentleman over there is an alder or a cork oak."

"It's a holm oak, Jacinto."

Evening was coming on as we slowly wended our way home. And the wonderful peace of that truly celestial sky and of the fields, where each small leaf seemed locked in quiet contemplation, caressed by the gently fading light, all of this seemed to touch Jacinto so profoundly that, in the silence into which we had lapsed, I heard him sigh with pure relief. Then, very gravely, he said:

"You say there's no thought in Nature—"

"Oh, no, not again! This really is too much! I—"

"But it's precisely because there is no thought that there is no suffering. We, poor wretches, cannot suppress thought, but we can certainly discipline it and prevent it from growing dizzy and exhausted, which is what happens in the furnace of the City, where thought invents pleasures that are never realized and aspires to certainties that are never achieved. That is what these hills and trees are saying to our watching, worrying soul: live in the peace of this vague dream and want nothing, fear nothing, resist nothing, and let the World roll by, expecting from it only a hum of harmony that lulls you to sleep in God's hand. Don't you think so, Zé Fernandes?"

"Possibly. But to live like that you'd need to enter a monastery and have the temperament of a St. Bruno, or else enjoy an income of one hundred and forty *contos* a year and the sheer audacity of certain people called Jacinto. More to the point, I'm completely worn out and starving hungry!"

"All the better for the trout and the roast kid awaiting us."

"Excellent! Who does your cooking?"

"One of Melchior's god-daughters. A sublime creature! You should taste her chicken soup or her chicken and rice! She herself is hideous, a squint-eyed dwarf, with one eye green and the other brown, but what a palate the woman has! What genius!"

He was right. Horace would have dedicated an ode to that kid roasted on a cherry-wood spit. And after the trout, after Melchior's wine and the chicken and rice—in which the sublime squint-eyed dwarf had been at her inspired heavenly best—and with the sweetness of the June night pouring in through the open windows and wrapping us in its black velvet, I felt so relaxed and so consoled that, in the room where coffee was served, I fell into the largest and most comfortable of the wicker armchairs and let out a bellow of sheer delight.

Then, wiping the coffee from my moustache, I said:

"Do you remember, Jacinto, when we used to trudge around Paris carrying a great weight of Pessimism on our backs, moaning on about everything being illusion and suffering?"

My Prince, who had been made still happier by the roast kid, was striding up and down the room, rolling a cigarette.

"Ah, that clever fool, Schopenhauer! And I was an even greater fool for believing him and letting him make me thoroughly miserable! And yet," he went on, stirring his coffee now, "pessimism is a very consoling theory for those who suffer, because it de-individualizes suffering, broadens it out into a universal law, makes it the law of Life, thus removing the sting of it being a personal injustice imposed on the sufferer by a hostile and very partial Destiny! The truth is that our ills taste more bitter to us when we contemplate or imagine our neighbor's good fortune, because we feel we've been singled out for Unhappiness, when we could, like our neighbor, have been born for Happiness. Who would complain about being lame if everyone was lame? And imagine the howls of fury that would issue forth from a man buffeted by the snow and cold and storm of a Winter organized by the heavens for him alone, while all around him the rest of humanity was bathed in the benign luminosity of Spring?"

"He would," I agreed, "have good reason to howl."

"And then," my friend went on, "Pessimism is an excellent thing for the Inert, because it attenuates the unfortunate sin of Inertia. If the only goal is a Hill of Pain, upon which the soul will inevitably stumble, then why bother coping with all of life's obstacles in order to chase after that goal? Besides, all the Poets and Theoreticians of Pessimism, from Solomon to that malign fellow Schopenhauer, sing their song or publish their doctrine in order to disguise the humiliation of their own miseries, subordinating them all to a vast Law of Life, a cosmic law, and thus adorning with a near-divine glow their tiny little misfortunes of temperament or of fate. Old Schopenhauer invented Schopenhauerism when he was a philosopher without a publisher and a teacher without students; he suffered horribly from terrors and manias; he used to hide his money under the floorboards. Existing as he did, in a state of constant fear and distrust, he wrote his accounts in Greek and lived in a cellar because he was afraid of fire; and he always traveled with a tin cup in his pocket so as not to have to drink from a glass that leprous lips might have touched! Schopenhauer was somberly Schopenhauerian. However, as soon as he became famous, his wretched nerves calmed down, and he found himself surrounded by good cheer and peace—and you could not then have found, in the whole of Frankfurt, a more optimistic bourgeois gentleman, beaming from ear to ear, as he savored the delights of the Intellect and of Life! And that other fellow, the Israelite, that pedantic King of Jerusalem. When did that sublime Rhetorician discover Illusion and Vanity? When he was seventy-five years old and found Power slipping from his tremulous grasp, and when his harem of three hundred concubines was clearly becoming surplus to requirements—ah, then he burst forth with his grand complaints! All is vanity and affliction of the mind! Nothing under the sun remains unchanged! It's true, my dear Solomon, everything passes, especially the ability to make the most of three hundred concubines! Had this ancient, bookish Asiatic sultan had his virility restored to him, would we now have his lament in Ecclesiastes? No, he would have issued a second triumphant edition of the ecstasy expressed in the Song of Songs!"

So spoke my friend in the night silence of Tormes. He may well have had other jovial, profound and elegant things to say about Pessimism, but I had fallen asleep by then, beatifically wrapped in Optimism and Sweetness.

It was not long, however, before a long, loud, healthy, genuine guffaw made me start awake and force open my heavy lids. It was Jacinto, sprawled in a chair, reading *Don Quixote*. Ah, happy Prince! He had preserved his keen ability to pluck theories from an as yet unripe corn cob and, by God's mercy, this had made the withered trunk flower again, and he had recovered the divine gift of being able to laugh at Sancho's buffoonery.

Taking advantage of my presence at Tormes and the two weeks of bucolic idleness that this imposed on him, Jacinto set about preparing the long talked about and long pondered ceremony, the reinterment of the bones of all those old Jacintos—those "respectable bones" as Silvério the administrator called them, with a bow, one Friday when he lunched with us, wearing a hideous double-breasted yellow velvet overcoat trimmed with blue silk! The ceremony had to be kept very simple because of the uncertain identity of the rather impersonal remains we would be laying to rest again in the chapel in the valley of Carriça, in that cold, bare, new chapel that still lacked a soul and God's warmth.

"Because as you will understand, sir," Silvério explained, using his napkin to wipe his broad, perspiring face and his vast black Turkman-like beard, "in that whole jumble . . . oh, forgive me, sir . . . in the confusion, when the whole thing collapsed, we couldn't tell whose bones were whose. In fact, to tell the truth, the tombs were so old and the names on them so faded that we didn't really know which of your worthy ancestors had been buried in the old chapel; now I'm sure they are all deserving of our greatest respect, but, if I may say so, sir, they were not in the best of shape. Then came the disaster and the jumbling up of the bones. And after much thought, what I decided to do was this. I ordered as many lead coffins as there were skulls found among all the rubble and the rubbish. There were seven and half skulls, by which I mean, seven skulls and one very small one. We put each skull into a coffin. Then . . . But what do you expect, sir?

There was no other way! I'm sure Senhor Fernandes here will agree that we proceeded properly. To each skull we added a reasonable proportion of bones. There really was no other way. Not all the bones were found, you see. For example, a lot of shinbones were missing. And it may well be that the ribs of some of these gentlemen have ended up with the skull of another. But who can tell? Only God. Anyway, we did what seemed prudent. And on the Day of Judgment, each of these gentleman will present himself with his own bones."

He uttered these macabre, grotesque—but always respectful—remarks almost majestically, fixing first me and then my Prince with his bright, beady eyes.

I agreed with the picturesque Silvério.

"You were quite right, Silvério. There is something terribly vague and anonymous about those ancestors! It's just a shame that Dom Galeão's bones should have gone astray."

"Oh, Dom Galeão wasn't buried here," said Jacinto. "I came here expressly to bury Dom Galeão, but it seems, fortunately as it turns out, that he wasn't buried in the chapel of Carriça."

Silvério gravely shook his sunburned head.

"No, we never had that honor. It's a hundred years, Senhor Fernandes, since a gentleman of the house has been buried in the old chapel."

"Where is he then?" I asked.

My Prince shrugged. He was somewhere around. In the church or the cemetery of one of the many parishes where he owned land. It was such a vast estate!

"So," I concluded, "since these are bones with no name and no date, what's needed is a very simple, very sober ceremony."

"Yes, a very quiet affair," murmured Silvério, taking a loud sip of coffee.

And the re-interment of those illustrious folk was, indeed, a very quiet affair, of sweet and rustic simplicity. Early one slightly misty morning, the eight little coffins—each covered with a red velvet cloth more appropriate for a fiesta than a funeral, each with a bunch of roses placed on it, and each containing its little pile of bones of uncertain origin—were carried out on the shoulders of the gravediggers and estate workers of Tormes from the Church of São José, whose bell tolled quietly in the misty sweetness of the morning, as soft as the singing of a sad little bird. Ahead of them went an elegant young man in a surplice, holding up an old silver cross; the hunched sacristan, his neck swathed in a vast blue-and-white check handkerchief, clasped the holy water vessel thoughtfully in his hands; and the good priest of São José, keeping his place in the breviary with one finger, mouthed a prayer, which filled the sweet air with still more sweetness. Jacinto and I walked immediately behind the last and smallest of the coffins, the one containing the smallest skull. I was encased in a too-tight black suit belonging to Jacinto and which had been plucked in haste from one of the bags sent from Paris, when, that same morning, too late to send to Guiães for a replacement, I realized that all my clothes were of colors suitable only for either festive occasions or pastoral pursuits.

Behind us came Silvério, looking extremely solemn in a vast starched shirtfront over which flowed his equally vast and very black beard. Next came Cricket, wearing a tailcoat; his large lips drooped, indeed, his whole person seemed to droop as befitted this melancholy ceremony set among the equally melancholy mountains; and over one arm, he carried an enormous wreath of roses and ivy. Bringing up the rear was Melchior, surrounded by a whole host of women, their faces lost in the shadows cast by their black headscarves, as they told their beads and muttered Hail Marys and occasionally sighed as mournfully as if they genuinely felt the inconsolable loss of those ancient Jacintos. Through meadows criss-crossed by streams that dawdled around the wooded hillsides and raced along the stony gulleys, the procession advanced, with, at its head, the tall silver cross that glittered sometimes in the occasional brief ray of light as the sun slowly broke through the dissolving mist. The low branches of nettle-trees and willows bestowed one final caress on the velvet cloths covering the coffins.

Sometimes a brook kept us company, glinting discreetly in the grass and whispering as if it were saying its own much happier prayers; and in the shady orchards, as we passed, the cockerels, perched on piles of cut undergrowth, sounded their festive bugles. Then, by the fountain of Lira—as we had already walked quite a way and wanted to spare our old priest—we took a short cut across a field of tall, almost ripe wheat, dotted with poppies. The sun was shining, and beneath the generous breeze, which had carried away the mist, the whole field undulated like a slow golden wave, on which the coffins bobbed like boats; and the cotton sunshade opened by the sacristan to shade the priest glowed just like another poppy, the largest and reddest of them all.

Jacinto nudged me:

"What a fine sight, eh! But that's Nature for you! How much grace and beauty in a simple reinterment of old bones!"

The new chapel, overlooking the Carriça valley, seemed solitary and bare in the middle of a churchyard that had not yet been properly smoothed and levelled, with not a blade of grass or cooling shrub to be seen; two young men were standing at the chapel door, holding bunches of tapers that Silvério was gravely handing out, bowing solemnly each time. Inside, the short candles barely lit up the interior, shedding only a sad yellow glow that paled against the strident white of the stucco walls and the cheerful light streaming in through the high polished windows. Around the coffins, which had been placed on benches covered by heavy velvet cloths, the priest was quietly murmuring in Latin, while, at the back, the women, faces almost covered by their black scarves, responded with a clear "Amen" then stifled a respectful sob. The priest took up the aspergillum and, in one final act of purification, sprinkled holy water over the uncertain bones of those uncertain Jacintos. And we all filed out past my Prince, who was standing timidly on the threshold; beside him stood Silvério, head bowed, vast beard pressing into his shirtfront and eyes tight shut as if holding back his tears.

In the churchyard, my Prince gladly lit the cigarette he had begged from Melchior and said:

"So, Zé Fernandes, what did you think of our little ceremony?"

"Very rustic, very sweet, and very cheerful ... in short, a delight."

However, at that point, the priest emerged, having removed his vestments in the sacristy and donned instead the loose lustrine jacket and battered broadbrimmed hat that his servant had brought with him in a cotton bag. Jacinto immediately went over to thank him for all the care he had taken, and for the hospitality and kindness he had offered the bones of his ancestors during the building of the new chapel. And the gentle old man, pale-complexioned, but still with rosy, childlike cheeks and an open smile that revealed healthy, white teeth, praised Jacinto for coming so far, for making such a long journey in order to perform the duties of a good grandson.

"They are only very distant ancestors, and now, sadly, very muddled up!" smiled Jacinto.

"All the more credit to you, sir. To respect a dead grandfather is common enough, but to respect the bones of a great-great-great-great-grandfather and so on unto the fifth or seventh generation . . ."

"Especially when one knows nothing about them and they did nothing worthy of note."

The priest smilingly wagged one fat finger.

"Ah, who knows, who knows? They may have been excellent men! And when one has lingered as long as I have on this earth, one ends up convinced that there is no such thing as a useless object or person. Only yesterday I was reading in a newspaper from Oporto that they have just discovered that long before the plowman comes along with his oxen and his plow, it's the worms who fertilize and work the land. So even worms are useful. There is nothing that is entirely useless. I was distressed to find a clump of thistles growing in one corner of my garden. Then I thought about it and ended up enjoying them cooked in a sauce. Your ancestors lived and worked and suffered here, that is, they served the land. And, besides, saying a prayer for their souls can only do them and us good."

And thus, gently philosophizing, we came to a plantation of oak trees where the priest's ancient mare awaited him, because the good man, after a severe attack of rheumatism the previous Winter, could no longer walk the rough mountain paths as once he did. In filial fashion, Jacinto held the stirrup to help the priest up. And while the mare, almost concealed beneath the priest's vast red sunshade, headed up the path, we hurried back through the Lombinha hills and the cornfields, because I was close to exploding, trapped as I was in my Prince's black suit.

"Now that those gentlemen are nicely settled in, Zé Fernandes, all that remains is for us to say an occasional Our Father for them, as the priest recommended, except I can't even remember how it goes."

"Don't worry, Jacinto. I'll ask Aunt Vicência to do the praying for us both. She says all my prayers."

During the weeks that I spent idling in Tormes, I watched fondly as a considerable change took place in Jacinto and his relationship with Nature. From that period of sentimental contemplation, in which he would pluck theories from the branch of any cherry tree and construct systems of thought upon the foaming waters of a mill-race, my Prince was gradually moving toward a desire for Action—a desire for direct material action, in which his hand, ready at last to apply itself to some superior task, would actually till the soil.

After so much talk, my Prince was clearly keen to create something.

One evening, as night fell, we were sitting in the orchard, beside the pond, while Manuel Hortelão, perched on a ladder propped against a tall orange-tree, was picking fruit; suddenly Jacinto said, more to himself than to me:

"It's odd, you know, but I've never planted a tree!"

"Well, it's one of three great actions without which, according to some philosopher or other, one can never claim to be a real man. Having a child, planting a tree, and writing a book. You'd better hurry up if you want to be a man. You might miss the chance to do a service to a tree just as you might to a fellow human being."

"Yes, in Paris, when I was little, I used to water the lilac trees. And in Summer, that's a real service! But I've never actually sown anything."

And as Manuel was coming down the ladder, my Prince, who—poor man!—never entirely believed in my agricultural knowledge, immediately demanded to know the view of that higher authority.

"Manuel, what could one plant in the garden now?"

With his basket of oranges over one arm, Manuel gave a slow smile, half-respectful, half-amused.

"Sow, sir? It's more a time for harvesting than for sowing. They're preparing the threshing-floor at this very moment."

"Yes, of course, but I don't mean corn or barley. Couldn't we plant a row of peach trees over there, by the old orchard wall?"

Manuel's smile grew wider.

"You could, sir, but you need to do that around about All Saints' Day or even Christmas. The only things we'll be sowing now are some cabbage, purslane, spinach, and a few beans when the soil's nice and cold."

With a wave of his hand, my Prince gently rejected such humble vegetables.

"Thank you, Manuel. Goodnight. Are those the oranges Melchior says are so sweet and juicy? Well, take some home for your children. Take as many as you like."

What he wanted was to plant a tree. His new love of the earth had begun gradually, perhaps while contemplating a tree in all its true majesty and enjoying its beneficent shade, the easeful cool of its rustling leaves, the grace and sanctity of the nests to which it gave shelter. And now he was dreaming of a Tormes thickly planted with trees, whose fruits and greenery, whose shade and nests and gentle rustlings would all be down to the work and care of his paternal hands.

In the grave twilight silence, he asked:

"Which are the fastest-growing trees, Zé Fernandes?"

"The fastest-growing tree is that ridiculous and extremely ugly creature, the eucalyptus. In six years, you could have the whole of Tormes covered in eucalyptus."

"Everything takes so much time, Zé Fernandes."

For, as I could perfectly understand, his dream was to plant seeds that would develop strong trunks and grow leafy branches before he went back to No. 202 at the beginning of the Winter.

"An oak tree takes thirty years before it reaches its full beauty! It's so discouraging! It's fine for God, who can afford to wait. *Patiens quia aeternus*. Thirty years! Thirty years for a tree to grow tall enough to shade my grave!"

"But it's still worth planting one. And it will be there for your children, Jacinto."

"What children? Where am I going to find *them*?"

"Well, it's the same process as with chestnut trees. First, you have to plant a seed—and there's no shortage of fertile soil around—and in nine months the plant will have grown. And the smaller and more tender the plant, the more you'll love it."

He folded his hands on his knees and muttered again:

"Everything takes such a long time!"

We sat on in silence beside the pond, in the cool sweetness of dusk, surrounded by the intense perfume from the honeysuckle growing up the wall, and we watched as the crescent moon rose up behind the rooftop.

It was doubtless this same haste to become not just a dreamer of Nature, but a creator, that sharpened his interest in livestock. During our walks on the estate, he repeatedly commented on how empty it was.

"What we need here are animals, Zé Fernandes!"

I imagined that he fancied a Tormes full of deer and peacocks, but one Sunday, as we skirted the broad plain of Ribeirinha, where water was always scarce and which was even drier than usual after that Summer's drought, my Prince stopped to consider the care-taker's three sheep cropping the scant grass.

And suddenly, he said almost sadly:

"Exactly! This is just the place for a vast, beautiful meadow, green and fertile, with flocks of white sheep, as plump as cotton wool balls placed on the grass! Wouldn't that be lovely? And it would be easy enough, don't you think, Zé Fernandes?"

"Yes. You could bring the water down to the meadow, and there's no shortage of water in the mountains."

And my Prince, linking this inspired idea with another far richer, larger one, remarked on how beautiful Tormes would be if those meadows, those green pastures, were filled by herds of cows—fine, fat, glossy English cows. Wouldn't that be a beautiful sight? To shelter those fine cows, he would build perfect corrals, of a light, useful design, all in iron and glass, ventilated by the fresh air itself and washed clean by natural streams. Superb, eh?

And then, with all those cows and all that milk flowing from them, what could be easier or more amusing, and indeed more moral, than to install a cheese dairy—in the fresh Dutch fashion, all white tiles and gleaming marble—and make Camemberts, Bries, and Coulommiers. That would be useful for the house and create gainful employment for the whole area!

"Don't you agree, Zé Fernandes?"

"Of course, and you have in abundance the four necessary elements: air, water, earth and money. With those four things you could easily create a large farm, and certainly a cheese dairy."

"Yes, you're right. I could even make a business of it. Obviously, as far as I'm concerned, the real profit would be the moral pleasure I would gain from the work and from filling my time usefully. But a proper cheese dairy would make a lot of money, as well as educating people's palates, encouraging other similar enterprises, and perhaps creating a whole new industry here. Once this new perfect dairy was in place, how much do you think each cheese would cost me?"

I closed one eye as I did my calculations.

"I would say that each cheese, one of those small round cheeses, say, a Camembert or a Rabaçal, would cost you, Jacinto the cheesemaker, between two hundred and fifty and three hundred *mil réis*."

My Prince recoiled, staring at me with bright startled eyes.

"What do you mean, three hundred *mil réis*?"

"All right, let's say two hundred. I'm serious! When you calculate the expense of channelling water to these meadows and reconfiguring the landscape, as well as buying those English cows of yours, building that porcelain and glass dairy and equipping it with all the right machinery, not to mention the general extravagance and the bucolic festivities, each cheese would cost you, the producer, two hundred *mil réis*. But you could doubtless sell it in Oporto for one *tostão*. Add fifty *réis* for boxes, labels, transport and commission, etc., and you would be making a loss on each cheese of a mere one hundred and ninety-nine thousand eight hundred and fifty *réis*!"

My Prince was not discouraged.

"Fine! I'll make just one amazing cheese a week on Saturday for us to eat together on Sunday!"

And such was the energy generated by his new Optimism, such was his eagerness to create something, that he immediately started tramping the estate, dragging Silvério and Melchior with him, up hill and down dale, in order to determine where—at his inspired command—green meadows would grow and where he would build those elegant corrals, glinting in the Tormes sun. With all the splendid confidence that comes with an annual income of one hundred and nine *contos*, there was no caveat, whether muttered with a smile by Melchior or spoken with a respectful yelp of alarm by Silvério, that he could not mildly sweep aside with a wave of his hand, as if it were the branch of a wild rose growing over a path.

Those rocks are in the way? Well, get rid of them! An importunate valley cuts across two fields? Fill it in! Silvério would sigh, wiping anxious beads of sweat from his swarthy pate. Poor Silvério! Rudely shaken from the sweet sloth of his old administrative duties, forced to calculate expenses which, to his thrifty country mind, seemed superhuman, and obliged to go panting after his master in the hottest part of the June afternoon, he had taken on the gloom that Jacinto had left behind him in Paris, and he was now the one to run weary fingers through his long dark beard. Finally, one afternoon, he vented his feelings to me as we sat at one end of the verandah, while Jacinto, in the library, was writing to his Dutch friend, Count Rylant, a majordomo at Court, asking him to send information about the design and costs of a perfect cheese dairy.

"The thing is, Senhor Fernandes, if all these grand plans go ahead, Senhor Dom Jacinto will be burying thousands of *contos* here in the mountains, thousands!"

And when I referred to my Prince's vast fortune and to the fact that such grandiose projects—which would alter the ancient face of the mountains—would be no more to him than repairing a single terrace, good Silvério, his long arms hanging dejectedly by his side, said:

"Exactly, Senhor Fernandes! If Senhor Dom Jacinto didn't have all that money, he would think twice, but no, he just plunges straight in. Not that I'm criticizing him. If I had his money, I'd probably plow it all into some hare-brained agricultural scheme too, but not here, Senhor Fernandes, not in a wild steep place like this. I mean, he owns that wonderful estate in Montemor, near the Mondego river, where he could plant a garden to rival the one at the Crystal Palace in Oporto! And then there's Veleira. Do you know Veleira, sir, over by Penafiel? The size of a whole county, it is. There the land is flat, the soil is excellent and it's all of a piece too, plus there's a house with a tower and everything. It's a real jewel, Senhor Fernandes—but Montemor is the place if you want fields full of English cows, a cheese dairy, a flourishing vegetable garden, *and* thirty turkeys in a pen . . ."

"But what do you expect, Silvério? Jacinto loves the mountains, and this is the family estate. This is where the Jacintos began in the fourteenth century."

In his despair, poor Silvério momentarily forgot the respect due to the noble house.

"I'm surprised to hear *you* coming out with such ideas, sir, in this age of liberty. It hardly seems the moment to be harking back to the nobility when all the talk now is of a Republic. Read *O Século*, sir, read the newspapers, and you'll see what I mean! And I'd like to see Senhor Dom Jacinto survive a winter here, with the mist rising up from the river in the morning, and the cold getting into his bones, and the storms uprooting whole oak trees, and rain and more rain causing landslides and mudslides. I reckon he should leave the mountains even if only for his health's sake, because Senhor Dom Jacinto isn't strong, you know, he's used to the easy city life. No, Montemor's the place, that's where he should go. You, sir, you're his friend and have some influence on him, you should keep nagging him until he agrees to move to Montemor."

Unfortunately for Silvério's desire for a quiet life, Jacinto had put down strong loving roots in his rough mountain home. It was as if he had been planted, like a cutting, in the ancient soil from which his race had sprung and as if the ancient humus were seeping into and penetrating him, transforming him into a rustic, almost vegetable Jacinto, as much a part of the earth and as rooted in the earth as the trees he so loved.

The other thing that bound him to the mountains was that he had found there—for all the social whirl in which he had lived in Paris—what he had never found in the City: days so full and so interesting and so delightfully occupied that he always entered them as if walking into a party or into heaven itself.

First thing in the morning, at six o'clock, while I was still in my room luxuriating on my cool corn-husk mattress, I would hear him clumping down the corridor in his boots, singing tunelessly, but clearly as happy as a blackbird. Moments later, with his broad-brimmed hat on, his cherry-wood stick in his hand, he would fling open my door, ready, with fresh reserves of enthusiasm, to set off along the now familiar mountain paths. And every day he would announce almost proudly, as if for the first time:

"I had the most delicious night's sleep, Zé Fernandes! In fact, I slept so serenely that I'm beginning to think I must be one of the Just! Plus—it's a glorious day. When I opened the window at five o'clock, I almost cried out with pure pleasure!"

In his haste, he wouldn't even let me linger in my cool bath, and as I struggled to get my parting straight, that man who had once owned thirty-nine hairbrushes would protest at such an effeminate waste of time, time that should be spent enjoying the potent joys of the earth.

But once he had patted the dogs in the courtyard and we had left the avenue of beech trees and before us lay the snaking paths of the estate—which seemed whiter in the morning greenery—all his haste vanished, and he entered Nature with the reverent slowness of someone entering a temple. He would repeatedly state that it was "contrary to Aesthetics, Philosophy and Religion to walk briskly through the countryside." Besides, with his growing and ever more refined bucolic sensibility, the briefest of beauties, be they of air or earth, were enough for him to stop awhile, enchanted. He could happily spend a whole morning walking through a pine wood, going from trunk to trunk, immersed in the silence and the cool and the resinous aromas, kicking aside pine needles and dried cones. He would pause by any running water, touched by its selflessness, as it rushed, singing, to the thirsty earth where it vanished and was lost. And I remember that, once, after Mass, he made me spend half a Sunday on a hillside, next to an old ramshackle corral, beneath a large tree, simply because all around it was stillness, apart from the gentle breeze, the soft trilling of birds in the branches, the murmur of a stream among the reeds, and, from the bushes nearby, the fine fresh perfume of their hidden flowers.

Whenever I, long familiar with the mountains, failed to fall into the same ecstasies that filled his novice soul, my Prince would roar as indignantly as a poet who discovers a grocer yawning over the work of Shakespeare or Musset. And then I would laugh.

"I'm sorry, my friend, but I'm just a small landowner. As far as I'm concerned, I don't care if the land is *pretty*, as long as it's *good*. Remember what it says in the Bible: 'You will work the fields with the sweat of your brow!' It doesn't say: 'You will contemplate the fields with the white heat of the imagination!' "

"Well, that's hardly surprising!" exclaimed my Prince. "What do you expect from a book written by Jews, by coarse Semites, always with one murky eye on the lucre! Take a look at that bit of valley down below and just for a moment try not to think about the thirty *mil-réis* profit you might get from it! You'll see, then, that its beauty and grace give far more contentment to the soul than thirty *mil-réis* ever will to the body. And in life, only the soul matters."

When we returned to the house, we found the windows pulled to and the floors dappled by the warm June sun whose heat, after lunch, kept us lingering in the library, yawning.

But my Prince's joyful activities did not cease or even slacken in that noontide heat. At that hour, while in the silent trees even the most agitated of sparrows were sleeping, and when even the Sun seemed to rest, transfixed by its own glittering light, Jacinto—his mind alert and eager, now that he had recovered the ability to enjoy things—happily took up his book; for in his house in Tormes, this owner of thirty thousand volumes was now, following his resurrection, the man who had only one book. That same Nature—which had broken the deadly bonds of tedium and spoken those lovely words: "Rise, take up thy bed and walk!"—had clearly also added the command *et lege*, and so he read. And liberated at last from the suffocating envelope of his vast Library, my happy friend finally understood the incomparable delight of reading a book. When, after Severo's revelations to me outside the smithy, I had first hurried to Tormes, he was just finishing *Don Quixote*, and I would hear him laughing out loud at the delicious and doubtless profound remarks murmured to him by fat Sancho astride his mule. Now, however, my Prince was immersed in *The Odyssey*, and was filled with amazement and disbelief to have found, midway through the journey of his life, that old wanderer, Homer!

"Oh, Zé Fernandes, how did I manage to get to this age without ever having read Homer?"

"You obviously had more important things to read—*Le Figaro*, the novels of Georges Ohnet . . ."

"Have you read *The Iliad*?"

"I am proud to say, my friend, that I have never read *The Iliad*."

My Prince's eyes darted fire.

"Do you know what Alcibiades did, one afternoon in the Portico, to a shameless sophist who, like you, boasted that he'd never read *The Iliad*?"

"No."

"He raised his hand and gave him the most almighty slap."

"Now hold on there, Alcibiades, because I *have* read *The Odyssey*!"

And I had, albeit hurriedly and with my soul distracted! He insisted, then, on initiating me and leading me through that peerless book. I laughed. And still laughing, still heavy with lunch, I finally gave in and lay down on the wicker couch. He sat at the table, upright in his chair, and having gravely, pontifically, opened the book as if it were a missal, began to read in a slow mournful chant. The great sea of *The Odyssey*—resplendent and loud, always blue, utterly blue, beneath the white flight of the seagulls, always rolling in and breaking softly on the fine sand or on the marble rocks of the Happy Isles—gave off a salty coolness, welcome and consoling in the June heat where even the mountains drowsed. The extraordinary ruses thought up by cunning Ulysses and the superhuman dangers he faced, his sublime complaints and deep longing for his lost homeland, indeed the book's whole plot, in which he confounded heroes, fooled goddeses, deceived Fate, seemed particularly delicious there in the countryside around Tormes, where one never needed subtlety or trickery, and where Life unfolded with immutable certainty, just as the same Sun rose each morning and where the fields of rye and corn, watered by the same waters, flourished, grew, and ripened. Lulled by my Prince's grave measured reading, I slowly closed my eyes. Suddenly, I would be startled awake by a vast tumult filling heaven and earth. It was the roaring of Polyphemus or the clamor of Ulysses' companions stealing Apollo's cattle. I would turn to Jacinto, wide-eyed, and murmur: "Sublime!" And the next moment, sly Ulysses, wearing his red Phrygian cap and with a long oar over one shoulder, would be eloquently wheedling clemency out of a prince or demanding gifts that should have been due to his host or perhaps craftily tricking a favor out of the gods. Meanwhile, Tormes slept on in the June splendor. Again I closed contented eyes beneath the ineffable caress of those long Homeric lines. And half-asleep, as if under a spell, I could always see before me, in divine Hellas, between the deep blue sea and the deep blue sky, a hesitant white sail seeking Ithaca.

After the siesta hour, my Prince would set off to the fields again. That was when he was at his most active, and he would return ardently to his "plans," to those lush fields and elegant factories that would bring a new rural magnificence to the mountains. Now he was filled with a longing for a garden of his own invention, a vast vegetable-cum-flower garden, in which all the vegetables, both classical and exotic, would grow proudly together in stately beds surrounded by hedges of roses, carnations, lavender and dahlias. Water would flow along lovely irrigation channels made of enamelled earthenware. The paths would be shaded by moscatel vines growing up pergolas faced with glazed tiles. My Prince had drawn a plan of this astonishing garden, in red ink, on a vast sheet of paper, and Melchior and Silvério, when consulted, contemplated it long and hard—one of them smiling and scratching the back of his neck and the other with his arms obstinately folded and a tragic frown on his face.

Like the plan for the cheese dairy, the chicken run, and another even grander plan for a dovecote so densely populated that, in Tormes, the evening sky would become one great white fluttering of wings, this plan never got beyond our pleasurable discussions or the sheets of paper on which Jacinto would sketch them out, and which remained piled up on the desk, platonic and immobile, between the brass inkpot and the vase of flowers.

No hoe broke a single clod of earth, no crowbar levered up a single stone, no saw cut through a single log in order to begin these marvels. Met by Melchior's staunch but slippery resistance and Silvério's respectful inertia, my Prince's plans were like handsome galleons that had run aground on the rocks or the mud.

It was best not to meddle with anything (cried Silvério) until after the harvest! And then (added Melchior with a smile that promised great things) "January was the month to begin work," because, as the saying goes:

> *To the workman you may open the door*
> *In the middle of January, but not before.*

Besides, for the moment, it was enough for my Prince—who was better at imagining things than putting them into practice—to savor the pleasure of coming up with the ideas for these projects and of pointing with his walking stick, over hill and vale, to the privileged places that his projects would beautify. And while he was pondering these transformations of the land, he started, in a very progressive and well-intentioned way, to get to know the simple men who worked it. On his arrival in Tormes, my Prince had felt strangely shy of the farmhands and day-laborers, even of talking to some young lad driving a cow to pasture. He would never pause to chat with the men, when, by the side of a road or in a field where they were weeding, they stood up, hats in hand, in a show of feudal respect. He was doubtless constrained by laziness, and perhaps by a certain reluctance to leap the gulf between his complex super-civilized self and the rude simplicity of those natural souls, but he was more concerned about showing his ignorance of agriculture and the land, or perhaps of appearing scornful of their work and their concerns, which to them were of supreme, almost religious importance. He made up for this reserve with a profusion of smiles and friendly waves, even taking off his own hat and bowing low with such extreme politeness that I sometimes feared he might say to the laborers: "A very good afternoon to you, sir . . . Your servant, sir."

But now, after spending several weeks in the mountains, and knowing (although this knowledge was still fairly sketchy) about sowing time and harvest time, and that fruit trees were always planted in Winter, he enjoyed stopping beside the laborers and watching them work and making vaguely encouraging comments like: "How's it going? . . . . Pleased to hear it. . . . This is a fine bit of land . . . That bank over there looks in need of some shoring up. . . ."

And each of these simple remarks was very sweet to him, as if through them he were entering into a closer communion with the land and affirming himself in his new incarnation as "a local man," and thus ceasing to be a mere shadow caught between two realities. Now he never passed a young lad driving his cows along the road without stopping him and asking: "Where are you off to? Whose cattle are these? What's your name?" And pleased with himself, he always praised the lad's easy manner and intelligent eyes. It also gave my Prince great satisfaction that he now knew the name of every field, spring, and boundary on his estate.

"See that pine wood over there, beyond the stream. Well, that's not mine, it belongs to the Albuquerques."

And given Jacinto's perennial good humor, the nights in the vast house passed quickly and easily. My Prince was a soul undergoing a process of simplification, and the smallest pleasure was enough, as long as it brought him peace and sweetness. It was with genuine delight that, after coffee, in his armchair, with the windows open, he would sit taking in the nocturnal serenity of the mountains beneath the starry silence of the sky.

He was so interested in the simple homely stories that I told him about Guiães, the Priest, Aunt Vicência, and my relatives in Flora da Malva that I ended up giving him a complete history of Guiães, with its flirtations, feats of strength, and quarrels over rights of way and water rights. Sometimes, too, we would settle down to a fierce game of backgammon, on a beautiful rosewood board with old ivory pieces, lent to us by Silvério. But nothing enchanted him more than to walk quietly through the large rooms of the house to a smaller room that gave onto the orchard and to stand there in the dark, leaning against the window, in quiet rapture, listening long and languidly to the nightingales singing among the orange trees.

: X :

Up until then, the weather had been wandering gaily about the mountains, all dressed in blue and gold, wearing an unchanging smile of dazzling light, kicking up dust along the paths, and bringing joy to all of Nature, from the birds of the air to the streams, but suddenly, on the morning of the day before I was due to return to Guiães, in one of those abrupt changes of mood that make it so very similar in temperament to Man, it turned up sad and frowning, wrapped in a gray blanket, plunged into a gloom so heavy and so infectious that all the mountains grew sad too. And no bird sang, and the brooks took refuge under the grass and silently wept.

When Jacinto came into my room, I could not resist frightening him a little.

"A southwest wind! Crows cawing in the woods! We're in for a lot of water, Senhor Dom Jacinto! Maybe two weeks of rain! Now we'll find out who is the refined lover of Nature, once the rain and the wind set in, and the hillsides turn into streams."

My Prince went over to the window, his hands in his pockets.

"The sky certainly looks very heavy. I've already asked for them to open one of my Paris suitcases and take out my raincoat. It doesn't matter, though; the trees will simply be all the greener. And it's good that I should know Tormes in its winter mode."

But since Melchior had assured him that the rain would only arrive in the afternoon, Jacinto decided to set out before lunch to Corujeira, where Silvério was waiting for him, in order to decide the fate of some very ancient, very picturesque, and very interesting chestnut trees, but which were also, alas, very rotten and threatening to fall down. And trusting in Melchior's forecast, Jacinto did not bother to dress for the rain. We had only gotten half way, however, when a kind of shudder ran through the trees, the sky turned black, and, suddenly, whipped up by the wind, a heavy slanting rain fell upon us, leaving us stunned and clinging to our hats, bewildered by the might of the tempest. We heard a shout, which the wind turned into a howl, and higher up, near a kind of hut, we spotted Silvério under a scarlet umbrella, waving to us and indicating the shortest route to that place of shelter. With the rain drenching our faces, we set off in that direction, skidding in the mud, hunched and stumbling, made dizzy by the storm, which, in a matter of moments, had flooded the fields, swelled the streams, washed away the earth from the terraces, set the trees waving their branches in despair, and turned the mountains black, wild, hostile and uninhabitable.

When, at last, beneath the vast umbrella with which Silvério was waiting for us at the edge of the field, we ran, dripping and panting, into the shelter of that unexpected haven, my Prince, wiping the rain from his face and neck, muttered faintly:

"Heavens, what ferocity!"

He seemed unnerved by this sudden, violent outburst from those hitherto friendly, welcoming mountains, which, in the last two months, had unalterably offered him only sweetness and shade, calm skies, gently rustling branches and discreetly murmuring brooks.

"Good God! Are there often storms like this?"

Silvério immediately seized upon this opportunity to terrify my Prince.

"Oh, this is nothing, sir, this is just a little game the Summer's playing. You should see it in Winter, though—if you're still here, of course. When it storms then, you can almost hear the hills shaking!"

And he explained how, on his way to Corujeira, he, too, had been caught out by the storm. Fortunately, that morning, as soon as he saw the scowling sky and saw the trembling leaves on the black poplars, he had taken the precaution of bringing his umbrella and putting on his big boots.

"I thought about sheltering in Esgueira's house, he's one of the tenant farmers—he lives in that house down below, the one with the fig tree—but his wife's been ill for some days now. And since what she's got might be catching, smallpox or something, I thought to myself: 'No, better safe than sorry!' And so I came up here to this hut. And hardly a minute had passed when I spotted you, sir. Fancy that! Anyway, you'd better get straight off home, sir, and change your clothes, because this rain's set in for rest of the day, I reckon, and for the night as well."

Just then, however, the rain falling from a very black sky became perpendicular, for the wind had dropped, and there was a patch of brightness beyond the river and the hills, like a gap between gray curtains slowly opening.

Jacinto was resting. I was still shaking myself and stamping my sodden feet, which were growing cold. And good Silvério, pensively stroking his black beard, amended his forecast:

"Well, perhaps not. It seems to be clearing up. Who'd have guessed it? The wind must have changed direction."

The "hut" consisted of a roof and two walls built at an angle out of loose stones—the rubble from some ruined shack—and supported by a prop. Just then it was home only to some wood, a pile of empty baskets, and an ox-cart, on which my Prince was now sitting, rolling himself a consoling cigarette. The rain continued to fall copiously, in long shining threads. And all three of us fell silent, absorbed in that inert, unthinking contemplation into which steady rain always plunges eyes and souls.

"Senhor Silvério," my Prince said, "what were you saying about smallpox?"

Silvério turned around, surprised.

"Me, sir? Oh, yes, Esgueira's wife. And it might well be. We get our fair share of illness around here, sir. Oh, the air is good, that's true, oh yes, there's clean air and clean water, but sometimes, if you don't mind my saying, sir, there's a lot of fever about."

"But isn't there a doctor or a pharmacy?"

Silvério gave the superior smile of one who inhabits a civilized region well provided with all amenities.

"Of course. There's a pharmacy in Guiães, close by the house of our friend here. A very knowledgeable man is our Firmino, eh, Zé Fernandes? Very capable. The nearest doctor is Dr. Avelino, and he lives about a league and half away, in Bolsas. But you see, sir, these people are poor. It's hard enough for them to earn their daily bread, let alone afford medicine!"

And again a silence fell in the shelter along with the growing chill from the drenched landscape. Beyond the river, that small promise of brightness between the two thick gray curtains had still grown no larger. The slope before us now ran with muddy rivulets. I was sitting weakly on a log, my hunger intensified by the wild weather. Jacinto, perched on the edge of the cart, his feet dangling, was stroking his damp moustache and feeling the bones of his face where, to my horror, the sad shadow of former days had reappeared, the shadow of No. 202!

Then from behind the wall of the hut, a boy appeared, very ragged and very thin, with a small, sallow, grubby face from which two large dark eyes were gazing at us, half in astonishment, half in fear. Silvério recognized him at once.

"How's your mother? No need to come any closer, stay where you are. I can hear you fine. How's your mother?"

I couldn't understand what the boy's poor pale lips were saying, but Jacinto was interested and asked:

"What's he saying? Let the boy come in. Who *is* your mother?"

But it was Silvério who respectfully explained:

"It's that woman I mentioned who's been ill, Esgueira's wife, in that house with the fig tree. She's got another younger boy as well. They certainly don't lack for children."

"But the boy looks ill as well!" exclaimed Jacinto. "He's so sallow, poor thing. Are you ill too?"

The boy said nothing, sucking his thumb and staring at us with sad, frightened eyes. And Silvério smiled kindly.

"No, this one's healthy. He's sallow and thin, right enough, but what do you expect, sir? Too little food and too little money. And when they do get some bread, it has to be shared out among them all. Oh, yes, there's a lot of hunger."

Jacinto suddenly jumped down from the edge of the cart.

"Hunger? So he's hungry, then? And hunger's commonplace, is it?"

His eyes were shining with horror and pity as he glanced from me to Silvério and back, asking for confirmation of this unsuspected misery. And I was the one who had to explain to my Prince.

"Of course there's hunger, Jacinto! Did you think Paradise still existed up here in the mountains, with no work and no poverty? There are poor people everywhere, even in the goldmines of Australia. Wherever there's work, there's a proletariat, be it in Paris or in the Douro valley."

My Prince made an anxious, impatient gesture:

"I don't want to know how things are in the Douro valley, what I want to know is if here, in Tormes, on my estates, on the lands that I own, there are people who work for me and who go hungry, and little children like this, starving. That's what I want to know."

Silvério was smiling respectfully at Jacinto's innocence and ignorance of the realities of country life:

"Naturally we have tenants on the estate who are very poor, sir— most of them are. That's how it is, and if we didn't give them a bit of help now and then, frankly, I don't know what would become of them. This Esgueira fellow, for example, has so many children he doesn't know what to do. You should see the hovels they live in too. They're real pigsties. Like Esgueira's down there, by the fig tree."

"Let's go and see!" said Jacinto with sudden determination.

And he left the shelter, without waiting for a pause in the rain, which was still falling, although more lightly now, more sparsely. However, Silvério anxiously barred his way, as if to save him from a precipice.

"No, sir, you are not going into that house! We have no idea what's wrong with his wife and, as I said before, better safe than sorry."

Jacinto remained unalterably polite and patient.

"Thank you for your concern, Silvério. Now open your umbrella and off we go!"

Silvério made a slight submissive bow and did as Jacinto had ordered, opening his vast umbrella with a thwack and sheltering Jacinto beneath it as we crossed the now waterlogged fields. I followed behind, thinking what magnificent alms the good Lord was sending to that poor couple through the agency of a remote gentleman from the Cities! Behind us followed the little boy, lost in amazement.

Like all the houses in the mountains, Esgueira's was built of stone, with no mortar, a flimsy roof, its tiles all mossy and blackened, with one window up above and a rough-and-ready door that served for letting in air, light and people and for letting out the smoke. And all around, Nature and Hard Work had, over the years, planted climbers and wild flowers, little bits of garden, flowering shrubs, added old moss-grown benches, and filled pots with earth in which parsley grew; there were babbling streams, vines twined around the trunks of elms; there were shady nooks and ponds, all of which made that place of Hunger, Disease and Sorrow seemingly a dwelling more suited to an eclogue.

Silvério cautiously pushed open the door with the point of his umbrella, calling:

"Maria, are you there?"

And the door opened a crack to reveal a very tall girl, dark-skinned and dirty, staring at us in astonishment with sad, serene, shadowy eyes.

"How's your mother? Open the door, girl. These gentlemen have come to visit."

And she slowly opened the door, saying in a weary, mournful, yet uncomplaining voice, accompanied by a vague, resigned smile :

"How do you think she is, poor thing? Very bad, very bad."

And from within, a slow, lethargic, muffled voice, that seemed to rise out of the earth, took up the desolate refrain:

"Oh, dear God, very bad, very bad."

Silvério, without actually moving from the door and holding his half-open umbrella before him like a shield against infection, replied consolingly:

"It won't be anything serious, Maria. She's just caught a chill, that's all." And over his shoulder to Jacinto, he said with a shrug: "As you see, sir, terrible poverty. It's even raining inside."

And there, on the one patch of beaten-earth floor visible to us, glittered a large puddle, formed by the rain dripping through the broken roof. The wall, thick with soot from the fire, was as black as the floor. And the filthy gloom within seemed cluttered, in dark disorder, with rags, broken pots, and detritus, among which the only clear, decipherable shape was a black wooden chest, and above it, between a saw and a lamp, a large scarlet petticoat hanging from a nail.

Jacinto, deeply embarrassed, withdrew, muttering:

"That's all right . . . that's all right. . . ."

And he strode off across the field in the direction of the hut, as if he were running away, and I followed after, while Silvério doubtless revealed to the girl the august presence of "the master of the house," because we heard her say mournfully:

"Oh, may the Lord give him good fortune! May the Lord be with him!"

By the time Silvério, striding along in his great boots, caught up with us in the middle of the field, Jacinto had stopped. Nervously fiddling with his moustache, he looked at me and said:

"This is terrible, Zé Fernandes, terrible."

Beside us, Silvério's great voice boomed out:

"What do you want? Go back to your mother!"

It was the little ragged, starving boy, who had attached himself to us, still staring at us in amazement, in the vague hope perhaps, that one of us, like gods encountered on the road, might give him either food or a little affection. And Jacinto, at whom the boy most persistently directed his sad gaze, and who felt horribly embarrassed and ashamed by the boy's dumb humility, could only smile and again mutter vaguely "That's all right, that's all right. . . ." And in the end, I was the one to give the boy a placatory *tostão* to get rid of him. But when he, grasping his one *tostão*, still continued to follow as if in the wake of our magnificence, Silvério clapped his hands and shouted, shooing him away like a bird:

"Go on, go back home! And take that money to your mother. Go on, off you go!"

"And now off *we* go to lunch," I said, looking at my watch. "It's going to be a fine day after all."

Indeed, a scrap of blue sky, washed clean and lustrous, gleamed now over the river; and the thick layers of clouds were rolling away, carried along by the wind, which was gently sweeping them, vacant and empty, into some hidden corner of the heavens.

We then made our slow way back to the house, up a steep path known to Silvério (and down which flowed a small torrent, leaping and chattering). Another light shower fell from each branch that we touched, and all around, the leaves glittered, green and refreshed, having drunk deep of the rain.

As we reached the end of the narrow track and were turning onto a wider path, between a terrace and a row of vines, Jacinto suddenly stopped and, slowly taking out his cigarette case, said:

"Look, Silvério, I don't want such poverty on my estate any more."

Silvério merely gave a shrug and an equivocal grunt of obedience and skepticism.

"First, though," Jacinto went on, "have Dr. Avelino go and see that poor woman. And then have someone fetch any medicine that's needed from Guiães. And ask the doctor to come back tomorrow and every day after that until she's better. Oh, and listen, Silvério, give all the poor people on the estate ten or fifteen *mil-réis* so that they can make some soup and buy a little decent food. Will that be enough, do you think?"

Silvério could not contain his laughter. Fifteen *mil-réis*! A few *tostões* would be more than enough. It wasn't a good idea to get people accustomed to such generosity. "They'll all start expecting the same treatment, they'll all come begging . . ."

"And they'll be given something, too," said Jacinto simply.

"As you wish, sir," muttered Silvério.

He stood stock still in the middle of the path, overwhelmed by such extravagance. I had to hurry him on impatiently.

"Come on, we can talk as we walk. It's midday, and I'm as hungry as a wolf!"

We walked on, with Silvério between us, thoughtful and frowning beneath the vast brim of his hat, his voluminous beard covering his chest, the huge scarlet umbrella under his arm. And

Jacinto, nervously tugging at his moustache—for he still feared Silvério—was nevertheless cautiously trying out on him a few more charitable ideas:

"And then there are the houses. That so-called house is a complete hovel! I'd like to give those people a better home. Presumably all the other tenants live in hovels too. What we need is complete reform! We need to build new houses for all the estate's tenants."

"*All* of them?" Silvério spluttered before lapsing into silence.

And Jacinto, terrified, stammered back:

"Yes, all of them, I mean . . . how many tenants are there exactly?"

Silvério made a sweeping gesture:

"Twenty or so . . . twenty-three, if I remember rightly. No, twenty-seven."

Then it was Jacinto's turn to fall silent, as if in recognition of the sheer scale of the undertaking. But he then went on to ask how much each house would cost. A simple house, but clean and comfortable, like the one Melchior's sister lived in, next to the wine-press. Silvério again started back in horror. A house like Ermelinda's? Did Jacinto really want to know? And he hurled a figure from on high, like an immense stone with which to crush Jacinto.

"Two hundred *mil-réis*, sir. At the least!"

I couldn't help but laugh at the excellent man's ominously threatening tone. And Jacinto, very gently, to appease Silvério, said:

"Fine, my friend. So that would be some six *contos de réis*! Let's make it ten, because I would also like to give each family some furniture and some new clothes."

At this, Silvério gave a terrified roar:

"But, sir, this is Revolution!"

And when Jacinto and I irresistibly burst out laughing at the look of horror in Silvério's eyes as he flung wide his huge arms—as if witnessing the collapse of a whole world—he pouted angrily and said:

"Oh, you may laugh, gentlemen! Houses for everyone, furniture, money, bedclothes, ten *contos de réis*! All right, I'll laugh too. Ha, ha, ha! What a joke, eh? What fun!"

And then, making a low bow, as if declining to take any responsibility for this act of grand extravagance, he said:

"After all, sir, you give the orders around here."

"I do, Silvério. And I also want to know how much rent these people pay, what leases they have, so that I can improve them too; because there's a lot that needs improving. Come and join us for lunch. And then we can talk."

Silvério was by then so saturated with horror and alarm that he did not even react to Jacinto's suggestion that the leases be "improved." He thanked him humbly for the invitation to lunch, but asked permission to go over to the wine-press first, to see how the carpenters were getting on repairing the spindle. It wouldn't take him a moment and he would then be entirely at Jacinto's disposal.

He set off down a path and jumped over a gate. We followed behind with steps made lighter by the approach of our much-delayed lunch, by the blithe reappearance of the blue sky, and by the blow for justice that had been struck against poverty in the mountains.

"Well, you certainly haven't wasted your day, Jacinto," I said, clapping my friend on the shoulder with undisguised affection.

"I never even dreamed there could be such poverty, Zé Fernandes. But having these houses, where children are going hungry, within sight of my own house, is just too terrible."

We were walking up the avenue of beech trees. Emerging from behind two large, cottony clouds, a ray of sun lit up one corner of the house at the far end of the avenue with a bright stripe of light. The cockerels were singing out loud and clear. And a sudden gentle breeze set the clean, shining leaves gaily jostling.

"Do you know what I was thinking, Jacinto? What just happened to you reminds me of the legend of St. Ambrose—no, it wasn't St. Ambrose. I can't remember now which saint it was. Anyway, this happened before he became a saint and when he was still just another sinful gentleman, who had fallen in love with a woman and given himself over to her heart and soul, even though he had only glimpsed her from a distance in the street. Then one afternoon, still enraptured, he followed her into a church and there, suddenly, she lifted her veil, unfastened her dress and showed the poor gentleman her breast eaten away by a cankerous sore. You were equally in love with the mountains, but without really knowing them, except in all their Summer beauty. And today the mountains suddenly showed you their great canker. Perhaps it's one step on the way to you becoming St. Jacinto."

He stopped to consider, his thumbs hooked in the armholes of his waistcoat:

"You're right, I did see the canker, but at least, thank God, it's one I can cure!"

I did not disillusion my Prince. And we both walked gaily up the steps to the house.

: XI :

THE DAY AFTER these large acts of charity, I returned to Guiães, but I so often rode the three leagues from our house to Jacinto's old beech avenue that my mare, whenever I failed to take that familiar turning, and guided her instead toward a familiar stable (where she was on intimate terms with Melchior's little horse), would neigh out of pure nostalgia. Even Aunt Vicência appeared vaguely jealous of that Tormes to which I was always racing off, of that Prince whose rejuvenation I was constantly celebrating—along with his charity, his delicious food, and his agricultural fantasies. One day, with just a pinch of salt and irony—all that would fit into a heart entirely full of innocence—she said to me, knitting rather more vigorously than usual:

"You should congratulate yourself! Now, even I am curious to meet this Jacinto of yours. Bring the marvelous boy over here!"

I laughed:

"Don't you worry, Aunt Vicência, he's coming for my birthday supper. We'll have a party, followed by a little dance in the courtyard, and invite all the great and the good from around and about. Who knows, we might even find Jacinto a bride."

And I had, indeed, already invited my Prince to this celebration.

It was important that the lord of Tormes should meet the owners of the other good families in the region. Besides, it was high time, as I told him jokingly, that he met a few women, some strapping lasses from those mountain mansions, because there was something very monastic and solitary about Tormes, and a man without a little of the Eternal Feminine to alleviate his solitude can become coarse and grow a rough bark like a tree.

"Tormes, your reconciliation with Nature and your renunciation of the lies of Civilization certainly makes for a lovely story, but what you lack is a woman!"

He agreed, laughing, and stretched out languidly in his wicker armchair.

"Yes, you're right, what this place needs is a woman, with a capital W, only I'm not sure about these local girls. I can't rid myself of the idea that they probably resemble vegetables. Healthy, nutritious and excellent for the cooking pot, but vegetables for all that. The women whom poets compare to flowers are always women from the Court, from the great capital cities, and it is they who have invariably inspired poets, from Hesiod to Horace. I mean there's no perfume, no grace, no elegance, no refinement in a carrot or a cabbage. I just can't believe these local women will be very interesting."

"Well, I'll tell you. Your nearest neighbor, Dom Teotónio's daughter, is, it has to be said—with all due respect to the illustrious house of Barbedo—a monster. And the Albergarias' sister, from Quinta da Loja, wouldn't even have tempted St. Anthony, especially if she took her clothes off—she's as thin as a string bean. She really *is* a vegetable, and not even a very nutritious one!"

"No, thank you, no string beans for me!"

"Then there's Dona Beatriz Veloso. Now she *is* pretty, but horribly well spoken. She talks like the heroines in novels by Camilo Castelo Branco. Ah, but, of course, you've never read any of his novels. And then there's her tone of voice, impossible to describe really, but it's the tone of voice actors use in the romantic dramas they put on at the Teatro de Dona Maria. But then you've never been to the Teatro de Dona Maria either. Anyway, it's quite ghastly! And she asks the most ridiculous questions. The hussy once asked me: 'Don't you get the most immense pleasure from Lamartine?' "

"And what did you say?"

"I just stared at her and said: 'Oh, Lamartine!' But she's an excellent creature really, poor thing! Then we have the daughters of João Rojão, two fresh, happy flowers, simple creatures who positively glow with good health; they even smell healthy. Aunt Vicência adores them. And of course there's Dr. Alípio's wife, who's a real beauty, a splendid creature! But then she *is* Dr. Alípio's wife, and you have now renounced the duties of Civilization. Besides, she's a thoroughly decent woman and totally absorbed in her two little ones, who resemble two Murillo angels. And who else is there? Ah, yes, to complete the list of female personnel, we have Melo Rebelo's daughter, from Sandofim, who is great fun and has lovely hair. She borders on perfection and bakes cakes as good as any made by an Ancien Régime nun. Júlia Lobo was very pretty, but she, alas, died. And that's about it. No, wait, there's the Flower of the Mountains, my cousin Joaninha, from Flor da Malva! And she really is perfection!"

"And how have you managed to resist, cousin Zé?"

"We're like brother and sister; we were practically brought up together. She's even more like family than you. And familiarity blurs the sexes. Her mother was Aunt Vicência's only sister, and she died very young. Joaninha was brought up in our house in Guiães almost from the cradle. Her father, Uncle Adrião, is a good man, an erudite fellow, an antiquarian and a collector. He collects all kinds of strange things: bells, spurs, seals, buckles—a most unusual assortment. He's been longing to come and visit you in Tormes, but the poor thing suffers with his bladder and can't ride a horse. And the road between here and Flor da Malva is quite impossible for carriages."

My Prince stretched out his arms in the perfumed shade.

"I'll obviously have to visit your uncle and Aunt Vicência. I really do want to get to know my neighbors, but later, when there's less to do. At the moment, I'm fully occupied with taking care of my own people."

And he was! Jacinto was like the founder-king of a new kingdom and a great builder. Throughout his domain of Tormes, work was being done to renovate the tenants' houses; some were being repaired and other older ones were being demolished so that larger, more comfortable houses could be built in their place. The roads were full of carts creaking under the weight of stone or of wood cut from the pine forests.

Pedro's tavern, on the edge of the parish, was full of unusual comings and goings, what with the glaziers, stonemasons and carpenters who had been engaged to carry out all the work. Pedro, shirtsleeves rolled up ever higher, was kept busy behind the counter filling bottles and glasses from a vast jug.

Jacinto, who now owned two horses, was up every morning, lovingly inspecting each building site. I, meanwhile, was uneasy, fearing that my Prince's old, obsessive desire to accumulate Civilization was about to burst to the surface again! The original building plans were constantly being enlarged and embellished. The windows, in accordance with centuries-old custom, were to have only shutters, but now Jacinto had decided that glass should be put in, even though the master-builder, with admirable candor, had told him that in a month there wouldn't be a single pane left. Rather than retaining the traditional beams, Jacinto wanted the ceilings to be stuccoed, and I could see that he had to make a real effort to keep within the bounds of common sense and restrain himself from installing electric bells in every house. I was not even surprised when, one morning, he declared that the reason country people were so dirty was that they didn't have anywhere comfortable to wash, which is why he was considering equipping every house with a bathroom. We were, at that moment, leading our horses down a steep, stony path; a light wind was rustling in the trees, and a stream was leaping, babbling over the stones. His ideas came as no surprise to me, but the stones, the stream, the trees, and the wind all seemed to be gaily laughing at my Prince. As well as these comforts, to which João the master-builder referred, wild-eyed, as Jacinto's "grand plans," Jacinto was pondering the good of his tenants' souls. He had commissioned his architect in Paris to draw up the perfect plan for a school that he wanted to build in Carriça next to the chapel that now sheltered his ancestors' bones. Then he wanted to create a library of picture books so that, on Sundays, those men who were now too old to learn to read would have something with which to entertain themselves. My heart sank, and I thought: "He's starting to accumulate Ideas again! The Book is beginning to invade the Mountains!" However,

I found other ideas of his genuinely touching, and I—and even Aunt Vicência—were very excited by his plans for a nursery school, where he hoped to spend happy mornings watching the children crawling about or stumbling after a ball. Our pharmacist in Guiães had agreed to set up a small apothecary shop in Tormes, to be managed by his apprentice, one of Aunt Vicência's godsons, who had published an article in the *Almanac of Memories* about popular festivals in the Douro region. And the post of doctor in Tormes had already been advertised with a salary of six hundred *mil-réis*.

"All you need now is a theater!" I said to Jacinto, laughing.

"No, not a theater, but I do have a plan to build a place where we could put on magic-lantern shows to teach these poor people about the great cities of the world and about Africa and perhaps a little history."

Even I liked that idea! And when I told Uncle Adrião, he, the worthy antiquarian, despite his rheumatism, slapped his thigh hard. "Yes, sir! A wonderful idea! It would be a brilliant way of teaching these illiterate people the history of the Bible, Roman history, even the history of Portugal, through images!" And he turned to his daughter Joaninha and declared that Jacinto was "a man of heart"!

And my Prince's popularity really was spreading throughout the region. In the words "May the Lord keep you safe, sir!" with which the women greeted him as he passed and in the way that they turned to watch him go, there was the earnestness of a prayer and a very genuine desire that the Lord *would* keep him safe always. The children to whom he gave coins could sniff out his presence from leagues away, and a motley crowd would gather around him: dark, grubby faces with eyes wide not with fear now, but with wonder. When, one afternoon, on the path leading out of the beech avenue, Jacinto's horse stumbled on some large boulders and fell, the very next day, a group of men came of their own volition to smooth the surface and put down gravel, horrified that their "good master" should have been exposed to such danger. The words "the good master" began to spread. The older parishioners never met him without exclaiming, some gravely, others with great toothless smiles: "Ah, our benefactor!" Sometimes, an old lady would run out from her garden or come to the door of her house if she saw him on the road, to call to him, waving her thin arms: "May God shower you with blessings, sir!" On Sundays, Father José Maria (a good friend of mine and a keen hunter) would ride over from Sandofim to Tormes on his chestnut mare in order to say mass in the chapel, and Jacinto was always there, in his family seat, like all the Jacintos of the past, so that the simple people would not think him a stranger to God. He was often given presents, which the tenants' older daughters or little children, blushing scarlet, would bring to him on the verandah: a pot of basil, a large bunch of carnations, and even, sometimes, a plump duck. Then biscuits and meringues from Guiães would be handed out to the children and, in the courtyard, jugs of white wine were passed around for the men. Silvério was already saying, in amazed tones and with renewed respect, that Senhor Dom Jacinto would soon have more votes than Dr. Alípio. And even I was impressed when Melchior told me about one João Torrado, an eccentric old man with a long white beard—a mixture of herbalist, animal doctor and soothsayer, who lived a mysterious existence high up in a cave in the mountains—who was declaring to anyone who would listen that the good master was King Sebastian returned to us!

: XII :

AND SO SEPTEMBER ARRIVED and with it my birthday, which fell on the third of the month and on a Sunday. I had spent all that week in Guiães, preparing for the grape harvest, but early that famous Sunday, I went up to my late lamented Uncle Afonso's bedroom and stood on the balcony overlooking the road that my Prince would come riding along in order to make his long-postponed visit to our house. Aunt Vicência had been rushing about from kitchen to pantry since dawn, because in her desire to introduce my Prince to all the local "personnel," she had invited to supper a few family friends, those who owned carriages or ox carts and could, on the safer roads, drive back home late after the dance that was to be held in the courtyard—which, to this end, had already been decorated with Chinese lanterns. However, at ten o'clock, I was gripped by despair when a servant from Flor da Malva brought a letter from my cousin Joaninha, announcing regretfully that she would be unable to come because her father had developed a boil overnight, and she didn't want to leave him. I rushed indignantly into the kitchen, where Aunt Vicência was overseeing the violent beating of some eggs in a vast terrine.

"Joaninha isn't coming! It's typical. She says her father has a boil. Uncle Adrião always seems to choose the really important days to have a boil or a pain in his side."

A look of concern filled my Aunt Vicência's round, kindly, red face.

"Oh, the poor thing! It must be somewhere that would make it painful for him to sit in the carriage for any length of time. *Poor* thing! Look, if you write a note back, tell him to put a poultice of rosemary leaves on it. That always worked for your Uncle Afonso."

I merely shouted from the window to the servant who was down in the courtyard, giving his donkey some water to drink:

"Tell Senhora Dona Joaninha that we're very sorry she can't come, but that I might visit tomorrow."

And I returned impatiently to the window because the clock in the corridor, which was always slow, had already chimed half past ten, and my Prince was going to be late for lunch. However, as soon as I reached the balcony, Jacinto appeared at the bend in the road, wearing a large straw hat and mounted on his mare, followed by Cricket, also wearing a straw hat and carrying a vast green sunshade, as he sat astride the packsaddle on Melchior's old mare. Behind them came a boy carrying a suitcase on his head. Overjoyed to see my Prince trotting toward my village home on the day of my thirty-sixth birthday, I remembered another birthday, his—in Paris, in No. 202, when, surrounded by all the splendors of Civilization, we had sadly raised our glasses *ad manes*, to our dead!

"*Salve!*" I cried from the verandah. "*Salve, domine Jacinthe!*"

And to welcome him I gave a spirited rendition of the national anthem.

"It's lovely here!" he called from below. "Your palace is quite superb. But where's the door?"

I was already rushing down into the courtyard, where Jacinto was dismounting and gaily recounting the agonies of Cricket, who had never before ridden a horse and had not ceased for a moment to complain about the perils of such an adventure.

That worthy gentleman, huffing and puffing, his skin shiny with sweat and looking somehow pale beneath his splendid blackness, kept exclaiming and pointing one tremulous hand at the poor mare (which, let loose, was standing thoughtfully, stock still, as if made of stone, on feet that seemed as fixed as boundary markers):

"You should have seen that creature, Senhor Fernandes! A wild beast, she is—never quiet for a moment, moving now to the left and now to the right, one foot here, another foot there, obviously trying to unseat me!"

And he could not resist giving the mare's saddle a vengeful prod with the point of his parasol.

As Jacinto climbed the elegant steps into the bright corridor, where at the far end the window was garlanded with climbing roses, he lavishly praised our house as a respite from the solid walls and great feudal doors of Tormes. And in the room reserved for him, he was full of gratitude to Aunt Vicência for the many little maternal touches—two Chinese vases filled with flowers on the chest of drawers, the fine canary-yellow Indian bedspread decorated with large golden birds. I smiled, greatly touched. Then we folded each other in a warm birthday embrace. "You're thirty-eight, aren't you, Zé Fernandes?" "Why I'm thirty-four if I'm a day, you brute!" And my Prince immediately opened his luggage, the sober suitcase of a philosopher, and offered me—as sly Ulysses always put it in *The Odyssey*—the noble gifts that were my due. These were a sapphire tie pin, a cigarette box made from brushed steel, a sprig of apple blossom in delicate enamel, and an antique carved paper knife from China. I protested at such prodigality.

"I found them in the boxes sent from Paris, which I ordered to be opened last night. And I took the liberty of bringing this small token for your Aunt Vicência. It's not worth a great deal, but it once belonged to Princess de Lamballe."

It was a small chased silver vessel for holding holy water, ornate and rather elegant in style.

"Aunt Vicência has no idea who the Princess de Lamballe is, but she'll be delighted! And it's reassuring too, because she suspects that, coming as you do from Paris, that land of impieties, you are not a religious man. But now—a quick wash and brush up and come down to lunch!"

Aunt Vicência seemed at first surprised by and then enchanted with my friend, whom she had believed to be a real prince—arrogant, unapproachable and difficult. When he presented her with the silver vessel—asking her humbly to remember him in her prayers—and with two long-stemmed roses, even fresher and rosier than the roses filling the table, the good lady, who had never received such a pious present, blushed prettily. What captivated her most about Jacinto, though, was his tremendous appetite and the enthusiastic conviction with which he piled chicken onto his plate, followed by great mountains of baked rice, then several helpings of beef and onions, all the while praising our cuisine and swearing he had never tasted anything so sublime. She positively glowed.

"It does a person good to see you eat, it really does! Now have another of these stuffed potatoes."

"I'll have two if I may! At such a perfect lunch table, my portions are always Gargantuan!"

"Now don't go quoting Rabelais, Aunt Vicência knows nothing of profane authors!" I exclaimed, equally radiant. "And try some of our white wine and praise God for ripening such a grape."

The lunch was a very jolly affair, very friendly and full of talk about the work Jacinto was carrying out at Tormes, about the nursery school that so enthused Aunt Vicência, about the coming grape harvest, about my cousin Joaninha, whose father was ill, and about the dreadful state of the roads. However, the most touching moment of all came when coffee was served, and the servant placed before Jacinto a saucer on which sat a cinnamon stick, his strange but customary cinnamon stick.

Aunt Vicência had remembered! She wanted him to feel as at home in Guiães as he did in Tormes, and the cinnamon stick was the sign that Aunt Vicência had adopted my Prince as her new nephew.

She then withdrew to the kitchen to prepare for that evening's banquet. We smoked a lazy cigar in the garden by the fountain, in the private shade of the cedar tree. Then, as proud landowner, I showed my Prince the whole estate, in pitiless, inexorable detail, omitting not a single field or stream or vine. And only when his face began to grow long and pale with tedium—and all he could squeeze out from his stunned and overloaded brain was a vague "Hmm, lovely! Beautiful!"—did I turn our steps back to the house, although not without first making a long detour to show him the wine press, the asparagus bed, and the site of a Roman castle.

When we went back through the garden into the cool drawing room, I managed to herd him, like a dumb beast, into my good Uncle Afonso's library, to show him our prize possessions, a magnificent copy of Fernão Lopes' *Chronicle of Dom João I*, a first edition of João de Barros' chivalric romance *The Emperor Clarimundo*, a copy of the *Henriade* signed by Voltaire, charters dating from the time of King Manuel, and other similar marvels. He sighed as he read the last piece of parchment and sighed again when I dragged him down to the cellar to admire the famous barrel which bore, in relief on the wooden lid, the complicated Sande family coat of arms. It was four o'clock, and my Prince looked glassy-eyed and pale. I fixed him with a fierce gaze, aware myself of its ferocity, and declared that we would now visit the place where we stored our olives. Jacinto, however, put his hand to the small of his back and murmured humbly, like a small child.

"Do you think I could sit down for a while?"

Then I took pity on him and loosened my grip and let him slouch after me to his room, where he immediately took off his boots, threw himself down on the cool cotton-upholstered divan, all the while murmuring in exhausted tones:

"A very fine estate!"

I generously allowed him to sleep and went downstairs to ensure that Gertrudes had set out the brushes and the towels in the room where the guests, who would soon be arriving, could wash their hands and brush off the dust of the road. Just at that moment, a caleche rolled into the courtyard, one of Dom Teotónio's old caleches, drawn by two chestnut mares. Peering out of the window, I saw, with relief, that he had come alone, wearing his white tie and his dustcoat, and without his ghastly daughter. I ran gaily into Aunt Vicência's room, where, with Catarina's assistance, she was hurriedly putting on her magnificent topaz bracelets.

"Dom Teotónio's here, Aunt Vicência, and without his daughter! You'd better hurry, because the others won't be far behind. Make sure Manuel is spruced up and wearing a proper starched tie. And let's see how the party goes!"

: XIII :

THE PARTY, ALAS, failed to sparkle. By the time my Prince entered the room wearing a white rose in the buttonhole of his black jacket, a white, embroidered double-breasted waistcoat, and a full white silk cravat pinned with a black pearl—an elegance that I suspected had its source in one of the newly opened boxes from Paris—the other male guests were already there, standing in a tight knot: Dom Teotónio, Ricardo Veloso, Dr. Alípio, plump Melo Rebelo from Sandofim, and the two Albergaria brothers from Quinta da Loja. Around the sofa where Aunt Vicência had installed herself was a smaller knot of chairs on which sat the ladies: Beatriz Veloso, her hair drawn up on the top of her head in a mass of curls, was wearing a dress of white muslin over silk, which made her look thinner and somehow airier; the two Rojão sisters (along with their aunt, Adelaide Rojão) were as red as roses and both wearing white; Dr. Alípio's wife was all in black and as splendid as a rustic Venus. And it was as if a prince really had entered the room, a prince from some northern country where all princes are magnificent, aloof, and terrifying. A silence fell, as if the oak-beamed roof had suddenly fallen in and had crushed us all; and every eye was trained on the unfortunate Jacinto, as when, on a Hindu hunt, a tiger suddenly appears at the edge of the forest. In the hasty, confused introductions I made as I led him around the room, his handshakes and his smiles, his murmured comments of "delighted to meet you" were full of genuine sympathy and simple warmth, but to no avail. The gentlemen remained very reserved, coolly observing this Prince who had come to live up in the Mountains; and the ladies huddled closer to Aunt Vicência, like sheep around their shepherd when a wolf suddenly hoves into view. Concerned, I singled out Dom Teotónio, the most ornamental of the gentlemen present.

"It was particularly kind of Dom Teotónio to come, Jacinto, because he rarely leaves his lovely house in Abrujeira."

The worthy Dom Teotónio, a former brigadier, smiled and smoothed his white moustache.

"So you came here straight from Vienna, did you?"

"No, I came straight from Paris with my friend Zé Fernandes."

Dom Teotónio insisted: "But you must often visit Vienna."

Jacinto smiled, surprised.

"Vienna? Why? No, I haven't been to Vienna for over fifteen years."

DomTeotónio murmured a slow "Ah!" and then fell silent, eyes downcast, as if pondering deep thoughts, his hands behind his back, beneath the tails of his long blue jacket.

Having observed this odd scene, I decided to try Dr. Alípio instead.

"The doctor, my dear Jacinto, is the most powerful man in the district."

The doctor bowed his handsome head with its beautiful black hair, so admirably smooth and glossy, but Aunt Vicência had, by then, gotten up from the sofa and was beckoning to Jacinto, because Manuel's large, stiff, scarlet figure had appeared at the door, silently announcing supper.

At the table (where the crème caramels, the dishes of sweet egg pastries and the old Madeira and Port wines in their thick cut-glass bottles all fused into a happy blend of rich, warm colors), Jacinto sat between Aunt Vicência and Luisinha—she was one of the Rojão sisters and my aunt's god-daughter, who, whenever she dined at Guiães, always sat beside her kindly godmother. The soup—chicken with noodles and rice—was consumed in a long heavy silence, and, anxious to break that silence and quite forgetting that I was at my own table in Guiães, I exclaimed:

"This soup is delicious!"

And Jacinto echoed my sentiments, declaring:

"Oh, indeed, divine!"

But since all the guests were clearly bewildered by my yelp of delight and by Jacinto's excessive enthusiasm, the bemused silence merely thickened into one of embarrassment. Fortunately, Aunt Vicência, smiling her kindly smile, remarked that Jacinto seemed to thoroughly enjoy good Portuguese food. And I, still eager to liven things up, didn't even allow my Prince to confirm his love of the local cuisine, but cried:

"He doesn't just enjoy it, he adores it! Well, after all those years of deprivation in Paris . . ."

Happily, I remembered the rice pudding prepared for Jacinto's birthday by the cook at No. 202, and immediately told the story in all its detail, exaggerating wildly and saying that the rice had even contained foie-gras, and that a tricolor had fluttered atop the ornamented pyramid, above a bust of the Comte de Chambord! However, that extravaganza of a rice pudding, so far from the mountains, provoked no interest at all and drew only a few polite smiles of agreement when I turned to the other guests, male and female, exclaiming: "Extraordinary, eh?" Dom Teotónio remarked mysteriously that "the cook clearly knew for whom he was cooking." And Dr. Alípio's beautiful wife, Senhora Dona Luísa, was bold enough to murmur:

"It must have looked charming and, who knows, perhaps it even tasted good too."

Then (in another absurd attempt to breathe life into the party) I launched into a wild, albeit friendly, attack on her for having thus defended such a profanation of our great national dish! Unfortunately, so loudly and energetically did I do so that the lovely lady retreated into her shell, silent and blushing, and looking even lovelier. And another silence fell upon the table, like a mist, until Aunt Vicência, ever providential, apologized to Jacinto for the absence of fish from the menu. But what could one do? Up there in the mountains, however much money you might have, it was impossible to find fish, apart from the salted variety. My excellent friend Rojão, in that particular way he had, with each syllable apparently lubricated with holy oils in order to flow more smoothly, commented that Senhor Dom Jacinto owned a long stretch of the Douro and had the right to fish for shad in it. Jacinto knew nothing of this right or of the existence of shad in the river. Dr. Alípio, however, was not surprised because those fishing rights, he said, had been sold to Cunha, the Brazilian, twenty years before, when Senhor Dom Jacinto was just a lad. And now, according to Dom Teotónio, they wouldn't be worth two *mil-réis* because there were no shad any more! And as the gentlemen around the table began a slow rural conversation about those long-vanished shad, the ladies took advantage of this lifting of the formal silence—which weighed heavy even on the chicken stew—to exchange a few whispered comments. Then, fearful that this rather dull fringe of desultory murmurings around the table would drag on, I again addressed Jacinto (in yet another attempt to enliven the party) and reminded him of the famous adventure: how the Dalmatian fish got stuck.

"That was one of the funniest things to happen to us in Paris! Jacinto had been given a very rare fish by the Grand Duke Casimiro, and so he put on a magnificent supper, to which the Grand Duke, the Grand Duke Casimiro, the brother of the emperor . . ."

All eyes turned to Jacinto, who was serving himself some peas, and Melo Rebelo almost choked as he took a hasty sip of wine and studied my friend to see if something of the Grand Duke had rubbed off on him. And I described, again in profuse detail, the fish stuck in the dumbwaiter, the Grand Duke fishing for it, the hook made out of a hairpin loaned by the Princess de Carman, the Duke de Marizac almost falling down the shaft . . . But no one laughed. Instead they listened reluctantly, purely out of politeness. In vain did I hurl the magnificent names of Grand Dukes and princesses at them, adding picaresque details. None of my guests knew what a dumbwaiter was or how a plate could possibly get stuck down a black well, and at the mention of the princess's hairpin, the Albergaria sisters lowered their eyes. So my delightful tale fizzled out, not helped by the cold water thrown on it by Aunt Vicência:

"Oh really, child, what nonsense!"

However, Jacinto had by now embarked on a long conversation

with Luisinha Rojão, who was laughing and talking brightly, and everyone, as if liberated from the solemn weight of his august presence, started their own discreet conversations, to which the Champagne, after the roast meat, lent more vivacity. The same fringe of murmured talk around the table, inconsequential and amicable, took over again. And I gave up all attempts to "liven things up." With the doctor's beautiful wife, I plunged into a discussion of the great social question of the time in Guiães: Dona Amélia Noronha's marriage to her farm manager. And I was still defending Dona Amélia and the Rights of Love when a silence spread around me, and I looked up to find Jacinto leaning toward me, glass in hand.

"To my old friend, Zé Fernandes, may you have many, many happy returns, always in the company of your aunt, to whose health I also have the honor to drink."

All glasses, in which the Champagne bubbles were now dying, were raised, accompanied by a murmur of friendship and good neighborliness. Indicating to Manuel that he should refill the glasses, I then rose to my feet, brushing back the tails of my frockcoat.

"Ladies and gentlemen, I drink to the health of my old friend Jacinto, who is honoring this, his brother's house for the very first time! What can I say about this man who is also for the first time honoring his own country with his presence? May he remain here in the mountains for many years, and may all of them be good years. To you, my friend!"

Another murmur ran around the table, quieter and more serious this time. Aunt Vicência clinked her almost empty glass with Jacinto's, who in turn clinked his with that of his neighbor, Luisinha Rojão, resplendent now and as pink as a peony. Then everyone, their glasses almost empty, drank to everyone else's health, including those of Uncle Adrião and the parish priest—both of whom were absent and both afflicted by boils. Aunt Vicência was just glancing about her, with that look that signaled a great getting up and scraping of chair legs on the floor, when Dom Teotónio, raising his glass of port, his other hand resting on the table, half stood up and, addressing Jacinto in a respectful, almost gruff voice, said:

"This toast is entirely personal, beween you and me. To the absent one!"

And he earnestly emptied his glass, as if he were making a statement. Jacinto drank too, bemused and uncomprehending. Then, at last, came the scraping of chair legs on floor, and I offered my arm to Aunt Albergaria.

And I only understood what had been meant when we were back in the drawing room, and Dr. Alípio, holding his cup of coffee and his cigar, gave me one of those keen looks that had earned him the nickname "Dr. Sharp," and said: "I just hope we don't see the gallows being built here again in Guiães." And with that same keen look he pointed me in the direction of Dom Teotónio, who had dragged Jacinto off to a window seat, where, with a devout and mysterious air, he was discoursing at length. Dear God, he was talking about *Miguelismo*! Good old Dom Teotónio had taken Jacinto for an hereditary, dyed-in-the-wool supporter of the pretender Dom Miguel, and suspected that behind his unexpected arrival on his Tormes estate lay some political mission, perhaps the beginning of an energetic propaganda campaign and a first step toward an attempt at bringing about a Restoration. Then I realized the reason for my guests' feelings of reserve toward Jacinto:

Liberal suspicion, the fear of a new and very wealthy presence at the elections, and a nascent irritation with those old ideas, embodied, or so they thought, in this extremely rich and cultivated young man. I was so surprised and pleased by this absurd idea that I almost spilled my coffee. I stopped Melo Rebelo, who had just placed his empty cup down on the tray, and stared in some amusement at "Dr. Sharp."

"You two don't really believe that Jacinto came to Tormes in order to stir up support for the Miguelites, do you?"

With utter seriousness, Melo Rebelo pressed his thick moustache to my ear and whispered:

"Some people even say that Prince Dom Miguel is staying with him in Tormes!"

And when I stood gazing at them openmouthed, the very sharp Dr. Alípio agreed.

"It's true. Disguised as a servant!"

As a servant? Good God! They must mean Anatole. Just then, Ricardo Veloso came up to me, took out a cigar and used mine to light it. Rebelo immediately invoked him as a witness. It was true, wasn't it? People were saying that Dom Miguel's son was in hiding at Tormes?

"Yes, disguised as a lackey," the worthy Rebelo immediately confirmed.

He lit his cigar, blew out the smoke and raised thoughtful eyebrows.

"If it's true, it seems to me downright impudent, not that I wouldn't mind having a look at him myself. They say he's a good-looking lad, handsome even. Then again, my Uncle João Vaz Rebelo, was hacked to pieces in the prisons of Almeida. And if all that business starts up again, it'll be a bad look-out for everyone. Now your friend . . ."

I said nothing. Jacinto had finally freed himself from old Dom Teotónio and, wearing the remnants of a smile and a look of bemusement, he joined me to vent his feelings.

"How extraordinary! I see that here, in the mountains, the good old ideas have been preserved without a line or a wrinkle."

Unable to contain himself, Melo Rebelo blurted out:

"Well, that depends on what you call 'good' ideas."

Infuriated by this whole ludicrous invention, which was surrounding my poor Jacinto with hostility and spoiling an otherwise pleasant birthday gathering, I said:

"Do you fancy a game of cards, Jacinto? No. Well, let's set up two tables anyway. Dom Teotónio is sure to want to play."

And I hauled Jacinto off to where the ladies were sitting, nestling once more in the shade of Aunt Vicência, who was settled in her usual corner of the sofa. They all fell silent and seemed to cower before my Prince, like pigeons spotting a vulture. And I left this fearsome man telling Dr. Alípio's wife (who was standing slightly apart from the other timid birds) how pleased he was to have the opportunity to meet his neighbors. She nervously opened her fan and smiled, and I am sure that in the City Jacinto had never seen redder lips or more dazzlingly white teeth. After organizing the card table, however, I had to take the place of Manuel Albergaria, who tended to dyspepsia and declared himself to be feeling "out of sorts" and in need of a little fresh air out on the verandah. Indeed, all the gentlemen were complaining about the heat, and so I ordered the servants to open the windows that gave onto the mimosa trees in the courtyard. Veloso, even while he was shuffling the cards, stopped what he was doing and blew out his cheeks as if he were stifling.

"It's dreadfully close. We could have thunder later on."

And Dr. Alípio, uneasy because he had an hour's journey back to his house and one of his mares was a little skittish, immediately ran to the window to scan the sky, which had grown black and warm and heavy.

"Yes, we're in for some rain, all right."

The branches of the mimosa trees shivered and whispered; and the air that stirred the curtains was warm and heavy too. In the other room, the same unease had arisen among the ladies, and Aunt Albergaria came in to tell her brother Jorge that it would be prudent to think about leaving, that it was growing dark. Dr. Alípio, taking out his watch, proposed that as soon as the game was over, they should all get ready to depart. Just then, Albergaria came in from the verandah, feeling less out of sorts, his dyspepsia relieved by a glass of gin, and took up his cards again, announcing that a terrific thunderstorm was brewing.

Going back into the drawing room, I found Jacinto gaily chatting to the ladies, who had by now lost their fear of him and were laughing and smiling, listening to the tale of his arrival in Tormes, with no luggage, no servants, and so woefully unprovided for that he'd had to sleep in a nightdress belonging to the caretaker's wife! Meanwhile, my poor birthday party was slowly unravelling. Aunt Albergaria prowled from window to window, worrying about the return journey to Roqueirinha and peering out at the sultry gloom. Slowly drawing on her gloves, Dr. Alípio's beautiful wife was asking if the card game was nearly over. Aunt Vicência had ordered tea to be served early, and Manuel, followed by Gertrudes carrying a tray of cakes, was already serving the ladies. Jacinto, standing up, was offering around cups and joking:

"Why all this haste? Why so frightened of a little thunderstorm?"

They retorted, quite at ease now and steadily warming to my Prince:

"That's easy for you to say, you'll be safe and dry under a roof!"

"How would you like to be heading off to Tormes in the dark?"

The games at the two card tables had finished, and the gentlemen went over to the windows and called down to the courtyard now plunged in gloom, where the carriages were ready and waiting.

"Put up the hood on the victoria, Diogo!"

"Light the big lantern, Pedro! The other lights by themselves aren't bright enough."

The maid Vicência arrived at the door with her arms full of shawls and lace mantillas. One of the Albergaria sisters would be travelling on the front seat of the victoria and so I ran to fetch my waterproof coat for her to wear if it should rain. And only Dom Teotónio, whose house was a mere half a league away down a good road, appeared to be in no hurry, and had again managed to button-hole my Prince, whom he led off into a solitary corner, where he engaged him in deep conversation, jabbing with one solemn index finger to emphasize each point. Aunt Albergaria called out that it had already started to rain, and the ladies all began bustling about, planting loud kisses on Aunt Vicência's cheek, while the men, in the hallway, were hurriedly donning overcoats.

Jacinto and I went out into the courtyard to accompany this unruly flight, and one by one, Dr. Alípio's dog-cart, the Albergarias' victoria, and the Velosos' vast old caleche rattled out into the night, followed by our wishes for a safe journey. Finally, Dom Teotónio drew on his black gloves and got into his caleche, saying to Jacinto:

"Well, my cousin and my friend, may God ensure that our meeting today and any future meetings prove to be of some benefit to this region of ours!"

Going back up the steps, my Prince was finally able to give expression to his bewilderment:

"That Teotónio fellow really is extraordinary! Do you know what he thinks? He takes me for a *miguelista* and imagines that I've come to Tormes in order to prepare the way for the restoration of Dom Miguel to the throne!"

"And what did you say?"

"I was so astonished, I couldn't even bring myself to disabuse him."

"Well, I'll tell you something else, my friend. All the other men think the same thing. They suspect that something's afoot and fear that scaffolds will again be built in Guiães. There's even a rumor that Prince Dom Miguel is hiding at Tormes, disguised as a servant. And do you know who he is? Anatole!"

"Amazing!" muttered Jacinto, his eyes wide.

In the drawing room, Aunt Vicência was disconsolately waiting for us with the lights still burning brightly in the peace and quiet of the abandoned party.

"Really! Fancy not even staying for a bowl of jelly or a glass of port!"

"Oh, it was all dreadfully dull, Aunt Vicência!" I exclaimed, glad to give vent to my own irritation. "None of the women would say a word, and the gentlemen all kept eyeing Jacinto most suspiciously."

Jacinto, greatly amused and quite sincerely, protested:

"No, on the contrary! I enjoyed it immensely. They're excellent people, so simple, and I thought the girls were just delightful, so fresh and jolly! I'm going to make some very good friends here—as soon as I've convinced them that I'm not a supporter of Dom Miguel."

Then we told Aunt Vicência about the extraordinary rumor doing the rounds and according to which Prince Dom Miguel was in hiding at Tormes. She laughed out loud. How ridiculous! How absurd!

"You're not a *miguelista*, are you?"

"No, madam, I'm a socialist."

I hurriedly explained to Aunt Vicência that being a socialist meant helping the poor, and the dear lady thought this to be the best and only true line to take.

"My Afonso, may he rest in peace, was a liberal. My father too; in fact, he was a friend of that great liberal hero, the Duque da Terceira—"

At that point, a loud crack of thunder rumbled through the black night, and a squall of rain drummed on the window panes and on the flagstones out on the verandah.

"Goodness me," cried Aunt Vicência, "those poor people! I do hope they'll be all right, especially the Rojão sisters in that victoria of theirs!"

And even before putting away the silver, she ran into her room in her haste to light the two candles she always lit at her little shrine, where she said a rosary or two with Gertrudes.

: XIV :

THE NEXT DAY, after lunch, Jacinto and I set off on horse-back for the long ride to Flora da Malva to find out how my Uncle Adrião and his boil were faring. I felt curious, almost uneasy, to see what impression my cousin Joaninha—the pride of our household—would make on my Prince. That very morning, as we were all strolling in the garden looking for a beautiful tea rose for my Prince's buttonhole, Aunt Vicência had so fervently praised the beauty, grace, charity and sweetness of her beloved niece that, in the end, I had told her off:

"Aunt, please! Such praise is fit only for the Virgin Mary! You're falling into the sin of idolatry! Jacinto will be terribly disappointed when he meets her and finds out she's only human."

As we trotted along the easy road to Sandofim, I remembered the morning when Jacinto had come across her portrait in my room at No. 202 and referred to her as a strapping peasant girl. Joaninha was certainly a strapping girl, but the photograph he had seen dated from her days of rustic vigor, when she was simply a lovely, strong, healthy mountain plant. Now she was nearly twenty-five and thought and felt for herself; her soul had grown gentler and more refined, adding a spiritual dimension to her rubicund splendor.

With the sky washed clean by the previous night's thunderstorm, and the fields left new and green by the light rain, the morning was filled by a cool and luminous sweetness in which, as old Euripides or Sophocles would have said, it was a delight to move one's body and to allow the soul to loiter, with no need to hurry and without a care in the world. There were no shadows on the road, but the sun was beating down on us very gently, its light as soft as an airy caress. To Jacinto (who had never before been here) the valley below resembled a painting by an artist from the French School of the eighteenth century, with its gently rolling fields, its peacefully flowing river, and its houses white among all those delicate shades of green, so friendly and so rich in promises of plenty and contentment. Our horses rode along at a pensive pace, and they, too, seemed to enjoy the delicious morning peace. And from some small, hidden, wild plant unknown to me came the delicate aroma I had so often noticed on that same road at the beginning of Autumn.

"What a glorious day!" murmured Jacinto. "This road to Flor da Malva is the road to Heaven itself! And what *is* that extraordinarily sweet perfume I can smell?"

I smiled to myself, then said:

"I don't know, perhaps it's the smell of Heaven!"

Stopping my horse, I pointed down into the valley with my whip.

"See over there, that line of elms and the stream, that's where Uncle Adrião's land begins. He has an orchard that produces the most delicious peaches in all of Portugal. I'll have to ask Joaninha to send you a basketful. And the jam she makes from those peaches, my friend, is positively celestial. I'll have to ask her to send you some of that too."

He laughed:

"That would be an abuse of cousin Joaninha's generosity."

And (for some reason) I suddenly remembered these lines from a romantic ballad, composed in Coimbra by my poor friend Procópio, which I then quoted to Jacinto:

> *Lady most fair,*
> *To thee I sing:*
> *"Accept this rose*
> *And this golden ring."*

"I think that might be a little excessive, Zé Fernandes, for just half a dozen peaches and a pot of jam."

We were still laughing when, at the turn of the road, we saw the long wall surrounding the Veloso estate and, beyond that, the chapel of São José in Sandofim. I headed at once for the main square and Torto's tavern, in pursuit of the particular white wine my soul always demands of me whenever I go there. My Prince said indignantly:

"Really, Zé Fernandes! Drinking white wine at this hour, when we've not long had our lunch?"

"It's an old custom of mine, stopping for a little glass of wine at Torto's tavern. It's for the good of my soul."

And so we paused outside, and I called for Manuel, who came rolling into view with his great belly and his bandy legs, and carrying a little green pitcher and a glass.

"Two glasses, Torto, my friend. The gentleman here will have the same."

After the feeblest of protests, my Prince took a glass, held the limpid, golden wine up to the light, tasted it, drank it down, and smacked his lips with relish.

"Delicious! I must have some of that wine at Tormes. It's perfect."

"Didn't I tell you? Fresh, light, aromatic, cheering—in short, pure soul! Fill our glasses again, Torto. This gentleman is Senhor Dom Jacinto, the owner of Tormes."

Then, from inside the tavern, a great voice boomed out, round and solemn:

"Blessed be the Father of the Poor!"

And there appeared at the door a strange old man with long white hair and a beard that seemed to cover most of his brick-red face; he was leaning on a stick and carrying a box on a strap worn crosswise over his chest; he fixed Jacinto with two small, dark, glittering eyes. He was João Torrado, the prophet of the mountains. When I held out my hand to him, he shook it, but Jacinto remained the focus of his wide, dark gaze. I ordered another glass of wine for him and introduced Jacinto, who had turned red with embarrassment.

"This is the owner of Tormes, who has done so much for the poor."

The old man reached out his arm, which emerged hairy and almost black from a rather short sleeve.

"Your hand, sir!"

And when Jacinto held out his hand, having first quickly removed his glove, João Torrado shook it long and thoughtfully, murmuring:

"A royal hand, a hand made for giving, a hand that comes from above, a hand that is now all too rare."

Then he took the glass offered him by Torto and very slowly drank down his wine. When he had done, he wiped his beard, adjusted the strap on the tin box he was carrying and banged the end of his shepherd's crook on the ground, saying:

"Well, praised be Our Lord Jesus Christ, who brought me here, for I have not wasted my day: I have seen a man!"

Then I leaned toward him and asked in confidence:

"Is it true you've been telling people that King Sebastian has returned?"

The picturesque old man rested his two hands on the crook and his bearded chin on his hands and, without looking at us, as if following the procession of his own thoughts, murmured:

"Maybe he has, maybe he hasn't. Who knows who comes and who goes. We see only the bodies, but not the souls within. There are present-day bodies with ancient souls in them. The body is the outer garment, the soul is the person. At the fair in Roqueirinha, who knows how many kings of old you might be bumping into as you push your way past cowherds. A vile body might conceal a lord!"

And as his voice trailed off, I glanced at Jacinto to share with him my amusement at these strange, soothsayerish comments, and asked the old man:

"But do you truly believe that King Sebastian did not die in battle?"

João Torrado eyed me distrustfully:

"These things are very ancient and not to be spoken of at the door of a tavern. The wine was good, and you are in a hurry! The flower of Flor da Malva has a sick father, but the sickness is already setting off down the mountain with the inflammation on its back. It's always good to meet someone who brings succour to the sad. Above Tormes a bright star is shining. So off you trot now, while the day is still fine!"

He ushered us on our way with one thin hand. As we were passing the cross in the square, his ardent voice rang out again with grave solemnity:

"Blessed be the Father of the Poor!"

Standing very erect in the middle of the street, he was holding his crook aloft as if directing the cheers of a whole people. Jacinto was filled with wonder that, in Portugal, there should still be someone who believed in Sebastian's eventual return.

"We all believe it, Jacinto. Whether in the City or the Mountains, we are all waiting for our personal King Sebastian to return. The Christmas lottery is really just another form of Sebastianism. Why, every morning, even when there's no mist, I peer out to see if my personal King Sebastian has arrived. Or, rather, my Queen Sebastiana. And what about you, you fortunate man?"

"Me? Waiting for a Queen Sebastiana? I'm too old for that, Zé Fernandes. I'm the last Jacinto, full stop. Tell me, what house is that over there with the two towers?"

"That's Flor da Malva."

Jacinto took out his watch.

"It's three o'clock. We've been on the road for an hour and a half, but it's been a delightful ride and most instructive. This really is a beautiful spot."

On top of a small hill, separated from the road by a grove of trees surrounded by a wall, stood Flor da Malva, with its long façade and its two towers — facing towards the east and the Sun — and with its windows on the verandah framed by glazed tiles. The great iron gate, with two stone benches on either side, stood at the end of the terrace over which a vast chestnut tree cast a deep, green shade. On the tree's strong roots a small boy sat waiting, holding a donkey by the reins.

"Is Manuel da Porta around?"

"He just this minute went up the avenue."

"Open the gates for us, will you?"

We rode up a short avenue of old trees to another terrace, where there was an ivy-clad shelter for the farmhands and a kennel out of which, chain jangling, sprang a mastiff, Tritão by name; but the creature soon quieted down when it recognized its old friend Zé Fernandes. Manuel da Porta was standing by the fountain, filling a large bucket, but he immediately ran to meet us so as to take care of our horses.

"How's Uncle Adrião?" I asked.

Manuel, who was extremely deaf, beamed and asked:

"And how are you, sir? Well, I hope. The last I saw of Senhora Dona Joaninha she was in the orange grove with Josefa's little boy."

As we walked down sandy paths lined with lavender and tall box hedges, I explained to my Prince that Josefa's little boy was Joaninha's godson and her pride and joy.

"My dear cousin may be single, but she has a whole family scattered around the parish. And it's not just a matter of giving them clothes and presents and helping out their mothers; she even washes the children, combs their hair, and takes care of them when they have a cough. Whenever I come here, she always has some child or other with her. At the moment, little José is her favorite."

However, when we reached the orange grove, beside the broad

path that led to the pond, I searched in vain through the trees, calling: "Joaninha!"

"Perhaps she's down below, near the pond."

We walked along the path lined with trees that shaded us with their dense, criss-crossing branches. Cool limpid water glittered in the stone irrigation channel. Entwined about the trunks, the wild roses were still as fresh as in Summer. And the little meadow in the distance glowed sweetly, all yellow and white with daisies and laxleaf.

The round pond had been emptied out to be cleaned, and was now filling up again with clear water, and even though it was still only shallow, the goldfish swam and leaped with joy to have recovered their tiny ocean. On one of the stone benches by the pond rested a basket full of cut dahlias. A boy, who was up a ladder pruning the camellias, had last seen Senhora Dona Joana heading toward the vine arbor.

We found the arbor still laden with black grapes. Some way off, two women were washing clothes under the shade of some vast beech trees. I called out to them: "Have you seen Senhora Dona Joana?" One of the women replied in a shrill voice, but her words were lost in the vast, sweet, luminous air.

"Let's go up to the house! We can't spend the whole afternoon hunting around for her."

"What a beautiful garden!" murmured my Prince, enchanted.

"Magnificent, eh? And well-tended too. Uncle Adrião has an excellent estate manager, not like your Melchior. He observes and learns and he works hard. Just look at those chives!"

We strolled through the vegetable garden, which was precisely the kind of vegetable-cum-flower-garden that Jacinto himself had dreamed of, its beds edged with lavender, and with honey-suckle scrambling up stone pillars to form cool shady paths. We walked around the chapel, too, where, to the right and left of the door, grew a tea rose, bearing a single bloom, and a vanilla bush, from which Jacinto plucked a sprig to sniff. Then we went out onto the terrace at the front of the house, with its stone balustrade all entwined with yellow jasmine. The French window stood open; in the immense reposeful silence in which the whole of Flor da Malva lay immersed, we went up the stone steps to the hallway, with its high panelled ceilings and long wooden benches, and where the paint on the Cerqueira family's complicated coat of arms was slowly fading. I pushed open the door of another room, where the windows—each with a canary cage—opened onto a verandah.

"How odd!" exclaimed Jacinto. "That looks just like the Nativity scene I have at home. And those are my chairs too."

On an antique sideboard adorned with antique bronzes stood a creche very similar to the one in Jacinto's library, and, like the worked leather chairs he had found in the attic at Tormes, the chairs here bore a coat of arms beneath a cardinal's hat.

"Honestly!" I cried. "Is there not one servant to be found?"

I clapped my hands, but the same sweet silence continued, made lighter and airier by the soft breeze from the garden and broken only by the canaries in their cages, hopping from one perch to another.

"It's like Sleeping Beauty's palace!" said Jacinto, almost indig-nantly. "Go on, shout!"

"No, I'll go and see if anyone's about."

Just then the door opened and my cousin Joaninha appeared, her cheeks flushed from her walk and from the fresh air; she was wearing a pale-colored dress, slightly open at the neck, which set off the white splendor of her skin and the undulating gold of her beautiful hair; she was smiling prettily, a look of surprise in her large, dark, luminous eyes, and she was carrying in her arms a small, plump, pink child, who was wearing only a skimpy shirt tied with large blue bows.

And so it was, on that September afternoon, at Flor da Malva, that Jacinto first saw the woman he later married, in the month of May, in the little tiled chapel, when the rose bush was in full bloom.

: XV :

AMID BLOOMING ROSES and fruitful vines, five years have passed over Tormes and the Mountains. My Prince is no longer the last Jacinto, Jacinto full stop, because that once dilapidated house now echoes to the lively footsteps of chubby, rosy-cheeked Teresinha, my god-daughter, and young Jacinto, who is a great friend of mine. Such is the perfection of Jacinto's moral beauty that the man who was once so picturesquely troubled by philosophical disquiet and by the torments of his restless imagination is now positively dull. He has become an expert on all things agricultural, and when he walks the estate with me and speaks sagely and prudently about such matters, I almost miss the old Jacinto who could pluck a theory from every branch and, sketching a plan in the air with his walking-stick, design a cheese dairy built of glass and porcelain that would produce cheeses costing two hundred *mil-réis* each!

Fatherhood, too, has awoken in him a sense of responsibility. He has an accounts book now, admittedly small and written in pencil and interleaved with all kinds of odd bits of paper, but therein income and expenditure are lined up like two disciplined armies.

He has visited his properties in Montemor and Beira, and repaired and furnished the old houses there so that his children, once they are grown, will find themselves with ready-made nests. However, I only realized how perfect and happy an equilibrium existed in the soul of my Prince when, having emerged from that first ardent love affair with Simplicity, he opened the door of Tormes to Civilization—just a crack. One afternoon, two months before Teresinha was born, the beech-tree avenue was filled by a long creaking line of carts requisitioned from all over the parish and piled high with crates. These were the famous crates that had been marooned all that time in Alba de Tormes, and which were now bringing the City to the Mountains. I thought: "Oh, no, my poor Jacinto has suffered a relapse." To my surprise, however, the more recondite comforts contained in those fearful crates were immediately relegated to the vast attics and to the dust of redundancy; and the old house benefitted only from a few rugs, curtains for those windows without any, and some comfortable armchairs and sofas in which, or so Jacinto imagined, he and Joaninha could more easily enjoy their repose. I attributed such moderation to my cousin Joaninha, who loved the rough bareness of the house at Tormes. She, however, assured me that this had been done on Jacinto's orders. Some weeks later, though, I again trembled. A foreman arrived from Lisbon, along with workmen and more crates, in order to install a telephone!

"A telephone in Tormes, Jacinto?"

My prince explained humbly:

"Just to my father-in-law's house, you understand."

That was a reasonable and, indeed, affectionate gesture. The telephone, subtly and silently, reached out another long wire to

Valverde. And Jacinto, holding up his arms in a gesture almost of supplication, said:

"Just to the doctor's house, you understand."

That, too, seemed a prudent move, but one morning, in Guiães, I woke to Aunt Vicência's cries of alarm. A mysterious man had arrived along with other men, bringing with them all kinds of wires, to install a telephone in *our* house. I calmed Aunt Vicência down, swearing that this new machine would make no noise, bring no diseases or attract thunderstorms. I then hurried over to Tormes. Jacinto smiled and, with a shrug, said:

"What do you expect? The pharmacy is in Guiães, as is the butcher's, as, of course, are you!"

It was a very brotherly idea, but nevertheless I thought: "We're lost!" Within a month, poor Joaninha would be grappling with a machine to do up her dress. But no! Summoned by Jacinto, Progress had climbed up to Tormes to install that one marvel, thinking perhaps that it had found a new kingdom to unravel, but instead, summarily dismissed, it had slunk silently back down the hill, and its stiff, grimy, metallic shadow was never seen again. Then I understood that the equilibrium of life had put down deep roots in Jacinto's soul, and with it Great Good Fortune—the princedom of which my Prince had so long been deprived. One afternoon, I met old Cricket—fully reconciled to life in the mountains, now that the mountains had provided him with children to whom he could give piggy-back rides—and as he sat, wearing a pair of large round spectacles to read his copy of *Le Figaro*, I remarked:

"I think we could safely say that Senhor Dom Jacinto is well and truly settled."

Cricket pushed back his spectacles and, holding up five fingers like the petals of a tulip, said:

"My master has blossomed!"

Cricket was right as usual! Yes, that withered branch from the City, replanted in the mountains, had taken root, sucked up the humus from that inherited earth, created sap, sent down more roots, thickened up, put out branches, and burst into flower— strong, serene, happy, beneficent, and noble, producing fruit and providing shade. Sheltered and nourished by that great tree, the one hundred families who lived round about all blessed him.

: XVI :

DURING THAT TIME, Jacinto had often spoken with pleasure of returning to No. 202 for a couple of months, so that he could show Paris to Joaninha, and I was to be their faithful companion, there to record my country cousin's reactions to the City! However, it was thought best to wait until young Jacinto turned two, an age at which he would be able to travel in comfort and point at the things of Civilization with his finger. But when, in October, he reached the desired age, my cousin Joaninha was filled by a terrible sloth and also by fear, of the train, of the noise of the City, of No. 202 and its splendors. "We're so happy here! And the weather's so lovely!" she said, putting adoring arms around her Jacinto's strong neck; and he immediately, blithely, abandoned the idea of Paris. "We'll go in April, when the chestnut-trees in the Champs-Elysées are in bloom!" But with April came that same weariness which left Joaninha immobilized on the divan, happy and smiling, her skin lightly freckled by the sun and her dressing-gown loose. So that happy adventure was put off for a whole long year. I had little to do at the time. The March rains guaranteed a good harvest. A certain Ana Vaqueira, red-faced and handsome, a widow who understood the needs of my heart, had left with her brother for Brazil, where he ran a store. Ever since Winter, my body had felt something like the beginnings of rust setting in, making movement difficult, and certainly a touch of mold was growing somewhere in my soul. Then my mare died. And so I left for Paris on my own.

As soon as I set foot on the sweet soil of France, my thoughts, like a dove to an old dovecote, flew to No. 202; this was probably brought on by the sight of an enormous poster on which a naked woman, with bacchantic flowers in her hair, was disporting herself, holding in one hand a foaming bottle and brandishing in the other, as if to display it to the whole world, a brand-new type of corkscrew. And what a surprise when, soon afterward, in the bright peaceful station of St. Jean de Luz, a slender, very elegant young man burst into my compartment and, on seeing me, declared:

"Hello, Fernandes!"

It was Marizac! The Duke de Marizac! No. 202 had come to meet me! With what gratitude I shook his slender hand, grateful to him for having recognized me. Throwing down in one corner his overcoat and the bundle of newspapers his valet had handed him, good old Marizac asked in the same tone of happy surprise:

"And how's Jacinto?"

I told him all about Tormes and the mountains, how Jacinto had fallen in love with Nature and then, more importantly, with my cousin, and about his two children to whom he gave piggyback rides.

"The cad!" exclaimed Marizac, his eyes fixed on me. "He actually has the nerve to be happy!"

"Oh, wildly, madly . . . there are no adverbs to describe it."

"How about 'indecently,' " muttered Marizac gravely. "The cad!"

I then asked about the friends of No. 202. He shrugged his shoulders and lit a cigarette:

"Oh, they're all still doing the rounds."

"And Madame d'Oriol?"

"The same."

"And Monsieur and Madame Trèves? And Efraim?"

"The same, all three of them."

He made a languid gesture.

"After five years, everything in Paris is exactly the same. Well, the women wear a little more face powder and their skin is a little less firm and the men are slightly more dyspeptic, but otherwise, everything is the same. Oh, there were the Anarchists, of course, and the Princess de Carman ran off with an acrobat from the Cirque d'Hiver, but that's about it!"

"And Dornan?"

"The same. I haven't seen him since Jacinto left No. 202, but I sometimes spot his name in *Le Boulevard* underneath some terribly precious lines of poetry—highly-wrought and frightfully subtle obscenities if you ask me."

"And the psychologist? Now what was his name?"

"The same. Still writing the same cheap literature for women— duchesses in chemises, souls laid bare, that kind of thing—and it sells too!"

I was enjoying myself, but just as I was about to ask after Todelle and the Grand Duke, the train drew into Biarritz station, and the delightful Marizac, snatching up his overcoat and his newspapers, and having first shaken my hand, leaped out of the door, which his servant had opened for him, and cried:

"I'll see you in Paris! You'll find me still at Rue Cambon!"

Left alone in the compartment, I yawned, filled by a strange sense of tedium and satiety, as if already surrounded by people I had seen too often and about whom I knew too much, and who, smiling wearily, kept repeating the same thing over and over. On either side of the train lay a broad, monotonous, unvarying plain, very precisely cultivated and very precisely divided up, all of the same light grayish green, where no flash of light, no bright flower, no slight gradient spoiled the discreet, orderly mediocrity of the scene. Pale, slender poplars in slender, regular lines bordered straight, clear canals. The dun-colored houses barely rose above the surface of the land, barely stood out against the faded greens, as if huddled in their own safe mediocrity.

And the smooth, cloudless sky above, with its dull sun, was like a vast royal robe washed and washed again until all the color and glow had vanished. I fell asleep in a state of sweet dullness.

It was a glorious May morning when I arrived in Paris. So cool and fresh, and the air so soft that, despite my tiredness, it was with reluctance that I plunged into the deep, dark bed in my room at the Grand Hotel, all hung with lavish velvet, thick braid and heavy tassels, like a dais at a gala. In this soft deep lair I dreamed that another Eiffel Tower had been built at Tormes, and that all the most respectable local ladies, even Aunt Albergaria, were dancing around it naked, waving huge corkscrews in the air. After the excitement of the dream, after my bath, and after unpacking my case, it was nearly two o'clock by the time I finally emerged from the hotel's mighty door and once again, after an absence of five years, stepped out onto the Boulevard. And it seemed to me that I had spent those five years simply standing at the door of the Grand Hotel, so wearily familiar to me were the strident roar of the City, the scrawny trees, the huge hoardings, the vast feathered hats worn over dyed yellow hair, the stiff overcoats sporting the cross of the Légion d'Honneur, and the boys touting for business in low hoarse voices, offering for sale packs of cards or boxes of matches containing obscene pictures. "Good God," I thought, "how long *is* it since I was last in Paris?" I bought a newspaper, *La Voix de Paris*, from a kiosk, so that I could read all the latest news over lunch. The kiosk counter was crowded with illustrated magazines, and on every cover was the same woman, always either naked or half-dressed, either showing off her thin ribs, like those of a starving cat, or displaying to the reader a pair of enormous buttocks. I murmured to myself: "Good God!" In the Café de la Paix, a pallid waiter, wearing a little face powder to conceal his pallor, suggested (since it was so late) a light lunch of fried flounder and a cutlet.

"And which wine, Monsieur le Comte?"

"Chablis, Monsieur le Duc!"

He smiled at my playful joke, and I contentedly opened *La Voix de Paris*. In the first column, I managed to make out, through some very contorted prose—which glittered like cheap jewellery—some tale of a naked princess and a heartbroken captain of dragoons. I jumped to the other columns, which were all full of the exploits of cocottes with high-sounding names. On another page, eloquent writers celebrated *digestifs* and tonics. Then came the crime section. "Nothing new there!" I flung down *La Voix de Paris*, and a fearful battle ensued between me and the flounder. The wretch, which had clearly taken against me, would not allow me to detach from its spine so much as a tiny fragment of flesh. It was as dry, burned, and impenetrable as shoe-leather, and my knife bent on it, impotent and tremulous. I summoned the pallid waiter, who, equipped with a sturdier knife, and pressing down hard on the floor with the heels of his buckled shoes, finally managed to wrench from the stubborn creature two strips of flesh, as small and thin as toothpicks, which I swallowed in one, and which did little to assuage my hunger. I finished the cutlet off in one forkful. This cost me fifteen francs. I paid with a good louis d'or and in the change—brought to me by the waiter with exquisite politeness—there were two forged francs. On that mild May afternoon, I sat out on a café terrace and drank a cup of coffee that was as black as a bowler-hat and tasted of broad beans.

I lit a cigar and contemplated the Boulevard, which, at that hour, was filled with the hustle and bustle of coarse sociability. The dense torrent of omnibuses, old carriages, carts and splendid pairs of horses rolled swiftly past, and a dark mass of humanity restlessly threaded its way past legs and wheels. This ceaseless movement and restless haste was bewildering to a mind which, for five quiet years, had become accustomed to the peace of the unchanging Mountains. I tried, in vain, to rest my eyes on some stationary object: an omnibus that had stopped, a fiacre whose skinny nag suddenly skittered to a halt, but some hurrying figure would always clamber into the carriage or a clutch of dark shapes would scramble hurriedly onto the omnibus, and the roaring and the rolling would start all over again. The tall buildings remained still, of course, like stiff limestone cliffs containing and disciplining the breathless torrent, but from street to rooftop and on every balcony there was signboard upon signboard, crowded out by other hoardings, and it tired me still more to think of the incessant labor, the unending, wearying scrabble for lucre that went on behind those decorous, silent façades. And then, while I was smoking my cigar, I was surprised to find myself filled with the very feelings that Jacinto had once experienced in the midst of Nature, and which I had found so amusing. There, at the door of the café, amid the indifference and haste of the City, I felt, as he had in the Country, a vague sad sense of my own fragility and solitude. For I was certainly adrift in an unfriendly world. I knew no one. Who cared about Zé Fernandes? If I felt hungry and asked for food, no one would give me half of their loaf of bread. However grief-stricken the look on my face, no one, in their haste, would stop to console me. And whatever excellent qualities my soul might have, what purpose did they serve if they bloomed only in my soul? If I were a saint, the multitude would care nothing for my saintliness, and if I opened wide my arms and cried out, there on the Boulevard, "O my brothers!" those same men—fiercer than the wolf of Gubbio poor St. Francis had to confront—would laugh and pass coldly by. Only two impulses, corresponding to only two functions, appeared to be alive in that crowd: the getting of lucre and of pleasure. Caught between them and infected by the contagion they gave off, my soul would soon shrivel up into a hard pebble of Egotism. Yes, all that would remain of the reasonably noble being I had brought with me from the Mountains would be that pebble containing the City's twin appetites: filling one's purse and satisfying one's flesh! The City instilled me with the same exaggerated emotions Jacinto had once felt in the midst of Nature. The Boulevard, it seemed to me, gave off a deadly breath exhaled by its millions of microbes. In every doorway some trickster seemed to be lying in wait to rob me. In every face glimpsed at a carriage window, I suspected a bandit. All women seemed to me to be whited sepulchres, containing only putrefaction. I considered with extravagant melancholy the skin and the shapes of that Multitude, their clever futile haste, their affected gestures, the immense feathers on their hats, their false, insincere expressions, the sumptuously padded bosoms, the hunched backs of old men peering in at obscene shopwindows. These were perhaps puerile feelings, but I felt a great need to escape back to the Mountains and let the pure air dry and finally peel away the scab of the City so that I could re-emerge human again and fully Zé Fernandesized!

Then, to drive away the bitter weight of solitude, I paid for the coffee and set off slowly to visit No. 202. As I passed La Madeleine, outside the omnibus station, I thought: "I wonder what's become of Madame Colombe?" And, wretch that I am, I felt rising up in my wretched self the brief hot breath of brute desire for that grimy scrawny creature. She was the puddle in which I had poisoned myself and which had wrapped me in the subtle emanations of its poison. Then, as I came out of Rue Royale into Place de la Concorde, I bumped into a robust vigorous man, who stopped, raised one arm, and exclaimed in a booming voice of command:

"Fernandes!"

It was the Grand Duke! The handsome Grand Duke, in a pale overcoat and honey-brown Tyrolean hat! I reverently shook his hand, again grateful to someone for having recognized me.

"And what about Jacinto? Is he in Paris too?"

I told him about Tormes, the mountains, Jacinto's rejuvenation in nature, my sweet cousin Joaninha, and the fine children to whom Jacinto gave piggy-back rides. The Grand Duke shrugged glumly.

"Oh, dear me! Ugh! Married and living in a village and with

children! The man's done for! Oh, dear, and he was such a very useful fellow, so amusing and with such exquisite taste! Just think of that delicious pink supper party he held! There's been nothing so brilliant in Paris since. And then there's Madame d'Oriol . . . I saw her a few days ago at the Palais de Glace. She's still a very tasty piece, though not really my type . . . too sweet, milky, and pomaded, too vanilla ice for my liking. But Jacinto . . . who would have thought it!"

"And what about you, sir, are you staying long in Paris?"

The formidable gentleman bent toward me, frowning, and said in a confidential tone:

"Certainly not. Paris has become utterly unbearable. It's ruined, totally ruined. One can't even eat well here! Nowadays, all one hears about is Ernest's in Place Gaillon; he used to be *maître d'hotel* at the Maire. Have you ever eaten there? No? Well, don't; it's frightful. But now, as I say, no one talks of anyone else. Where does one eat? At Ernest's. I had lunch there only today. Dreadful! A *salade Chambord* that was a disgrace, an utter disgrace! Paris is finished! There are only a handful of theaters left. And no decent women. Nothing. Mind, there is a review worth seeing in one of those little theaters in Montmartre, the Roulotte: *Come On, Ladies!* it's called. Most diverting and plenty of naked flesh on display. Celestine has a song in it, half-sentimental, half-filthy, 'Love in the Ladies' Room' it's called, but it's very funny and rather saucy. So where are you staying, Fernandes?"

"At the Grand Hotel, sir."

"Hm, not a bad billet. And how is your King?"

I bowed my head:

"His Majesty is well."

"I'm glad, Fernandes. Anyway, good to see you again. Dreadful news about Jacinto though. Go and see the review I mentioned. She's got fine legs, that Celestine. And it's a catchy little number, 'Love in the Ladies' Room.'"

He clasped my hand in his iron grip, then clambered into his victoria and gave me a friendly wave, for which I was obliged. An excellent man, the Grand Duke! Feeling more reconciled to Paris, I crossed over to the Champs-Elysées. Along its fine, noble, green length, where the chestnut trees were already in flower, velocipedes raced up and down. I paused to contemplate this new ugliness: the innumerable bent backs and skinny legs pedalling along, knees akimbo, on two wheels. Old men with scarlet necks pedalled plumply by. Lanky ne'er-do-wells, with thin shanks, whipped past. And heavily painted women, wearing boleros and bloomers, sped rapidly along, savoring the equivocal pleasure of speed astride an iron frame. And at every moment, some fearful new machine would pass, steam-driven victorias and phaetons— with a whole complicated mechanism of tubes and boilers, taps and funnels—rolling along making a terrific noise and giving off the most awful stink of petroleum. I continued on to No. 202, thinking wryly: "If only a Greek from the time of Phidias could see these graceful new modes of transport!"

At No. 202, as soon as old Vian the porter recognized me, he greeted me with touching joy. He wanted to know all about Jacinto's marriage and his dear children. And it was a source of delight to him that I should appear just when they were beginning the spring cleaning. However, when I entered the beloved house, I felt my solitary state even more keenly. There was not a trace in it of anything that would revive my old comradeship with my

Prince. In the hallway, great pieces of canvas covered the heroic tapestries, and the same dull fabric concealed walls, upholstery, and the long ebony shelves in the Library, where the thirty thousand volumes, like an assembly of learned doctors, seemed cut off from the world by the final curtain that had fallen on them once the drama of their force and authority was over. In Jacinto's study, the rabble of instruments and apparatus—which I had quite forgotten about—had vanished from the ebony desk, and all that remained, perched on pedestals and pillars, was the array of rigid, metal machines, carefully dusted, their gears, tubes and wheels glinting—dead, cold and inert as are all objects fallen into disuse—like museum pieces, examples of the defunct apparatus of a lost world. I tried to use the phone, but it wouldn't work; the electric switch lit not a single lamp; the universal forces, dismissed like servants, no longer served No. 202. And as I walked through the rooms, I really did feel like someone visiting a museum of antiquities and that in years to come, other men, with a purer and more exact understanding of Life and Happiness, would, like me, visit these rooms crammed with Supercivilization and, like me, scornfully shrug their shoulders at the great illusion that had ended and now lay forever useless, like so much historical debris to be swept away beneath a sheet of canvas.

When I left No. 202, I took a fiacre and drove up to the Bois de Boulogne. After a few moments in the decorous silence of the Avenue des Acacias, broken only by the squeak of brakes and the slow crunch of wheels on sand, I began to recognize the same motionless figures, the same smiles, the same layers of face powder, the same drooping eyelids, the same flashing eyes, the same waxen immobility! The editor of *Le Boulevard* passed in a victoria and fixed his smoked-glass monocle on me, but remained otherwise impassive. Madame Verghane's furiously black hair seemed even more furiously black among the harmonious whites of dress, hat, feathers, flowers, lace and bodice, beneath which her vast bosom rose and fell like a wave. Beside the path, beneath the acacias, Dornan, his bulk spread over two chairs, was sucking on what remained of his cigar. Madame de Trèves was smiling the same smile of five years before, with slightly deeper lines on either side of her dry lips.

I headed off to the Grand Hotel, yawning, as Jacinto used to do. And I concluded my day in Paris at the Théâtre des Variétés, my senses dazed by a very sharp, much acclaimed and glitteringly Parisian comedy, the plot of which turned entirely on a Bed, upon which frolicked a succession of women in chemises, fat men in their underwear, a colonel with a poultice on his buttocks, cooks wearing embroidered silk stockings, and other noisy, frisking people, all alive with lust and knavish tricks. I drank a melancholy cup of tea in Julien's surrounded by a rough lugubrious rabble of prostitutes sniffing out their prey. Two of these women—with their greasy, copper-colored skin, slanting eyes and hair as coarse and black as a horse's mane—had all the feline allure of the Orient. When I asked the waiter—a fearsome creature, as pale and flabby as a eunuch—where they were from, the monster explained in a hoarse whisper:

"They're from Madagascar. They were the very first import when France occupied the island!"

My next few days in Paris were days of immense tedium. Along the Boulevard, I saw the same luxury goods in shopwindows that had bored me five years before, without a hint of any new spark or fresh invention. In the bookshops, finding no book worthy of the name, I leafed through dozens of yellow volumes which, when opened at random, exhaled a warm bedroom smell and a whiff of face powder from between lines written in an effeminate mannered style, as elaborate as the lace on a nightdress. At supper, in whichever restaurant I entered, I found, adorning and disguising both meat and poultry, the same sauce, which looked and tasted like hair oil and which, in another mirrored gilt-edged restaurant earlier in the day, had ruined my fish and vegetables. I paid enormous prices for bottles of our coarse, rustic Torres wine, ennobled with the title of Chateau This and Chateau That and coated in fake dust. At night, in the theaters, I found the Bed, the usual bed, as the sole and central aim of life, attracting, as a dunghill attracts flies, a whole swarm of disoriented people, frantic with desire and uttering very tired old jokes. The sordid nature of the Plains made me seek better, more spiritual air on the Heights, in Montmartre, and there, in the midst of an elegant multitude of Ladies, Duchesses, Generals and all the City's other personnel, I was greeted from the stage with great streams of obscenities that made the hairy ears of overweight bankers tremble with pleasure and the false bosoms of Noble Ladies breathe harder beneath bodices made by such couturiers as Worms or Doucet. And I withdrew, sickened by that Bedroom stench, feeling vaguely dyspeptic from all those hair-oil sauces, and, above all, dissatisfied with myself because I was not amused, because I did not understand the City, and because I wandered through it and its Superior Civilization with all the ridiculous reserve of a Censor, of an austere Cato. "How can I not enjoy myself," I thought, "in this delicious city?"

Had the mold of old age already entered my soul? I passed the bridges which, in Paris, separate the Temporal from the Spiritual; I plunged into my dear sweet Latin Quarter; outside certain cafés, I evoked the memory of my beloved Nini; and, as before, I idly climbed the steps of the Sorbonne. In a lecture theater, from which came the sound of whispering, a thin man, with a very broad white forehead—apparently made to give lodging to high pure thoughts—was speaking about the institutions of the Ancient City. However, as soon as I entered, his elegant, limpid words were drowned out by shouts, howls, and stamping, a rancorous tumult of bestial mockery from the youths crammed into the seats, the youth of the University, the sacred Spring in which I myself had once been a withered bloom. The Professor stopped and cast about him a cold serene gaze, then shuffled through his notes. When the grunting had subsided into a suspicious murmur, he began again with the same serenity. His ideas were both considered and substantial and expressed in pure strong language, but immediately there burst forth a furious blast of whistles, howls, whinnies, and cockadoodle-doos, from mouths cupped by scrawny hands eager to strangle ideas. Beside me, an old man with a heavy cold sniffed and shrank inside the high collar of his check macfarlane coat and regarded the tumult with a baleful eye. I asked him:

"What do they want? Do they dislike the teacher? Is it political?"

The old man shook his head and sneezed.

"No, it's always like this now, in all the classes. They don't want ideas. I think what they want are songs and other such rubbish. They just love making fun."

Then I roared indignantly:

"Silence, you brutes!"

And a little abortion of a boy, sallow and grimy, with long hair and wearing enormous glittering spectacles, got up, fixed me with his eye, and yelled:

"Filthy Moor!"

I raised my great countryman's fist, and the wretch, hair flying, blood all over his face, fell to the floor, like a soft heap of old rags, whimpering desperately, while the hurricane of howls and cocka-doodlings and whinnies and whistles wrapped once more about the Professor, who stood, arms folded, waiting with the same simple serenity as before.

It was then that I decided to leave the tedious City, and my one happy, enjoyable day was the last, spent buying extravagant pres-ents for my dear ones in Tormes, complicated toys courtesy of Civilization: steamships in steel and copper, equipped with real boilers so that they could be sailed on ponds; lions made of real lion skins and that emitted terrifying roars; dolls dressed by La-ferrière with phonographs in their bellies.

And finally, one afternoon, I left, having first said farewell to the City from my window overlooking the Boulevard:

"Goodbye, then, because I won't be back! You won't catch me again stuck in the mud of your vice and the dust of your vanity! And whatever good qualities you may have—whatever clear ele-gant genius—I will receive in the Mountains by post!"

And one Sunday afternoon, leaning out of the train window, as the train glided along the edge of the slow river in a silence made entirely of blue sky and sun, I spotted on the platform of the oth-erwise empty station the Lord and Lady of Tormes, along with my god-daughter Teresa, flushed and wide-eyed, and brave little Jacinto, who was brandishing a white flag. The happy delight with which I embraced and kissed that dearly-beloved tribe was not unlike that of someone returning alive from some distant war in Tartary. In my joy to be back in the Mountains, I even planted a kiss on Pimenta, who, vast and obese as ever, was urging the porter to take care of my luggage. Jacinto, looking magnificent in broad-brimmed hat, jacket and gaiters, embraced me again:

"So how was Paris?"

"Ghastly!"

And I again opened my arms to young Jacinto.

"So why the flag, my little man?"

"It's the castle's flag!" he declared, his fine large eyes very serious.

His mother laughed. Ever since that morning, as soon as he knew about Uncle Zé's arrival, he had been clutching that flag, made for him by Cricket, and had not let go of it once; he had lunched with it in his hand and carried it down to the station.

"Bravo! And you, cousin Joaninha, you look magnificent too! True, I have just come from all those faded Parisian complexions, but nevertheless, you look splendid! And how are Uncle Adrião and Aunt Vicência?"

"They're both fine!" cried Jacinto. "And the mountains, thank God, are prospering. And now let's go back up to Tormes. You're spending tonight in Tormes so that you can tell us all about Civilization."

In the courtyard, underneath the fig trees—a glad sight—three horses were waiting and two handsome white donkeys, one with a little seat for Teresa and the other with a wicker basket in which heroic young Jacinto could sit, each donkey being led by a servant. I had just helped Joaninha onto her mount when the porter appeared, bearing a bundle of newspapers and magazines I had left in the carriage—it was the nonsense I had bought at the Gare d'Orléans, full of naked women, tawdry stories, and the usual Parisian erotica. As soon as Jacinto saw it, he said, laughing:

"Throw it away!"

I did as he said and threw that foul matter from flighty Civilization onto a pile of rubbish in one corner of the courtyard. And then I mounted my horse. As I turned to begin the steep ascent up to the mountains, I looked back to say goodbye to Pimenta, whom I had forgotten all about. The worthy stationmaster was bent over the rubbish heap and picking up, dusting off and lovingly gathering together those pages fresh from Paris, full of the seductive delights of Paris life.

We began the ride back in single file. The afternoon heat of Summer was beginning to abate. A breeze wafted the perfumes of wild flowers to us, as if giving them to us as gifts. The branches stirred as if waving a welcome, their leaves bright and glossy. All the birds were singing in a babble of joy and praise. The streams that ran leaping and glinting seemed to shine more brightly and to move more swiftly. The distant windows of the lovely houses flashed golden in the sunlight. The mountains offered up their true eternal beauty. And at the head of our party, in all the greenery, fluttered the white flag that young Jacinto kept firmly grasped in his hand. It was the "castle's flag," he had said very gravely. And it did seem to me that, along those paths, through gentle rural Nature, my Prince, burned brown by the mountain sun and wind, my cousin Joaninha—that tender smiling mother—the two representatives of their blessed tribe, and I—far now from bitter illusions and false delights—were treading an eternal soil, eternally solid, with a contented heart, and that God was contented with us too, as we serenely, confidently climbed up to the Castle of Great Good Fortune!

Afterword

Eça wrote this novel in 1895, when he was living and working in Paris. In 1892, he had visited the house and estate his wife had recently inherited in the Douro valley, in the north of Portugal. His responses to these two very different places seem to hold the key to the origin of *The City and the Mountains*. Eça had long wanted the post of consul in Paris, but once there, took little part in Parisian society and wrote to a friend: "[the city] has grown very coarse as regards manners and ideas, and it's completely black!" Writing to his wife from their Portuguese estate, Quinta da Vila Nova, he praised the wild beauty of the country-side, but commented:

> One of the drawbacks is the terrible squalor in which the local people live. There is genuine poverty here, which is the reverse side of all this beauty. The houses in the village and the tenants' houses are out-and-out hovels, not even fit for cattle—and this is entirely the fault of the landlords. Now that I have had a chance to observe it more closely, I am truly appalled.

Out of his twin ambivalence toward city and country comes this spry and strangely modern satire split neatly into two halves. In the first half, set in Paris, Eça describes a society obsessed with technology and money, a society divided into those who have too much and those who have almost nothing. In the second half of the book—which is, in many ways, a paean of praise to the natural beauty of the mountains and to the simple country life—a similar division exists. Jacinto and his neighbors live comfortable lives in large pleasant houses, but the tenants on Jacinto's estates exist in the most abject poverty.

Jacinto—the novel's hero—is an idealist, a seeker after truth. His personal philosophy—Absolute Knowledge x Absolute Power = Absolute Happiness—lets him down, as do his many machines and gadgets. When he arrives in the Portuguese countryside, happiness, he finds, comes in the form of home-made chicken soup, a sky thick with stars, and crisp clean sheets on a hard bed. For an idealist, however, that is not enough either, and he has to find a purpose in life, a way of being useful.

Eça was a self-proclaimed realist. In 1878, he wrote to his friend Rodrigues de Freitas: "What do we want from Realism? . . . We want to take a photograph, I very nearly said draw a caricature of the old bourgeois world, sentimental, devout, Catholic, exploitative, aristocratic, etc. And—by mocking and ridiculing it and holding it up to the scorn of the modern democratic world—prepare its ruin." And this, in effect, is what he does in both halves of the book. He pokes fun at Paris's empty-headed men and women, at so-called psychologists, at symbolist artists and decadent poets, at the many "isms" pursued by the spiritually bankrupt. More importantly, he is scathing about the indifference of the haves to the sufferings of the have-nots, who keep the former in luxury. He is equally scathing about the terrible poverty in which rural laborers live, a poverty that is accepted as normal by Jacinto's administrator, Silvério. Indeed, when Jacinto declares his determination to take drastic action to improve his tenants' lives, Silvério roars: "But, sir, this is revolution!" There is no suggestion from Eça that other landowners will necessarily follow Jacinto's example—he is too much of a realist for that—but there is a sense that individuals can create their own small revolutions.

Eça's realism, especially in his later works (for example, *The Mandarin*, *The Relic*, and *The Illustrious House of Ramires*), often exists in parallel with his liking for fantasy, and there is in *The City and the Mountains* the thread of a fairy-tale alongside the social satire. In Jacinto we have a kind of modern-day fairy-tale prince (Zé refers to Jacinto from the start as "my Prince") who must go through many trials—exploding water-pipes, recalcitrant dumb-waiters, the melancholy of surfeit—before he finds his promised land and his princess. The book is strewn with all kinds of clues to this other side of the novel: the references to Don Quixote and Sancho Panza, to Ulysses and his return home to Ithaca, to Virgil and the bucolic ideal, to the hypothetical return to Portugal as savior of a resuscitated King Sebastian, there are sermons on mounts and spiritual awakenings, and there is, last of all, the silent house where, just before Jacinto finally meets his princess, he declares: "It's Sleeping Beauty's palace!" Jacinto is a prince in exile—both from his own country and from his own values. Only by returning to his own country can he find himself and his true purpose in life.

It is perhaps this combination of satire, fairy-tale, and social comment that makes the novel such a delight and such a surprise too, one in which we are startled to recognize many of the malaises that afflict contemporary urban society—starless city skies, pollution, noise, endless, futile bustle, and—still—that divide between the haves and the have-nots.

It should perhaps be pointed out that Eça died before he had fully revised the proofs of the novel, and that the last page of the proofs was, in fact, missing. The ending we have now was supplied by Eça's close friend and fellow writer, Ramalho Ortigão, and one does wonder what Eça would have made of the rather over-sugared final paragraphs. Perhaps an ending truer to Eça's warmly satirical imagination is to be found in the almost-final scene in which the station master eagerly sifts through the rubbish in search of the scandalous Parisian newspapers discarded by Zé Fernandes. The City's seductive powers, it seems, remain undimmed.

—*Margaret Jull Costa*